The Weight We Carry

CHRISTINA CONSOLINO

Black Rose Writing | Texas

The author grants the final approval for this literary material.

First printing

This is a work of fiction. Names, characters, businesses, places, events, and incidents are either the products of the author's imagination or used in a fictitious manner. Any resemblance to actual persons, living or dead, or actual events is purely coincidental.

ISBN: 978-1-68513-290-3
PUBLISHED BY BLACK ROSE WRITING
www.blackrosewriting.com

Printed in the United States of America
Suggested Retail Price (SRP) $21.95

The Weight We Carry is printed in Minion Pro

Cover by Kiwi Cover Design Co.

*As a planet-friendly publisher, Black Rose Writing does its best to eliminate unnecessary waste to reduce paper usage and energy costs, while never compromising the reading experience. As a result, the final word count vs. page count may not meet common expectations.

For Melina, without whom this novel would never have been completed.

And for Dee, whose dedication, enthusiasm, and love for her residents shows in every single action she takes.

PRAISE FOR

The
Weight
We
Carry

"*The Weight We Carry* actually made me feel lighter—Consolino beautifully captures the frustrating, heartbreaking reality of dealing with aging, failing parents."

—Katrina Kittle, author of *Morning in This Broken World*

"With insight and love, Christina Consolino balances both the happy and the difficult moments while looking to the future and the possibility of renewal. *The Weight We Carry* is a gift."

—Jenn Bouchard, author of *First Course*

"*The Weight We Carry* provides a window into the struggles that adult children face and sustains hope for not only surviving but thriving; this important novel will remain in my heart for a long time."

—C. D'Angelo, award-winning author of
The Difference* and *The Visitor

"Consolino highlights how identity and sense of belonging tug at the fabric of family, particularly during a time of crisis, [and] provides us with closure that is both sweet, satisfying, and honest. A must read!"

—Elizabeth Sumner Wafler, author of *A Cleft in the World*

"With dignity and insight, Consolino explores the possibility of an unconventional happily ever after, regardless of age and physical or mental agility. A compelling, timely story that will resonate with readers."

—**Jill Caugherty, author of**
The View from Half Dome* and *Waltz in Swing Time

"Unique to *The Weight We Carry* is its emphasis on the stressful process before official diagnoses are made. Marissa's anxious caretaking of her parents and their complicated response to losing agency are sure to connect with readers."

—**Amanda Fields, co-editor, *My Caesarean***
and Editor in Chief, *Literary Mama*

"I wanted so badly for Marissa to get an afternoon to herself with a good glass of wine and a great read. I hope the same for you, dear reader, and a crisp rosé and this book are my recommendations."

—**Erin Flanagan, Edgar-winning author of *Come With Me***

The
Weight
We
Carry

"To love a person is to learn the song that is in their heart and to sing it to them when they have forgotten."
–Arne Garborg

CHAPTER 1: HER

The woman stared at the monarch butterfly perched outside the kitchen window screen. Thin, jointed legs. Long black antenna. Brilliant orange wings with white spots along the outer edges. She didn't know what attracted the butterflies to that spot, but it didn't matter. Joy arrived in all shapes and sizes, and that creature alone brought peace to her kitchen. Looking away, she moved the pieces of her handmade confections on the platter, finding a spot for each among the crevices of the flat, ceramic flower. Caramels enrobed in dark ganache sat next to cream-filled milk chocolates, and pieces of cocoa toffee crunch lounged near the layers of coconut clusters and mounds of petite candied roses.

She paused in her work, stepping back to admire the beauty of the art she'd pulled forth that morning. The stream of June light threading through the blinds of the kitchen highlighted the tray of treats, and beyond it, the butterfly still stood, immobile, as if inspecting her handiwork too. The corners of her mouth turned upward. *I've still got it*, she thought and then wiped her fingers across the stained kitchen apron she'd bought thirty years ago. Every holiday or family gathering since then, she spent far too much time making her candy tray look impeccable. When she was finished with it, the large platter of delights would hold not only a spread of dipped chocolates but also a trove of delicious nuggets that collectively resembled the flower garden beyond her house.

She walked around the tray, assessing its fullness and whether the choices could all be seen by the chooser, and there it was—a small gap of space at the rear. A spot large enough to hold several more cranberry clusters or maybe her favorite candy—the milk chocolate raspberry cream nougat. But what did she usually put there? The dark chocolate fudge? Or her special cocoa-coffee truffles? The tick of the clock's second hand strummed a steady beat, and a cold sweat broke out across the back of her neck. Her family would arrive soon; she didn't have time to waste.

The candy timer buzzed as the woman gently positioned five white chocolate truffles—one for each of her grandchildren—in the open space. *It's perfect*, she thought, and a slow warmth spread throughout her chest at the image of her grandsons and granddaughter. Her fingers smoothed back the stray hair that had fallen over her eyes, and she adjusted her glasses. A niggling feeling, something she couldn't identify, boiled in the pit of her stomach, but she forced a smile across her once youthful face. When she glanced one last time out the window, the monarch had disappeared.

CHAPTER 2: FRANK

Two things were on my mind that day: Antonio and the Stanley Cup Finals. Hockey wasn't my favorite sport, but my brother had loved it. The year he died—1955—his beloved Detroit Red Wings had won the cup in April. Two months later, he was gone. Thoughts of Antonio always haunted me on the day he died, masking everything else, and no passage of time made it better. As I sat on the wide front porch of our southwestern Ohio home, he seemed to be everywhere: in the reclaimed oak posts and beams, the stain and grain of the wood. All things my woodworking craftsman brother would have appreciated. Angela and I had added the porch to the original house shortly after we moved in. She and I had shared countless cups of coffee out here. Read innumerable newspaper articles. Held many conversations. Things Antonio couldn't do. When would my memories of him begin to fade? At seventy-seven years old, my days were numbered—something my body kept telling me. Which is why I'd just finished making an appointment with my general practitioner for a month out.

Earlier in the year, I'd taken a stumble, just enough to send me in for testing and frequent checkups. Marissa would text or call later to confirm I'd made the appointment. She tried to make sure the whole family took personal health seriously. Some of us were better at listening to her than others.

Wind ruffled through the deep green blades of grass and the leaves of the full maple trees that ran the edge of our yard. Our Bellbrook property extended an acre on all sides of the house—enough room for me to feel sometimes as if the land went on forever. My ears picked up the honks and hums of the distant traffic a couple of streets over, and I breathed in a large gulp of air as a timer rang inside the house. Angie was done with her break, getting the rest of her orders ready for the day. She ran a licensed candy business out of the home and had more candy orders than she knew what to do with at times. Summer seemed to be the worst candy season of all. "I get so backed up when the weather is like this," she'd always say. Wasn't that just an excuse? When was the last time she wasn't backed up?

The timer rang again.

"Angie?" I called, hoping my voice would find its way through the open windows to the back of the house. "Angie? Can you hear that?"

Nothing but the timer again.

I pushed up on the porch swing arms, my muscles groaning at the change in position, but crashed against the seat back. "Last time it was the legs. This time, the arms," I mumbled. "Come on, body, don't fail me now."

All my life I'd heard people talk about what happens as you get older: forget words, misplace items, use a calendar for appointments. Bile ducts get blocked, arteries clogged. The ticker can lose its ability to keep time. Knees creak and shoulders grumble at wake-up time in the morning. But so far, my only issues had been diabetes and this (sometimes) muscle weakness in my limbs.

With a deep breath, I gently hauled myself off the cushion. A couple of slow shuffles to the wall and I stood at the open door, looking to the kitchen at the rear of the house. Angie was there, head in the refrigerator.

"Hey, Ang," I said as I approached. "That timer needs to go off. Did you forget you set it—"

Angie righted herself and whirled around to face me. "I know, Frank. And no, I did not forget." She nudged the refrigerator door shut and moved to the cabinet, then picked up the timer.

"You okay, hon?" In her hand, the timer dinged again, and a pot bubbled on the stove. "Doesn't this noise get to you?"

"I'm fine. Just busy. You know how it is in the summer."

"Busy, busy. You're always busy," I mumbled.

"What did you say?"

"Nothing. It just seems like that's all the time. Have you thought—"

"You know what, Frank?" She tossed a worn kitchen towel over her shoulder, wiped her silver hair away from her face, and forced a smile as she set the timer. "Can you please leave the kitchen? You know how I feel about you being in here. It's all just too…too much."

Knowing better than to argue with Angie, I pursed my lips, grabbed the latest *Boones* magazine, and headed toward the garage. An old picture in the corner of the hallway mirror caught my eye. *The kids.* Then my gaze bounced to my face's reflection in the mirror. A full head of hair, as gray as an Ohio winter sky, but a face as weathered as my hands, which were littered with liver spots. *Hey, at least I'm alive.* A tightness settled in my chest at the thought of my brother, long gone—

The timer rang out again.

"Angie!" I yelled. "Are you going to get that this time?"

"Yes, Frank. Just… Go do what you need to do," she called. "That magazine—it's got an article you might like in it."

A quick glance at the cover of *Boones* revealed a title: "What Legacy Do You Want to Leave Behind?" Legacies—money, reputation, all sorts—concerned me, almost to the point of obsession, Angie claimed, but I didn't want to think about my own demise. Not yet. I had more life left to live.

"Ang? I'm going out back. I want to see if that gutter is still giving us problems. Yesterday's rain might tell us."

"Okay," she called. "Don't do anything stupid."

•   •   •

As I stood on the ladder and looked at the still problematic gutter, my mistake stared me square in the face. Only eight rungs stood between me and the ground, but for me, going up was always easier than going down. I patted my pocket, reassured by the cell phone. Thought about calling Angie to help me, but she'd be furious with another interruption. I could manage eight rungs.

Gripping the ladder sides, I lifted my right leg and moved it down a step—*thunk*—then followed with my left leg. *One down, six to go.* I repeated the action again, making it to the next step as a fly buzzed in my face. *I can do this.* The phone in my pocket vibrated, and I lurched, trying to find purchase on the step that followed, but my foot never connected. So I brought it back up, and a tingle ran up my left leg as I urged it to follow my command. A tremor ran through my entire lower half. I crumbled, falling to the ground and knocking the wind out of my sails.

"Ang?" I called, grateful for the ability to speak. "Angie? Can you hear me?" That damn timer rang again. She'd never hear me. Not with the drone of the neighbor's lawn mower. The bubbling pot on the stove. The sheer amount of space that separated us. Though my legs still refused to cooperate, my fingers fully worked. I pulled the phone out of my pocket and dialed 911. Waiting for the ambulance to arrive, one question came to mind: Would I be back from the hospital in time to watch the final cup game?

•   •   •

"Mr. Raffaelo?" A woman in blue scrubs stood in the ER bay doorway, her gaze boring into mine. "Mr. Raffaelo? You okay? I'm here to take vitals and ask you a few questions."

"Thanks." I nodded.

We went through a host of procedures I'd come to expect from medical personnel: a check on weight loss or gain, height, and temperature, my blood pressure, pulse, and reflexes. The woman checked off each item in time while I focused on the hospital sounds around me. A ding. A whistle. The squeal of a medicine cart. The howl of— *God no.*

"Okay, Mr. Raffaelo," the woman said. Her identification tag held a self-portrait and the word NURSE and then the initials, RN. Maybe she'd lost her permanent tag. "We have a couple more things we need to go through, and then the doctor will see you."

"Okay, shoot." I pulled the blanket over my chilled legs.

"What's your full name?"

"Francesco Silvio Raffaelo." Why the hell did I have to go through all this *every single time* I saw medical personnel? Shit, if I couldn't remember my name...

NURSE jotted letters onto a paper. "And when were you born?"

"May eighth, nineteen thirty-eight, in Columbus, Ohio."

"Thank you—that answered my next question." Again, she scribbled something on her paper. What about computers? Seeing as it was 2015... *I could be in trouble.*

"And where do you live now?"

"Bellbrook, Ohio. Do you need my address?"

"Yes. Thank you." She tapped the clipboard and jotted down my answer. "Mr. Raffaelo, are you married?" NURSE smiled this time.

"Why are you asking? Are *you?*" I toyed with NURSE for only a moment because her warm eyes iced over quickly, making me scramble. *So much for trying to be funny.* "Yes, to Angela, since 1965."

"And what's the exact date of your anniversary?"

Why that question? My mind wandered to a favorite picture—me in my uniform and Angela in a frothy white dress reminiscent of the desserts she would eventually create. Her eyes sparkled, and a single tear had trickled down my face, only to be snatched away by Angie's thumb as we said our vows.

And the flowers: red ranunculus and orange poppies had dotted Angela's bridal bouquet and the spaces around the altar. Her decision to include those flowers had driven her mother nuts. She said Angie would "look like a harlot" with those red flowers in her hands. But Angie had insisted and even bought her own bouquet. The pride I felt when I looked at my girl was a feeling I'd never forget.

Tap tap tap. "Mr. Raffaelo? What's your anniversary date?" NURSE asked again.

Another image appeared in my mind. The paper invitation enclosed in a glass frame hanging on our foyer wall. Our wedding had been quite the party. Over one hundred friends and family had gathered to see an airman like me get married to the prettiest gal around. Despite our difficulties, I'd marry Angela all over again.

Everything else appeared in my mind—the people, the weather, the dress, the flowers, the cake, for God's sake—but I could not recall our wedding date, one of the happiest days of my life.

Just yesterday, I'd misplaced my wallet and now this. My fingers shook. "I don't know," I whispered. "I can't remember."

CHAPTER 3: MARISSA

The call from Dad's number came in as I was shuttling Cam and Eli to swimming lessons. Finally, the perfect summer day—almost aqua sky and cottony, white clouds. A day away from the clinic, time to spend with the boys and let them burn off their boundless energy. My time with the kids was precious, too important to miss. Once I saw who was calling, I should have let voicemail pick up.

But the voice on the line wasn't Dad's at all. "Marissa Raffaelo-Moretta?"

"Yes? May I ask who's calling? This is my father's phone number." A beep sounded in the background, almost like a—

"This is Holly, your father's PCA at Miami Valley Hospital. He's doing okay, but I wanted to let you know he's here."

Flashes of shiny steel and grim faces filled my thoughts. "The hospital? What happened?" My pulse thumped, and my gaze flicked to the rearview mirror: cars lined up behind me as I slowed, hoping to find a stopping spot on the roadside.

"He was brought here after a fall. He's alert, and that's all the information I have, but your mother—Angie, I think—wanted me to call you."

"Is she there too?"

"Yes."

"And how is Dad?

"Would you like to speak with him?"

The bleak roaring inside me waned. "Yes, yes, I would, and thank you, Holly. Thank you."

A quick tapping noise sounded over the line, and then heavy breathing.

"Dad? Is that you?"

"It is." His voice almost creaked in the reply.

"What happened?"

"What happened? I'll tell you what happened." He slowly filled me in on the details, from the moment he fell to the questions the nurse asked to the current idea that he wanted to get out of "this damn hospital" to a new fear about what he might have: dementia.

I stared out the car window as cars coasted by, brilliant spots of color against the emerald backdrop of the woods. *Life moves on, even if individual people seem to repeat the same actions.* "All right, Dad. I'm sorry this happened to you. A few things though. Are you okay? Are you in pain? What made you fall? And did the doctor say you *have* dementia?"

"The doctor didn't say anything, dammit! I haven't *seen* any doctor yet, and if you ask me, it's taking too long for them to get here." Dad paused, and a thickness settled into his voice that wasn't there before. "But I couldn't *remember*. These fucking legs, and now I've got dementia. I just know it."

Fucking? Dad normally stuck with less egregious curse words—maybe it was worse than I thought. But Dad's backstory made me hesitant. He'd called me several times over the last few years about one perceived health crisis or another. A year ago, he claimed to have melanoma. Instead of coming by to tell me his news, he'd called me and said, "Marissa, I have cancer." No greeting. No beating around the bush. Scared the shit out of me. After a few torrid days—hours that seemed to have no end as I tried to gather medical information for Dad between my job and parenting duties—it turned out Dad had misunderstood everything his doctor had told him.

A few weeks later, Dad had moved on to the next (non)crisis: brain cancer. Too bad my brothers weren't medical professionals; they had more patience for dealing with my father, and at least Nico, the perpetual bachelor and baby of the family, had more time. Gabe? Currently stationed with the military in Germany and the father of three young children. Well, he'd be less useful.

"You're almost eighty years old for goodness' sake!" I slapped my hand to my forehead, astounded at Dad's ability to draw incorrect conclusions when he had no evidence. What had happened to the father who required positive proof before he'd believe anything? The man who always said, "I'll believe it when I see it." That man was long gone and oddly enough, I wanted him back.

In the back seat, Cam and Eli continued to toss miniature dinosaurs back and forth and discuss the attributes of the butterfly ("They smell with their feet!" and "Their wings are made of scales!"), oblivious to the conversation with my dad. We'd just spent time examining the chrysalis nestled inside the boys' butterfly garden kit. They'd peppered me with questions: When will the cocoon be ready? What's it made of? What will the butterfly look like? Will we be able to hold it? Equal parts grateful for my inquisitive boys and irritated by all the questions, I had jumped for joy when the clock struck the hour—time to get ready for swimming lessons.

Biting my tongue, I said, "Dad, listen. I know that fall must have been scary for you, but let the doctors check you out. Let's see *why* you fell and if something is wrong. And then, if you think dementia is a problem, we'll look into that too. What do you say?" I glanced down at my lap, where my hand tangled with the pink frayed end of my sundress. A bad habit I hoped the boys didn't pick up.

"But what if I have it? What if I have dementia? And your mother here, she's not being helpful." Either the line cracked, or Dad's voice did.

Cradling my head in my hands, I wished Dad could see me as I rolled my eyes along with my shoulders. He'd give me that sheepish look he always gave when he finally realized how inane his behavior was. Enough time or energy did not exist to go through this with him so often. "You know, you're at a hospital *right now*. Why don't you mention it to the doctor when they come in."

"But…"

"Listen, I'm sorry, but I can't discuss this. We're in the car on the way to the boys' swimming lessons. I can come by, but it will have to wait until afterward." Talking to Dad at this stage in his life was like talking to the boys: it required a firm, no-argument voice, forced me to pull out my authoritative, professional persona, and distance myself from this man, this conversation so I could continue with my day. It was like playing parent to *my* parent, an awkward and disturbing feeling for me.

Dad hadn't been home much when we were kids; he couldn't comprehend the need to get outside and run around or the trouble two little boys, ages four and six, could get into. And Cam. He'd been diagnosed with a tree-nut allergy when he'd gotten into a cashew jar at almost a year old. It was clear within moments that those nuts were not friends. We'd hauled him to the emergency room and then the next day to an allergist. After a detailed personal and family history, a battery of tests, and plenty of tears, tree nuts were pronounced a life-threatening hazard. Limiting such products at home wasn't a problem, even after Eli arrived. Thankfully, while Cam was sensitive and could go into anaphylactic shock if he ingested tree nuts, he didn't have an issue with being in the same room as a jar of almond butter, even if it was open. Still, I left my beloved nut butters at work, as did Will. And if we succumbed to a sandwich while on duty, we showered at the rec center before we came home and left the dirty work clothes and scrubs in the laundry room.

That level of alertness and how it weighed on me—Dad would never have understood. Plus, I craved the forty-five minutes to myself. God, how I longed for the time—along with a glass of red wine—but that wouldn't happen at three-thirty in the afternoon.

"Well, that won't work, will it, Angie?" Dad's voice meandered from the phone, as if he were holding it out to Mom. A tap and ding sounded in the background, hospital noises that could be anything. "Tell her we need her here."

A light scuffing sound echoed on the line, and then Mom's voice, thin and weak. "I think you should come over. It's bad...it might be bad."

"It *might* be bad, or it *is* bad? Which is it? Look, I don't mean to be ungrateful, but it's hard to pick up every time—"

A beep rang out, then the crash of a metal cart, followed by a "shit," possibly voiced by Dad. "Marissa?" he said. "You better get over here. Please. Something's not right. I can feel it."

Dad rarely said please, so what did this mean? Talk about the sandwich generation: I was it. Stuck between obligation to my parents and the desire to give my kids a lovely memory of swimming on a summer day. I glanced back again at the boys, who still played together quietly. "Let me get the kids situated, and I'll be right over. You're still at the emergency room, right?"

"Yes," Dad whispered. "Come soon. We *need* you."

"You need me or my expertise?" Either way, I'd be there, but his answer would be telling.

"*You.* You'll get whatever needs to be done, done, and...maybe you can bring your husband. He'll figure out what the problem is."

Will and I had both attended Ohio State for our post-baccalaureate programs, but my work involved all the body systems—the letters PNP, standing for pediatric nurse practitioner, sat behind my name. To anyone else, those letters meant something. Somehow, though, Will's letters—PhD, that he could be called "doctor" and I could not—held more weight for Dad. Will ranked higher than I did and probably always would.

"We'll get to the bottom of this. If the docs haven't come by before I get there, I can assess you too," I said.

"No need, honey. The docs and Will can do just fine."

My phone pinged with a text from Will. *Perfect timing*. With his schedule—his research involved time-sensitive experiments he still liked to perform himself—he rarely contacted me midday, but he had flexibility, and every once in a while, he reached out.

Will: *Guess what? I'll be home for dinner tonight.*

Me: *Great. Except I might not be. I need to get to the hospital for Dad. Maybe we'll be eating with my folks tonight.*

Will: *So maybe I won't be home. *wink emoji**

Me: *Ha! Can I drop the kids off with you? Do you have time? I don't want to take them to the hospital.*

Will: *Of course. You okay?*

Me: *Yep. Was headed to the pool with the kids. We didn't get there. But they're doing well. Maybe they can show you their talents next weekend? Are you working? And the cocoon—fingers crossed that this one emerges as a butterfly.*

Will: *No, not working. So yes to the pool. Can't wait to see them. I'll cross my fingers about the butterflies. What's their fascination with them anyway? But the only talents I want to see are *yours* you know.*

Me: *Insert eye roll here. As for the butterflies? Not sure. Maybe it's in the genes. Mom has always loved them. And the butterfly garden setup is pretty cool. Thanks so much. Love you.*

That Will Moretta, always the flirt, even years later. His words about the kids rang through my mind: *Can't wait to see them.* Dad had never said anything like that, at least not out loud. Did he look forward to seeing us? Had we made him proud? As the middle child, I played mediator so often—between Nico and Gabe, between them and Dad— my perspective felt skewed. Our familial connections had never seemed especially strong or unbreakable, and I'd craved a support level that maybe they couldn't give. But Will? I'd found a guy unlike my father, and though we had our moments, contentment filled me.

My phone pinged again. A rare text from Dad: *Are you coming?*

CHAPTER 4: FRANK

Angela placed a hand on my shoulder as I stared at the television monitor mounted high on the wall. Then she handed me a plastic cup of water and sat next to me in the metal chair. The hard, gray seating would bother Angie's back. Like always, she'd find a way to get back home or be anywhere but stuck here in this dreary box. But having her there felt right. She said nothing at first, just reached out and covered her hand with mine.

Once I had steadied my breathing even more and thought about what I wanted to say, I turned my head and looked into her eyes. "Did you see it?" I said.

"See what?"

"That pamphlet in the ambulance. The one about dementia…"

"We're here because you fell, Frank. I don't think—"

"But the other day—" Something clogged my throat. Just saying the words, that my mind might be leaving me, seemed wrong. Legs be damned. Without a mind, well, there was no sense in living.

"What aren't you telling me, Francesco?" The full first name. She only used it when she felt angry or worried or both. Just like Antonio. Right then, I didn't want to be a Francesco; the name held too much potential that had never been realized. I had always been just Frank. A retired air force guy who liked big trucks, the newspaper, a good baseball game, money, and a round of golf. But Angela could read me. She always had, from the moment I met her all those years ago.

"I only got a brief glimpse, but I saw...what the dementia signs are, all that jazz."

Angela's hand stilled over mine, and her shoulders stiffened. She went from looking directly at me to focusing across the way, her face stoic as she glanced at the washed-out cell phone notice on the wall. "I don't think you have it, Frank."

I flipped my palm and grabbed her fingers between mine, giving them a light squeeze. "What makes you so sure?"

"Sometimes women just know. Plus, my mom had it, remember? I spent enough time with her before she passed to know what dementia looks like. I don't care what the...paper said, and God only knows how you focused on that coming over here. You don't have dementia. That's final."

She patted my hand one time, rose from her chair, and kissed me on the forehead, ending the discussion, like always. It was a kiss she would have given the children or the grandchildren. One meant to mollify me.

All it did was make me angry.

How *could* she be so sure? She was so entrenched in her chocolate business, we barely saw one another except for a few scattered moments throughout the day, at dinnertime, and then again at sundown. Any time I ambled into her kitchen, she'd shoo me away or ask me to go somewhere else, saying she couldn't concentrate with me present. I was used to that behavior. But Angie *couldn't know* if I had dementia; she was too busy to notice.

My attention strayed to the television again; Angie had turned it on to the news, which featured a segment about summer days. The camera panned over several local farms, and I marveled at the tall green grass on the screen. We'd had a large amount of rain the last few weeks, and no matter how many times I sat on my riding mower, I couldn't seem to keep up with our lawn. Gabe had suggested hiring a service, but the feel of riding a tractor... It reminded me of the days when I was a kid and had dreams of being a farmer, complete with horses, cattle, poultry, and my brother as a sidekick. It reminded me of what never came to fruition.

•   •   •

Marissa flew into the room with splotchy red cheeks, a concerned look on her face. "Dad? How are you doing? What was the beep and crash on the phone? Are you okay?" She moved to my side, took a hand, and stroked the back of it. Her fingers helped warm the skin there—too much coldness here in the ER.

"Where's Will?"

Marissa's brow furrowed. "Will? He's with Cam and Eli..."

"Did you at least bring the big car? If so, we can get out of here. You ready to go, Angie?" She'd have candy orders to fill or weeds to pull. The usual litany of tasks she often listed when I asked, like a never-ending hamster wheel. Angie nodded but said nothing.

Marissa did though. "Wait a minute... I'm a little confused." She looked at the machine monitoring my vitals, then back at me. "You just asked me to come over here because you thought there was something seriously wrong. You told me you needed me here. If you don't need me here, what was that all about?"

"I'm feeling fine now, so I think we can go."

"But have you seen a doctor yet?"

"Well, no, but do I need to?"

Marissa smiled tightly, glanced at the tiled ceiling, and squeezed my fingers. "Listen, if Mom thought you needed to call 911 and take an ambulance to get here, then yes, I *do* think you need to get checked out."

"*I* called 911, not your mother."

"Okay, but either way. You're here now, and those legs have been giving you trouble lately. Let's see if the docs have any news. What do you say?"

"And what about Will?"

Marissa let go of my hand and crossed her arms over her chest. Then a knock sounded on the door jamb. *Speak of the— Nope.* Luke Butterfield, an old family friend, poked his head in.

"Luke! What are you doing here? It's good to see you. How long has it been?"

"Frank, let's just call it too long, how about that?" He extended his hand and shook mine, gentler than he might have in the past. Then he nodded at Marissa and leaned down, pulling Angie in for a hug. "Of course, I'd rather have seen you at the house, but I was here for orientation and overheard the last name. So of course I had to come see you."

Marissa smiled, and her stance relaxed. "You took the job! That's great news."

Back in the day, the kids had spent a lot of time with Luke. For a while there, I'd considered the possibility of Luke and Marissa together. Alas, they'd been fast friends, but nothing had ever developed. "He's like a brother," Marissa had said. Eventually, Angie and I came to accept that fact, but until Will came along, we had hoped.

A huge smile stretched across Luke's face. "I did—I meant to tell you all, but it's been hectic—and though I'm not *technically* working right now, and I haven't been given a badge yet, let me check you out. Purely off the record, of course. We need to still listen to what the attending will say."

I nodded. "Of course."

As Luke washed his hands, I glanced at Marissa, whose smile had turned to a scowl. This jumping around of behavior, cold to hot to cold. Where was it coming from? "What's the problem?" I asked. "You look upset."

"Upset? I *am* upset." She glared at Angie, who did and said nothing, and then directed her stare back at me as she gripped the bed rail. "You call *me* and tell me to scurry over, like it's a huge emergency. Never mind that you had me worried. Then when I get here, you tell me everything's okay and you want to leave and you don't need *me* to check you, but *Luke* can?"

"And?"

"You're kidding, right? If you don't know what's wrong with that, then I won't tell you. Instead, I will excuse myself for a moment while you visit with Luke." She let go of the bed rail then pulled the curtain over, yanked the door open, and left without looking back.

Luke raised his eyebrows. "I think she's upset, Frank."

"Why?"

"I suspect that's between the two of you." Taking the stethoscope from the IV pole next to me, Luke tapped the drum and then placed it against my heart. The cold made me shiver.

CHAPTER 5: MARISSA

My right eyelid twitched—a telltale sign of my annoyance—as I walked down the empty hall and into the restroom. After locking the door, I shut my eyes and imagined being at the pool with the kids, pulling my favorite lounge chair—tangerine bunting with huge cobalt nautical stripes—as near to the pool as a chair could get but far enough from the small crowd of children there for swim lessons. About twenty feet to my right at my imaginary pool, both boys dipped their feet into the crystalline water as their instructor motioned with his hands to get in. A stray beach ball, propelled by the strong summer breeze, bounced by my feet and skittered against the fence, causing a tree swallow that had been perched on the edge of the chain link to take flight. The imaginary heated aromas of sunscreen and chlorine floated in the air and caressed my senses, and within moments, the tension that had been sitting on my shoulders eased.

Maybe I would be the same way at Dad's age. Call the boys all in a panic, wondering if my demise was imminent. But would I dismiss my children's knowledge and wisdom so easily? A daughter wasn't a part of my equation, but I sure as shit knew that if I did, I would hold her with the same regard as the boys. But Dad...

Years ago, Dad had lectured me about the difference between boys and girls. "The male brain is wired differently," he said, mired in the binary way of thinking. "The male brain—it can do different things. We see things in a more systematic way and, better, I think. We don't rely on emotions so much."

Even then, Dad's statement shocked me, stunning me into silence. Neither Gabe nor Nico had come to my rescue that day. My only reprieve had been Mom's rare comment, muttered after tears welled in my eyes.

"Your dad's full of shit, Marissa," she whispered. "You're only nine, and I'm sorry to use that language, but it's true. It might not always be wise to believe what he says."

But what kid doesn't believe her father? If he had so little confidence in me, in my training...

Oh, why did I let him get to me this way? Maybe it was Dad's age, maybe it was narcissism on his part, a focus only on him and his desires. Maybe crabbiness pervaded me because I wanted to be with my boys. Maybe I was tired of having my skills dismissed. Whatever the case might have been, I needed to step up, play the proper role: supportive daughter and informed clinician. I shrugged my shoulders, washed my hands, and headed back to Dad and Mom.

Pulling the door open, I looked around at the brightly lit space, still devoid of a doctor. The staff would get two more minutes to send someone in before I hunted them down. Throwing my credentials around wasn't something I did often, but I knew how hospitals ran. The more letters after your name, the more they were willing to listen, and if those two letters were *M* and *D*, well then, you were usually in luck. I didn't have those, but Luke did, and I'd use them to our advantage.

Just like when we were younger, Luke tucked himself next to me and whispered into my ear. "Your Dad looks fine, honestly, though I am concerned about the falling. By the way, where's Nico? Did he arrive yet?"

Well, that was a non sequitur. "Did Dad or Mom call him? In the rush to get over here, I didn't message him or Gabe. Oops."

A bit of color flushed Luke's cheeks, contrasting with his blue stripe button-down. "Uh, I got a text he was on his way over. Thought it would be nice to say hi to four-fifths of the Raffaelo clan, you know?"

The last we'd all seen Luke was at his first interview in March. Since then, when he was in town, he begged off meeting up with Will and me. "Too busy, not enough time to fit you in," he said. Since we were good friends and knew we'd see him eventually, Will and I gave it no thought; I assumed Nico hadn't either.

I shot a heads-up text to Nico and Gabe. "Well, I haven't seen him yet, but I'm going to the desk to find out when we'll be speaking to the doctor in charge." I took two steps to the right and looked up at Luke.

"Want me to go?" he said.

Luke meant well, but I didn't need help, yet. "Nah. Just stay here and be with them, will you please?"

Leaving Luke with my folks, I walked to the nurses' station, which sat empty. The beeps and whistles, shoes scuffing against the linoleum, wheels creaking on the carts that moved down another hallway—they all filled the air. A hospital had always comforted me, the smells and sights included, but when you were there for a loved one, everything changed. This time, the antiseptic smell irritated my nose, and the whir of the automatic doors harassed my nerves. Tired and grumpy, I wanted to know more about my dad. Tapping my fingernails against the counter, I took a deep breath. *Where is everyone?*

A few minutes passed, and a brown-haired nurse rounded the corner, an apology on her lips. "I am *so* sorry. We had a code blue. I'm sure you can appreciate that."

"Not a problem. I'm just curious what you can tell me about Frank Raffaelo. I'm his daughter."

"Are you on the release form?"

"I would hope so. Can you check?"

She clicked open her computer program and scanned the documents. "And your name is?"

I held out my ID for her. "I should be there."

She nodded. "Okay then. I don't have much, but the doctor is on his way down. Doesn't look like he broke anything, but he was disoriented upon arrival. They're keeping him for observation, maybe a few tests. He was also dehydrated, hence the IV."

I thanked the nurse, and by the time I made it back to the room, the doctor had just arrived. A quick introduction to the doctor, which indicated my relationship to Frank and Angie.

"I was just telling your husband here—"

A rush to correct *that* impression. "Luke isn't my husband, just a dear friend. My husband is at home with the kids."

"Oh, my mistake, my apologies. Anyway, I was telling Dr. Butterfield that Mr. Raffaelo is, for the most part, okay. He can be discharged at any time." The doctor jotted down a few notes on paper and then moved toward the computer used to chart everything.

Confusion settled on my shoulders. Had he just said— "Wait a minute. Discharged? Are you kidding me? Do you even know *why* he fell?"

"Well, no, but it says in his chart that his vitals are okay, his blood work looks good, a little low on sodium, maybe, but that can be fixed, and he's diabetic. It could have been a hypoglycemic episode that caused him to fall. We see things like that all the time."

The doctor's nonchalance exasperated me. "And you're not concerned with trying to find out the cause? What if it happens again?" I asked.

He stayed silent as a redness stole over his cheeks. Of course, I didn't give him time and jumped to the next complaint. "This isn't the first time he's fallen, Doctor. And with all due respect, your people did nothing then. I can't let you do nothing this time. Did he experience leg weakness?"

"I can't be sure. I didn't ask him."

Where did this guy go to medical school? "Then let's do it now." Turning toward Dad, I directed my questions to him. "Did your legs feel weak before you fell, or were you dizzy?"

"I wasn't dizzy," Dad said. "I know what dizziness is. My legs felt...unsteady, like they couldn't support my body, and I fell. I couldn't...couldn't make my feet do what they were supposed to do. I tried, but..."

"And how are your legs now, Dad?"

"I have no idea."

I looked at the doctor. "Did you test his leg strength? His reflexes? Believe me, I *want* him to be fine, and I'd love for him to go home tonight. But has he tried to support himself yet?" Each of my questions kept time with the vitals monitor.

Dad answered that question himself. "Nope. I haven't done much moving from this bed."

"And do you think you can?"

"I'd like to try. I'm already tired of being here. And tonight's the last game of the cup finals."

Oh for the love of.

The doctor shook his head but agreed with me. "Okay," he said. "Mr. Raffaelo, let's see if you can make it to the bathroom in the hallway. That's not far, but if you can get there in one piece, that will tell us something."

Due to the number of blankets and monitor attachments, Dad had a bit of a time adjusting himself, but eventually, he pulled his legs over the bedside. "Okay, here I go!" he said as his toes hit the floor.

CHAPTER 6: FRANK

The room spun into chaos as my entire body tumbled, the edges of my vision fading in and out. The people in the room moved quickly to get me back onto the bed. My legs paid no attention to my mind, and the doctor gently positioned my limbs and tucked me under the thin covers. What had happened? What did this mean? My life as a golfer—was it over? My independence—would that be gone? These legs—they threatened everything good about my life.

I looked at Marissa, who fumed, her cheeks all splotchy and red once again, like she was going to let loose at any moment. Luke placed a hand on her arm and stood with a placid face, as though he was ready to talk her down. Angie sat still in her chair, a deer in headlights. And the doctor? He wrinkled his brow. With what—confusion?

"That felt like what happened on the ladder," I said. "I just couldn't support myself anymore."

"So, Doc... What say you?" Marissa asked. "I'm thinking that he's not being discharged tonight, and that's final."

The doc didn't know what hit him, that's for sure. He turned around and mumbled, "I'll be right back."

Marissa stood with her hands on her hips, her stance wide, a fighting form if I'd ever seen one.

"Dammit," I whispered. "I want to go home." I'd never liked hospitals. Too many friends had come and gone from house to hospital over the years. Most of them went in and didn't come out. I wasn't ready to part ways with my life yet. A weight settled right on my chest, unrelenting, tiresome. If I wasn't careful—

"Dad." Despite the heat in her eyes, Marissa's tone was soft. "I want you to go home, but you can't right now. We don't know what's wrong with your legs. We need to find out what's causing the weakness, but barring that, we at least need to let you recover." She stepped closer to me and looked directly into my eyes. "Have you seen yourself?" She searched the room for a tabletop mirror. When she didn't find it, she pulled out her phone and snapped my picture. "Look." She thrust the phone in my face.

Was that me? A face, drawn and pale, like someone who'd just finished boot camp. "Well, it has been a long day."

"I knew you'd say that, Dad. Please..." She put a gentle arm on my legs. "Let's speak to the doctor, see what he says about anything else that might be wrong, and we'll go from there. I don't want you to go home and fall again, and on those legs, you might do that."

"But—"

Luke stepped forward, eyebrows lowered, a frown on his face. "Mr. Raffaelo, Frank, with all due respect, you need to listen to Marissa. I'm in complete agreement with her. As a physician and someone who's known you a long time, a friend. You need to be *here*—not at home. And once we know more, we'll see what happens."

Luke was a good kid. Always had been. That third son to me. In all these years, I had yet to hear a word come out of his mouth that wasn't the truth. I needed to trust them both. No matter how hard that might be.

"That's *fine*," I said. "I'll try to get some rest. But Angie?" I turned my head toward her. "What about you? Do you want to go home?"

Angie shook her head. "I'm fine." She pulled her purse against her chest and rested her head against the wall. We didn't need any words then to communicate our worry; it hung there, tangible, in the atmosphere—

"What's up, bitches?" Nico rushed into the room, cardboard drink holder with three coffees in hand. He'd been entering rooms that way for a while. The tone, the words, the smug look—everything bothered me. He glanced at me, then Marissa, Angie, and Luke. A smile spread across Nico's face, one that reminded me of my brother.

"Coffee? I don't need coffee," I said. "I need rest!" My breathing hitched. A hiccup caught in my throat. I swallowed, or tried to, but that heaviness chipped away at my sternum.

"Sorry, Dad, it's not for you. Not yet. If they say coffee is fine, and you want one, I'll go get you one. It's for the rest of us. We might be here a while, you know?" Nico passed the coffees around, thankful murmurs following. "Mom, I didn't get you one since you don't like coffee. But if you want hot cocoa or something, just say the word."

Angie pursed her lips and voiced my thoughts. "Nico, how many times do I have to tell you to watch your language! It's, it's so...crass."

Despite my fatigue, I looked at Nico, who straightened his spine. "Mom, that's who I am. Take it or leave it."

"I just think that this isn't the time or place—"

"You know what? When *is* the time or place? Why do we always have to—"

Marissa tipped her chin at Nico. "This coffee tastes great. Where'd you find it?" She peeked at Nico over her cup's edge and then slid her glance to Luke.

We all knew what she was doing: diffusing the situation, like she always did. I breathed a relieved sigh, but moisture beaded on my skin. My whole body cooled as a fog populated my brain. Nico's voice trailed away. And then, the blare of my monitors—

"Shit," Marissa said and plunked her coffee on the side table. "Sorry, Mom. Nico, get out of here. We might all be too much for Dad. Wait for me outside. We'll give Dad time to settle and update Gabe." The noise continued to blast away at my skull, like shell casings that kept on coming. Her warm hand rested on my forehead, and soon the cadence of the beeps slowed. "Breathe calmly and deeply, Dad. You're fine."

"Am I?"

"You will be. This is stressful to your body, and you're right—you need rest. I'm going to leave Luke here with you for a few minutes, and I'll be right back." Marissa leaned in and patted me on the knee.

"You'll be fine all right," Luke said and took a sip of his beverage. "Just you, me, Angie, and this latte. Life is good."

With one last glance, Marissa slipped out of the room, and I scooted my body back against the pillows. The softness formed around me. *If I shut my eyes and go to sleep, maybe I'll wake up in my house, in my bed.*

CHAPTER 7: MARISSA

Pressing Gabe's number on my phone, I hauled Nico to the small reception area around the corner. Gabe picked up on the second ring just as Nico winked at me. Germany was six hours ahead, so my older brother should be chilling for the night, unless one of the kids was having trouble sleeping. I had a full schedule the next day, the always jam-packed Tuesday, so informing Gabe and getting Dad's situation ironed out took priority over Nico's attention to Luke's coffee preferences. That didn't mean I wasn't curious. *How did he know he liked lattes?*

"Dad fell when he tried to put weight on his legs," I said to Gabe on speaker.

"I know—you texted me," Gabe replied. A bleat and crash sounded in the background, and Gabe grunted. "I'm done for on this game! Hold on, let me pause, and then you'll have my full attention."

"Sorry to interrupt, but I'm talking about a few minutes ago." I filled Gabe in on what had just happened, to which Nico, a born realist with a good amount of common sense said, "I missed that. They wanted to discharge him already? That seems premature."

"Well yeah, I agree. And I know Dad wants his autonomy, but he fell last year, and I think we need to push for answers this time. His vitals look okay right now, for his age, but—"

"No, I get it," Gabe said. "What can I do?"

Nico and I looked at one another and shrugged. "Probably nothing," I said. "We figured we'd at least let you know what was happening."

"Appreciate that, and if there's anything I can do, tell me. Make calls, whatever support you need."

Gabe had been an outstanding big brother over the years, mainly protective, sometimes informative. He'd taught me how to drive on back roads and offered to beat up a bully when I was in middle school. Of course, he'd given me a rough time about past boyfriends and choosing OSU, but Gabe was someone anyone could count on. He'd even travel in a heartbeat if we needed him. The military might have something to say about that though...

"Getting back to Dad is what we need to do. Luke is handling the situation, but it's not his place."

Gabe's voice sounded surprised when he said, "Luke? What's he doing there?"

I glanced up at Nico, who had taken a sudden and distinct interest in his phone. "We'll give you those details at another time, but Luke is back—got a job here."

"Ah, yes. I remember now. Well, it'll be good to see him the next time I'm on leave. We'll talk soon, I guess. Tell Dad and Mom I'll be in touch."

The call ended as one from Will came in. Waving my hands at Nico to head back to Dad, I whispered a hello and asked if the kids were okay.

"Yes. You won't believe this, but they fell asleep in Cam's room, and I'm resting in the bed for an afternoon siesta." Will let out an exaggerated yawn. "It's lonely here without you."

While a bed to myself delighted me, Will preferred me in it, and when we slept in the bed together, he'd always sling at least one arm over my body, snuggling in as far as he could without causing me discomfort.

I laughed. "You'll be fine. I'll be home tonight, and if not, it's one night, Will. *One* night. So what's up?"

He was just calling to check in, which warmed my heart, but I had nothing substantial to report. Then I mentioned that consults might be in order and rehab could strengthen Dad's legs and prevent future falls.

"I agree, but what does that mean for you? For Nico? I don't want you to take too much on, Mar, like you always seem to do."

"Not sure what that means for anyone. And as far as taking too much on—you love me for it."

"I do."

I sighed. "Remember when we said those words? That was a great day, wasn't it?"

He yawned, which sounded genuine this time. "It was."

"Honestly? Go take a nap. I mean, a real sleep. The rug rats will be up soon, and then you'll really be tired out. And, hey, did you see my note about the chrysalis? I'm not so sure what do do with it. Can you look, maybe check out the instructions—they should be near the box, maybe on the mantle. I'm not sure what we're doing wrong with these caterpillars. I'd love to see them transform as much as the boys would."

"Will do. Maybe the company sent a bad batch. We'll investigate, and before you say it, I know—don't let them know I'm investigating. Stealthy is my middle name, remember?"

Talking to Will always brought my blood pressure down, and despite the stressful situation, our chat helped gather the enormous amount of information bouncing around inside my brain. After hanging up with him, I scrolled through the calendar on my phone, looking at my appointments and such for the next several weeks. Here we were on June 15. If I could take time off to help with Dad this week, he might recover better and sooner. Will and the kids might have to adjust to a different schedule, but we still had a lot of summer left, and they'd always been resilient. I could hope for the same this time.

With that thought in mind and a desire to stretch my legs, I turned right instead of left out of the reception area and took the long way back, listening to the hospital's busy thrum. My mind wandered to the boys; they'd miss me if I wasn't back by dinner, but my bet was on a trip to the Cloverbell Diner—our favorite nut-free place—for chocolate chip pancakes. A warmth bloomed in my chest, and I pulled my phone out of my pocket to look at a few swim pictures from two days before. In one, Eli stood at the south end of the rectangular pool, wrestling with his goggles, and in another, water dripped from his dark lashes onto his dimpled cheeks. In that moment, he looked a lot like Dad had as a kid, something I hadn't noticed before. The next photo caught Cam at the crest of a cannonball. The glee on his face reminded me of Nico, and I zoomed in on the picture—

"Oof." My phone spilled, and I looked up at the obstacle in my way: Nico and Luke, entwined in a hug, Nico's back to me, Luke's eyes bright with surprise. My jaw dropped, and I stood there, heart thudding, mind trying to process. I kept my gaze trained on them as I bent to pick up my phone. "I'm...what...I'll be..."

Luke stepped back from Nico, his cheeks the color of the barn on my parents' property, but he didn't take his hand off Nico's arm. Nico blinked and gripped Luke's fingers.

"I'll see you back in the room, Nico." Turning on my heel, I slipped my phone back into my pocket, placed a hand over my heart, and giggled. What the hell had I just walked in on?

Behind me, Nico called. "Marissa! Wait!"

I turned. Luke was no longer there. "Wait for what?"

"I can explain."

"I'm guessing that's how you know about the latte preference, but please—don't feel you need to explain. Not right now. I'm not gonna lie. I'm surprised. Even though we've been friends forever, I had no idea Luke was gay. On the other hand, I'm not surprised at all. But I already have too much in here," I tapped my head, "to deal with anything else right now. Don't take this the wrong way, but since I have the medical experience, why don't you go home?"

Nico tugged at his shirt collar and tapped his fingers against his phone; he was agitated. About me catching him with Luke? About Mom and Dad? The energy to ask didn't exist.

"I'll call you when I know something—if we get any information," I said. "No sense in both of us being here, and you can take a shift another time."

Nico leaned in and patted my shoulder. "Are you sure? Please don't say anything to Mom or Dad—I'm not ready. I mean, we had *that* conversation already, but the whole Luke thing...might not go over well. And not that I want to talk about it, but with you, it would be easier. Maybe you can be a part of the trial run." His cheeks flared scarlet, and his gaze bounced from wall to wall, very uncharacteristic of my always suave, always collected brother. Very telling too.

My curiosity was piqued, but I hadn't lied. Only a certain amount of information would fit into my brain. The details could wait, but a gleeful bubble spread through my chest at the thought of Luke and Nico. "I'm sure. Just go."

With a deep yawn, as if this stressful afternoon had been too much for him, he nodded. "All right. We'll talk later. Now it's time for me to weave some dreams."

He hummed a few bars of the old Gary Wright tune. He was the master at doing such things, suggesting a catchy song in the middle of conversation.

Maybe I should have thanked him for maintaining levity, but a groan escaped me. "First, it's not even dinner time. And second, no, you didn't."

His voice resonated against the hospital walls as he warbled the corny lyrics about the night and morning light with a wicked gleam in his eyes.

"I'll help you get to that morning light all right, Nico. If I were you, I'd go before I change my mind and grill you till the cows come home. Because don't think that I don't have a billion questions about you and Luke."

Nico saluted and walked away, whistling. He looked back once and winked at me.

I gave him the bird.

CHAPTER 8: HER

How many times had they been at the hospital in the last few years? *Too many to count*, she thought, as she laid her head back against the cold wall. Staying here too long would eventually drive her batty, but for now she could play content. Closing her eyes, she thought about all the orders she had to fill at home and the list on her well-worn calendar, and one word came to mind: *busy*. That's what she was. Too busy to be sitting with him in a hospital room with chalky walls and weird smells.

What had he done this time to fall, and when would he ever learn? Her mother had warned her about men like him, told her they'd always know better no matter what happened in life. Ha! He might think he knew better, but... She thought back to the day they met; she'd been smitten. And why? What made her want to throw away her own plans to stay single? On days like this, when so much rattled inside her head and her lists overflowed, she rued the day she ever said yes to him. Cursed the day she'd had children. The children who seemed to push their noses where they didn't belong. And yet...

As her daughter came back into the room, she looked up at her, a far more capable woman than she'd ever been at her age. Looked at the scowl on her face, the worry lines, the way she pursed her lips. Maybe something *was* wrong with him; maybe this hadn't been his fault. If that were the case, then what? Should she be scared? Should she be upset?

The woman shook her head and concentrated on the television screen, the newscaster's mellow tone. Her mother had talked to her about that too. "Ignore what you can while you can, and sometimes, the fear becomes more manageable," she'd say. Those days were in the past though, and Mom had been gone a while. Hadn't she?

CHAPTER 9: FRANK

Making it home to watch the last game of the Stanley Cup Finals never materialized. Late that afternoon, an unfamiliar doctor wearing black plastic glasses loomed over me. Next to him, Marissa had a frown on her face. The room's stillness gnawed at me. The calm before the storm, as my mother used to say. My sudden cough disrupted the quiet.

"I've asked for it all, Dad. A neuro consult, an endocrine consult. The doctors here aren't happy with me, but you can't go home. Not yet—how are you going to get to the bathroom?" Marissa said.

Always questions from that kid. Good, common-sense inquiries and a need to understand the world. Like Antonio and his quest to make sense of his surroundings. He'd failed, and I'd failed him, but... Why did this have to happen today of all days? Couldn't I just wallow in my sadness without having to overthink things? And why was it that when shit hit the fan Antonio came to mind? I blinked, forcing myself to answer Marissa's question: "Your mom can help me."

Marissa glanced over at Angie, who still sat hugging her purse, narrowed eyes, thin lips. Probably tired at this hour. "Uh, of course I can help him," she said.

Angie's words lacked confidence. One of three things could be at play: she didn't want to help, she didn't think she could help, or she was petrified by the idea of helping a grown man to the bathroom. But she'd changed diapers for three kids and several grandkids. The least she could do would be to assist her husband. Maybe I had misinterpreted the look on her face.

Marissa's voice rang sharp against the hospital walls. "Dad, see? I don't mean this to be harsh, but you need someone who's strong and knows what they're doing." She looked quickly at Angie. "Sorry, Mom." Then she directed her gaze back at me. "I really think rehab will be the best place for you."

Rehab? What the hell? No one had mentioned rehab to me before. I'd heard of rehab, and though I didn't know exactly what went on there, I had to get home. *My home.* Not to a place called "rehab" with people I didn't know. People I didn't care about. Chances were, if I went there, I'd never go back home. Like those pets you take to the veterinarian's office and then— I buried the thought. That wouldn't happen; I wouldn't allow it, and neither would Marissa. My gut told me so. But I knew how to play Marissa's game. Give her a bit of what *she* wanted and eventually, I'd get what *I* wanted. "What happens at rehab?"

"They can work on strengthening your legs and get you walking again."

Walking *again*? Like I couldn't walk now? *Christ. I couldn't walk.* How had this happened? I'd taken all my medications the way I was supposed to. Exercised every day. Lived a good life. What else was I supposed to do? Was this God's way of getting back at me for failing Antonio? For failing Angie? The kids? Why was I thinking of failure and legacies and end-of-life things now? Did being inside the cockpit of a hospital do that to you? That, along with years of military training—how many times had the drill instructor yelled about smelling like failure? My last meal rose in my throat. "No, your mom can help me."

I glanced at Angie, hoping she'd jump in on the conversation and defend me. Say she would help in whatever way she could. Even though she'd already *said* she'd help, she needed to stand resolute about it, be a strong soldier. When I looked at her, though, doubt set in. *Would* she be able to help me? And what about the doctor... Why wasn't he saying anything?

Marissa forged ahead instead. "No, Dad, she can't help you. She can't lift you out of the bed to get you to the bathroom. She can't help you shower. I'm sorry to say it—Mom can do many things, but what needs to be done now doesn't fall on that list of capabilities. And *you* can't fix things. I'm your POA, and I'm your concerned daughter, so my guess is the choice will be out of your hands: it's rehab or you stay here in the hospital."

Marissa crossed her arms over her chest, a scowl front and center on her face. Boy could she be a hard-ass when she tried. Was she this bossy with her patients? She'd have made a good military member. Where had the little dark-haired girl I'd raised gone? She had to be in there somewhere. I just had to find her.

"Can't *you* understand, Marissa? I want to go *home*." I pulled at the bed's dingy plastic railing and concentrated on it. Anything to keep my anger at bay. "Home to my couch. My kitchen. My porch. My *television*. Home to my food and bed. Home to—"

"Yes, I *can* understand. But can *you* understand? You can't walk, Dad. *You can't walk!*"

Her voice shook as she said the words, and she stormed out the door. The doctor wordlessly followed her. A dead silence settled on the room, and the air crackled with negative energy. Angie just kept blinking her eyes under the strong fluorescent lights. An aide popped her head in and back out again, not even asking if I needed anything; had she witnessed the entire scene? Too bad if she had. I didn't do anything wrong. Neither did Marissa, technically, unless you counted yelling at your father as a transgression.

"Frank?" Angie whispered.

"Yes?"

"What's going to happen?"

"I'm not sure. I want to get out of here, but I don't know if Marissa will let me do that." To be fair, it wasn't all her fault, maybe not her fault at all. But she made a good target right then.

"Well why not?" Angie's voice was quiet, as if not to disturb any last shred of peace.

"Weren't you listening? She just went through why not."

"I *was* listening! It's just that... She talks so fast. You look okay. Why can't we go home?" She leaned back against her chair again and tipped her head up, looking at the lights. She closed her eyes and breathed deeply.

I mimicked her actions before speaking once more, trying to draw strength from deep within, like Antonio used to do. "I'm working on it, Angie. I'm working on it. We'll see what we can do. But my guess is I won't be heading back home anytime soon."

"Well, I need to get home. I have orders to fill."

My head fell against the pillows, and I clenched my jaw. *Those orders.* Why was it always about her goddamned orders? Did she not notice the bandages on my arm and the hospital bed? The hisses and beeps and hums. What in the hell? "Then go, Angie. Just go. Nico's here somewhere, and so is Marissa. Luke might even still be around. I'll be *fine.*"

"If you're sure."

I'm not sure, but it seems you can't be bothered to be here. "Yeah, I'm sure."

"All right then. I'll see you later."

Angie leaned in and kissed me, and I smelled the vanilla scent in her hair. It made me miss home, and I hadn't been gone that long. Positive thinking on my end—that I'd be heading home in just a few hours—wouldn't make it so, but I concentrated on that idea anyway. Fatigue settled in as I adjusted myself against the mattress, leaned my head back, and closed my eyes. While thoughts of Antonio usually camped in my brain's far corners, the mentions of him and this horrible, awful, day brought him fully into my dreams.

He stood silhouetted at the lake near our old house. Towel in hand, foot on the largest boulder lining the beach. Full of strength, vitality that fifteen-year-olds possessed. Next to him, body coiled, poised to hit—an unknown boy. He yelled words I couldn't hear at Antonio, but they rushed me all the same, moving from the tips of my toes to my kneecaps, then to my shoulders and fingers.

"What's going on?" I shouted. "What are you saying?"

No reply came. The boy extended his arms, pushing against Antonio's chest. I rushed forward, but an invisible barrier kept me from reaching the scene.

"Antonio!" I yelled.

The boy's voice carried over mine. "What's wrong with you? We don't mess around with people like you. It's *unnatural*." He sneered and pushed Antonio again.

My brother gritted his teeth and bent at the waist, as if he was going to charge the boy. Before he could do that, the boy snapped him with his wet towel, and bright red spattered across Antonio's chest. The crimson stain spilled outward, over the rocks, the sand, the boy. And then: a shove from the boy that toppled Antonio, and a resounding *crack* echoed as Antonio's head hit the boulder. "That's what you get for going after my brother, jackass," the boy said. "*See you in hell.*"

When I woke up, my skin felt clammy, and Antonio's face wasn't the only one still floating in my mind. Nico's hung there too.

CHAPTER 10: MARISSA

That conversation with my parents hadn't been my finest moment. Walking away in anger still seemed to creep back during stressful times even though I'd been working on that default response for years. I should have excused myself for a second time, concentrated on something good—the kids, the butterflies, vacations at Hocking Hills, Will—but reflexes can be difficult to retrain. *Just like old dogs.*

As I looped through the gleaming hallways thinking about the apology I should provide and where to go from there, the need to connect with my kids grew. I ducked into a quiet alcove and hit the button for a video call.

Will answered right away with a smile on his face. "Perfect timing! I want to head to the basement to put the laundry in the dryer. You can talk to the boys while I do that. I'll be right back." He winked and handed the phone over to Cam and Eli, who must have been right next to him on the couch.

Their faces filled the screen as I called a quick "Thank you!" to Will. Then, a chubby little finger came into view. I laughed. "Excuse me, but why are you thrusting your finger in my face?"

Eli poked his own face back to the phone. "Sorry. I wanted to show you where I'll put the butterfly when it hatches."

"When it hatches?" Surprise filled me. "You've already thought about where it's going to hang out once it's here?"

An enormous smile broke out across Eli's face. "Well, yeah."

"What he doesn't have," Cam said as he took the phone so both boys were visible, "is a backup plan for if it dies."

Eli gasped and turned toward Cam. "Don't! That's mean. It's not gonna die. It's just not."

"Come on, Eli. We haven't had one live yet. How do we know this one will?" Still holding the phone, Cam crossed one arm over his chest and glared at his brother. He looked so much like Will, another laugh threatened to escape; I knew better.

Eli wrinkled up his nose and stuck out his tongue at his big brother, which caused Cam to jab him in the arm, then the leg—

"Boys, listen." Both sweet faces gazed at me. "You're excited about the butterfly, and we'll chat all about its life cycle soon—birth, death, yes, Eli, even death—but right now, I just want to speak with *you*. I miss you. Can this wait until later? And can you please, *please* try to be kind to one another? You're the only siblings you have, you know."

"You say that a lot, Mom. How do you know?"

"How do I know you won't have any more siblings?"

"Yeah."

I shook my head. "Do you ask your Dad the tough questions too?" I knew they did, but this was one I didn't want to touch alone. "Why don't you ask your father that when he comes back?"

"Ask me what?" Will said.

"Aha! Now, I can say *you* have perfect timing!"

I assured Will I'd be home that night, most likely after the kids had already gone to bed. A quick round of air kisses to the boys and a lingering "I love you" to all three of my men, and the tension with my parents had lifted. The only thing left was to get in touch with rehab facilities. The social worker on call would do the same for us, but first-hand information would be good.

Assuring me that Dad would be in hospital for testing for at least two days, maybe three, the nursing staff provided a few rehab facility phone numbers, and several hours later, I had spoken to three. By then, the allure of home called to me. Luke had volunteered to stay with Dad—after shutting down my attempt to get information out of him about Nico—so I could get home before the entire night had passed. I cleared my schedule for the next day, hoping I'd easily juggle visiting Dad or Mom or both and taking care of the boys. At the moment, however, getting back to my house, my bed, sounded glorious. *Shit.* Maybe I was more like Dad than I thought.

My footsteps rang in the silence as I tiptoed from the garage through the kitchen, up the stairs, and into our bedroom. Even at this late hour, the shower was running. Change of plans: Will would appreciate a nice end to his overly long day. I dropped my clothes at the bathroom door and pulled back the shower curtain. Will gasped then smiled and reached for my hand. Stepping into the tub, I pulled the curtain closed behind me and hauled his body against mine.

Afterward, I stumbled toward the bed, towel still wrapped around me, and snuggled underneath the rumpled covers. The shower steam kissed my face as Will exited the bathroom, and then he leaned in, brushing his lips against my forehead. "Thanks for the surprise," he said.

Barely able to speak, I mumbled what I hoped came out as "I'll talk to you later" and "I love you" and then—nothing.

•　　•　　•

The next morning, the bright light streaming across the burgundy comforter announced I'd slept far longer than I should have. Summer meant a little less routine for the kids, but they had to be awake by now. So where were they, and what had they gotten into?

I threw back the covers, then moved to the bathroom, where I splashed cold water on my face and brushed my teeth. The toothpaste's minty freshness provided a quick burst of false energy, and I reached for my robe on the back of the bedroom door. After sliding my feet into my slippers, I padded down the stairs, listening for life from below.

Rounding the corner, I was surprised by Luke playing with my children in the family room. They sat on the multicolored rug, chess set on the coffee table, the kids engrossed in the moves. Cam had his hand posed over a rook while Eli sat in Luke's lap, accessing the chess board. How had Luke gotten in here? Had Will let him in? And who was staying with Dad?

He must have sensed me before I said anything because suddenly, Luke said, "Hey, how'd you sleep?"

"Great, thanks. With all the stress of yesterday and getting back late, I'm surprised I feel somewhat refreshed." A heat spread through my cheeks at the thought of *why* I hadn't gotten more sleep. "Felt a little like the power nap, and I haven't done that since nursing school. My job has been kind. What are you doing here, and how much sleep did *you* get?"

"Enough. I'm here because Nico's with your Dad, and I thought you could use help with something. I asked Will if you'd need a hand."

Letting the Nico comment go for a moment, I said, "The babysitter should be here soon. And," I looked at my watch, "she should be here already. Boys, did you—"

"Will called her off, Marissa. Gave her a little about what happened. Said you'd get back to her soon about needing her this week. He texted you all this."

I placed my hands on my hips and tried to keep the annoyance out of my voice. "Of course, I need her. Calling off for an entire week will never happen."

"I know. I also know better than to tell you to calm down, so just imagine whatever you want there. I do believe, however, that your husband was trying to be kind."

He was. "I *know.* Sorry. Too little rest agitates me." *As does thinking about what we need to do for Dad.* Hopefully we would have the three days the hospital spoke of. That would get us through Thursday. But would rehab take him—that would have to be approved—and for how long? Had anyone bothered to investigate the problem yet? Could *anyone* tell us if his issue was muscular or neurological or something else?

I could have stood in the family room for hours, going over in my head all the questions to ask, but that would get us nowhere. Instead, prying jumped to the forefront of my mind as a means of distraction from the impending shitshow with Dad. "So, Luke..." The scarlet tanager on the back patio caught my eye. "What's this about—"

"Nope. Not going there."

I turned toward him. "Why not? We've known you forever, it seems. Will we ever go there?"

"Maybe. Yes. Eventually."

Sigh. "You always were wonderful with one-word answers. But you know I won't drop this. I care about you. You get that, right?"

Luke had the decency to cast his eyes away and shake his head. "Yes, I know. But I think you need to talk to Nico first. It's...complicated."

And it probably was. Back in high school, even in college, nothing had given me the impression that Luke had any interest in men. Nothing. I could only guess that the journey toward that realization was something he wasn't yet ready to share. But old friends often hold a tether to a person's heart. To think that maybe this old friend would become an official part of the family? Well, that held a lot of appeal. Respect for both Nico and Luke and their boundaries meant being nosy would have to wait, again.

I clapped my hands together. "Boys, have you eaten yet?"

Cam and Eli looked up, eyes wide, and nodded.

"They had a snack after I got here," Luke said. "Fruit and a few crackers." He moved one of the chess pieces, and the boys groaned.

"And when did you get here? Before or after Will left?"

"Just as. The boys were still sleeping too. Will and I crossed paths. He was going to leave a key under the mat, but I told him that your dad had given me one already." Luke pointed to a pawn, silently giving a clue to Cam, who seemed flummoxed.

"What? When?" Why would Dad have given him a key?

Luke held up his hands, palms facing outward. "A bit odd, yes, but it was at the hospital. He worries about you, whether you realize it or not. Thinks you work too hard."

I shrugged then adjusted my robe, which had slipped off my shoulder.

"Hey now, he said it would be easiest. Gave me the babysitter's name, too, though I didn't need it. He's a wealth of information, that Frank."

Yeah. Dad gave a ton of information—maybe too much—to the people he liked. Sometimes, I thought he liked Luke better than Will. Knowing he gave Luke a key? That notion might be right. Maybe Nico had nothing to worry about, and Dad would accept Luke with open arms. He already loved him, after all. "All right. Well, I appreciate you getting here. I appreciate you letting me sleep. And I appreciate all that you're trying to do. But Nico, Gabe, and I need to make decisions about what's going to happen. As long as Dad's in rehab, I'm not worried. But—"

"But you want to figure this out."

"Exactly. I'd also love for people to let me finish my sentences." My smile would soften that tiny blow.

Luke hung his head before looking back up at me. "I'm sorry. And power in numbers, Marissa. You, me, Will. We all know how the body works or how to find answers. Let's put pressure on these people and see what they can tell us. If they can't tell us, then let's get him somewhere else."

Will wasn't a health professional, per se, but his background in the biological sciences lent a knowledge of the human body that most people did not have. So Luke made sense. "Okay, but breakfast first. Let's go out."

Eli's eyes lit up. "The Cloverbell?"

A quick side-eye to the boys. "Even though you went there last night?"

Both boys nodded, gleeful smiles broadening their faces. And people wondered why it was so difficult to say no to these littles. I'd say yes to just about anything to keep those smiles on their faces. Always.

Luke smiled, too, eyes crinkling, cheeks dimpling like they might if he were laughing with Nico. And again, the thought hit me straight in the chest: *Luke and Nico? Really?* Somehow, that idea just kept bouncing around in my brain. I needed to speak with Nico, and soon.

Being hungry and tired meant that not cooking breakfast sounded like a wonderful idea. Cam made sure the epi pen was in my bag, Eli made his bed, and I quickly cleaned up and threw on clothes, peeked at the cocoon—still nothing—then hustled the kids into the car, allowing Luke to ride shotgun. It wasn't until we left the diner that I noticed the missed call: *Mom.*

CHAPTER 11: FRANK

My original plans for a Tuesday in June did not involve lying all day in a hospital bed, watching looped highlights of yesterday's game. The game I missed. With Nico next to me as a guard, I wouldn't be moving from the dungeon any time soon. Or at least not soon enough for me. He still clung to the belief—put there by Marissa—that I'd be headed to rehab. I still clung to the belief that I could go home.

An itch broke out on my shoulder, and I tried to move my legs. They felt heavy and full, as if leaded shrapnel had filled them. Crap, maybe Marissa was right. How could I go home if I couldn't get out of bed myself? Furthermore, how had I gotten here? To this point in my life.

Antonio. The air force. Marriage to Angie. The kids. I tried to keep my faith foremost in my mind. Sure, I'd had my moments, my sins—who didn't?—but I'd learned my lessons and moved on. My thoughts landed again on the idea of punishment. It was easy to believe that; I'd failed Antonio after all. Marissa would scoff and say that God didn't punish and that my body had some issues. She'd tell me to focus on the positive. Stop worrying about irrelevant things. But they weren't irrelevant, were they? Because if God was trying to teach me something, or if the universe was speaking, then this could happen again.

"Hey, Nico," I whispered, and he opened his hazel eyes and looked at me. I'm not sure what he'd been doing all night, but he didn't look good. Tired. "I need to use the restroom."

"Uh, Dad. That's why you have a call button." He pointed to the bright red button hanging next to my bed.

"But I want *you* to help me. I need to see if my legs work."

Turmoil filled his face. He knew if he made a misstep, he'd have Marissa, Will, *and* Luke on his back. Not to mention the medical professionals helping me. On the other hand, maybe he understood about pride.

Outside my door, the nurses' station bell had rung three times before Nico said anything. "We can try one time, and if you're not strong enough, you're going back into bed, and you're pushing that damn button." Another point to the beastly button.

It was better not to balk. "Okay."

Nico helped me swing my legs around and then placed his hands underneath my armpits. He wasn't the tallest of the bunch—a little under six feet, shorter than Gabe—but he had a strength that came from working out. He had time. No family, no kids. A job and... What else? I straightened my body out and tried to put weight on my legs. One moment, I was looking into Nico's eyes. The next, I was sitting on the bed again.

"And this is why you're here and hopefully going to rehab, Dad."

I could do nothing but shake my head.

Nico called for the PCA, who helped me to the restroom and then gave me a bedside commode. Then he told me to "sit tight" because he was going to text the social worker about what rehab facility I'd be headed to.

"I don't know if you'll have your own room or which facility can take you or how long you'll be there, Dad," Nico said.

No room to argue. Could Angie stay with me? And how much was a rehab stay going to cost me? I'd worked long and hard for my money. The last thing I wanted to do was waste it on rehab.

"I know exactly what you're thinking, Dad," Nico said as we waited for the return text. He lifted his voice over the chatter in the hallway and vent system hum, which were about to drive me up the wall.

I'd rather be sitting on my porch, listening to the neighbors' lawn mowers. Sipping coffee. Legs outstretched. "Oh yeah? What am I thinking about?"

"You're wondering what all this will cost you."

How did he know that? Nico hadn't been the best student, and he seemed lazy at times. Sure he'd eventually done fine for himself—he'd graduated college, got a master's while teaching high school social studies. Something, I was told, Nico did very well. One of the most respected and liked at the school, in fact. "Uh, yeah. I am. Among other things. How'd you know?"

Like he did as a teenager, Nico rolled his eyes. "Because we're more similar than you'd ever care to admit, and right now, that's what I'm wondering." He held up a stack of UNO cards, still one of his favorite games.

I chuckled, both at his answer and at the cards. "One game. But aside from the eyes, you and I are nothing alike." He was so different from me. Physically, emotionally, intellectually. Always high strung and easy to ignite. Much like Angie, much like Antonio. And he possessed a passion for art. Not to mention he liked men. Speaking of, why *did* he like men? Was it something we did? When he was a freshman in college and found the guts to talk to Angie and me, he hadn't blamed us.

We'd been sitting on the porch, cold lemonade in hand, listening to the wind rustle the dry grass. Nothing but relaxation, though Nico had a terrified look on his face. He'd told me he wanted to talk, that he had something to tell me, tell us. Angie always had orders to fill, but that day, Nico waited until she was at a good stopping point. Had I known what he was going to say? I'd always suspected that Nico was different, but being gay never entered the picture because being gay... Well, I didn't *want* him to be gay. I'd seen what happened to boys who admitted to being gay. Bad things. Horrendous things. And Nico? Well... But I wasn't completely surprised when Nico blurted out, "I'm gay." Essentially two words. No beating around the bush.

"I've thought about how I'd tell you guys this for so long," he'd said, his voice trembling. "I wasn't sure *how* to say it, so I figured the fewest words might be best."

That day, he'd have rambled on had I not stopped him. "You nailed that, Nico. Two words. That's all it took. So let me be as clear—I'm sad you said it."

Nico visibly recoiled and wrinkled his brow. "Wait. *Sad* that I used the words or that I *am* gay?"

He posed a good question then, and like the coward I was—*still am?*—I said nothing, just looked away, unable to voice my fears for this kid. The fears that had morphed into a nightmare that haunted me for years. Still did.

Instead, Angie said, "Are you *sure* you're gay?"

Nico's face paled as white as the clouds I used to fly through before he let loose a brittle laugh. "Mom? Are you serious? Am I *sure*? No, it's just a phase." He rolled his eyes and paced on the porch, his footsteps ominous. "I kind of hoped you'd figure it out. I know it goes against what *you* believe, but for as long as *I* can remember, something inside my heart spoke to me. It basically said, 'You like boys.' And I've never doubted that fact."

"*Never*? What about that girl you dated in high school?" Angie said.

"That girl? You mean Sadie Rollins? She was a good friend. A very good friend, someone I tried hard to like in that capacity, mostly to appease you."

Nico had looked away then, and I knew he'd spoken the truth. I loved my kids, my son. Seeing him happy was important to me. But this? What a bitter pill to swallow. "This is a lot for your mother and me to think about. We'll be in touch." Such formal words, and yet taking them back was impossible.

Nico walked away, head hanging, shoulders slumped, hands in his back pockets, a proverbial cloud over his head. He got into his car and drove away.

We never talked about that revelation again.

Nico had that same stance as my focus returned to my youngest child, so anchored and so adrift at the same time. Had my words hurt him now like they might have then? What did he want? What would make it better? Should I—

Nico patted my knee and nodded. "We can revisit this another time, but if you want to know how I'm similar to you, I'll tell you. I value the same things: a good work ethic, family, and money." He nodded his head again, placed an emphasis on the word *money.*

"What do you mean about that last part?"

"Well, it seems like it's always about the money for you. Isn't it?" he said as his fingers twirled a red nine over and over. He usually won UNO. Today would be no exception.

"Yeah, money's important. When you don't grow up with much... You know, I've been working since I was eight—"

"All right, Dad. You've been working a long time. I get that. But here's what I know. Today you might go to rehab," he held up a finger, "and you're wondering how many dollars it's going to cost." He added a second finger. "You want to know the bottom line, and you don't want to pay it." Third and fourth finger. "You and Mom have money in the bank—"

"Yes, we have money in the bank. But we'll need that for so many things."

Nico flipped his thumb out and waved his open hand in my face. "You know that old saying, don't you? You can't take it with you?" He waited for me to nod. "Well, you can't. Having all the money in the world won't do you any good from beyond the grave."

"Geesh, I'm not there yet," I said between gritted teeth.

"And if you go to rehab—one of the good facilities—it will be a long time before you get there!" He dropped the stack of cards on the side table and whirled around to look out the window.

Was this Marissa standing here? Maybe she'd spoken to Nico, or maybe they, too, were more similar than I thought. A sinking feeling thrashed against my entire body as the shrapnel coalesced and pressed me to the bed, holding me there: I'd be going to rehab today whether I wanted to or not.

It was going to be a long couple of weeks.

CHAPTER 12: MARISSA

Before I had the chance to give Mom a call, my phone rang. I'd barely run my finger over the call button when her voice boomed throughout the car.

"You know what they're doing with your dad?" she asked.

"I hope they're sending him to rehab. That's what I want them to do." A quick glance to the rearview mirror showed no one behind me. This stretch of road always seemed empty, something I didn't mind since someday, the boys would drive on it, alone.

"What? You asked them to do that? Why?"

"We went over this yesterday, Mom. You can't help him as much as he needs you to. If the man can't walk, he can't go home."

This conversation deserved more than my thirty available seconds. "Let me call you back when I get home, after I've gotten the kids involved in something. But remember this: the best thing is for Dad to go to rehab. I'll take him there myself if I have to."

She hung up without saying goodbye, and I laughed at myself, the image of me trying to get Dad into rehab all by myself. It could be accomplished, but I'd prefer the help. And who would help me? Sometimes I felt like the Little Red Hen with my family. Counting on

Will was easy; but everyone else? They usually figured I'd get it done, so they asked me to do it. Why didn't I say no? Why didn't I say no now? Because Dad's health depended on this stay at rehab. An image of monkeys on bicycles popped into my head, and I laughed again.

"What's so funny?" Luke asked. He'd been uncharacteristically silent until then, keeping his gaze on the passing storefronts and gas stations.

"Just thinking of that phrase, not my circus, not my monkeys. And grateful that you're here. We're all grateful."

"I'm happy to help. Your parents mean something to me. When I think of family, I think of them."

At a red light, I snuck a sideways glance at Luke. The sun illuminated his profile, which struck me as beautiful. A silhouettist would give anything to create a cut-out of that man. But that man—the same one we'd known for so long—might be the love of my brother's life. "And is that the *only* reason?"

Luke turned then, his full gaze meeting mine for a fleeting moment. What would he say? I wanted to know the truth. I'd found my love years ago in Will, and I wanted my younger brother to find what we had, what Gabe and Sarah had. Luke blinked twice, honesty shining in his eyes. "I'd be lying if I said yes, your parents are the only reason, but I'm going to say yes out of respect for Nico."

I sighed. "You didn't."

Luke's high-wattage smile lit up the car. "I did."

He'd always been a little wily, but two could play this game. "You know what kudzu is, Luke?"

"The plant?"

"Yeah, the plant. The coiling, climbing plant."

"I've heard of it, but that's about it."

The light turned green, but I threw one more glance his way. "Why don't you and Nico look it up later. You might find it listed under *invasive species.* Once it takes root, it's difficult to get rid of, sort of like me and my curiosity. Plan for more questions later."

Luke's laughter filled the car as I pressed my foot to the accelerator.

. . .

After getting the kids settled with a few board games at home and the promise of a look at the butterfly garden, I took a seat in the kitchen and called Will at work.

"Hey, babe," he said. "How'd you sleep?"

"Pretty well. Someone tired me out."

"I'm not sure how to take that," Will said. "Do you mean me or your dad?"

"Ugh, thanks for *that* visual." My head fell into my hands.

"You're welcome. Listen, I had to get in early, but my schedule is pretty light for a Tuesday. Do you need me for anything?" Sometimes, Will had his head in the clouds, and he'd only focus on his own tasks, but today wasn't one of those days.

"We're good for now. I'm not sure what we're going to do, but if we need you, I'll let you know. The reason I was calling is to say thanks for orchestrating the lie-in, as the Brits like to say."

"Why do they say that?"

"No idea, but it was nice." My gaze flicked to Luke and the boys as they played a game of Apples to Apples Junior, one of their favorites. "The boys are having fun with Luke, and I don't know if I told you or not, but I'm pretty sure Luke and Nico are an item."

"Huh. That makes sense to me."

"It does? I mean, I'm fine with it, too, but I guess I never—"

A beep sounded on the line's other end. "Gah. That's the timer. I need to run. Anything else you wanted to tell me?"

"Nah. My brain's a little foggy. Seems someone kept me up a little later than he should have."

"And we're back to that. Isn't that my role?" His laugh washed away any lingering fatigue.

After finishing the call, I thought about bringing the boys and the game with me to the hospital, but then a better idea surfaced. "Who wants to go to Grandma's house?" I asked as I moved into the family room. The boys looked up, smiles on their faces. "If Grandpa is going to rehab, we can put together a few things for him."

"What's rehab?" Cam asked.

"Can I play with the yoga ball?" Eli shouted.

"Yes, you can play with the ball, both of you, and we'll explain about rehab on the way over. Luke? If you want to come with us, you're welcome to."

●　　　●　　　●

Mom opened the door, apron in hand, deep lines across her forehead. "You didn't need to knock—you know that." She pulled the door open farther, allowing the boys to scamper in.

"Mom, I don't live here anymore." In fact, I hadn't lived there for twenty-four years. We'd moved into the house the summer I turned fourteen, the year I entered high school. The year everything would be different, or so I hoped. A time in my life when I believed in magic and making myself someone else, someone I wasn't, someone I wanted to be. When I figured that if I didn't feel loved, I could change myself—a metaphorical caterpillar and butterfly, perhaps?—and find that love. Before I understood that to be someone else, you needed to understand who you were, what the problem was, and what could be done about it. And that if you didn't feel loved, perhaps it wasn't all your fault.

But I was still young then, naive and oblivious, and four years in that house tortured me. Tension between Nico and Dad. Gabe and his wild ways. Mom with little time for a teenage girl who didn't belong at school or anywhere else. No one got me, and they didn't care to get me either. And that's what hurt the most. That no one took the time to find out why depression and anger and melancholy trailed me like lost puppies. No one thought to ask, "What can we do to help?" No one bothered at all.

Once inside the foyer, I tossed my bag into the corner before turning toward the kids. In Grandma's house, shoes had to come off, pronto. Miraculously enough, Cam and Eli had already done so and were running toward the kitchen—*treat heaven* as they called it. They probably figured Mom had something brewing back there, chocolate fondue or molten lava cake—nut free, of course—something sinfully delicious they didn't get enough of at our house. I shut the door and glanced up. Mom still stood there, directly in front of me, looking lost as she stared at Luke.

"You okay, Mom?"

A quick blink of her eyelids, and she was back. "Sure. And you? How are you, Luke?"

"Great, Angie. Good to see you again." He pulled her in for a hug and lingered a moment. "I'll go keep the boys occupied, if that's okay."

"Thank you." I turned to Mom. "What can I do to help?"

"I think I've got things under control, but... Let's check." A soft smile turned the corners of her mouth upward, but her eyes looked more tired than the last time I was here. She leaned in hesitantly to hug me.

"Lots of orders to take care of?" I pulled from her embrace.

"You know how summer is. And, I have those plants I don't like waiting for me. All around the house."

I stifled a chuckle low in my throat. The way Mom brought up those weeds *every* time I spoke to her, you'd think they'd be nine feet tall by now. Encouraging a simple fifteen minutes a day of weed pulling as a means toward a nice-looking landscape had fallen on deaf ears. Or she could subscribe to Will's landscaping method—mow over everything in the path. Apparently, she didn't want to listen to either of us.

"Mom, seriously, the kids love to pull things. Ask them to come out and help. You can pay them in cookies, as long as you're careful about Cam's allergy. I won't mind a little indulgence a couple of times this summer."

She seemed to consider what I said but moved toward the back of the house without a word. The sound of the boys roughhousing in the great room that opened off the kitchen filtered to my ears, and I imagined them, all knees and elbows, rosy cheeks and wide grins. Their voices put a smile on my face, which contrasted with the coolness of the air-conditioning. The chill raised goosebumps on my arms, and they stayed there when my gaze landed on the paper and magazine piles scattered across the credenza in the foyer. Hadn't we been here for dinner a week ago? There'd been no piles at that point. Maybe they'd cleaned up for that dinner and here we were, surprising Mom with a visit.

In the center of the dining room table sat two paper stacks, but I also glimpsed a box in the corner, tucked next to the tall hutch. That hadn't been there a week ago either. I lifted the box's corner to reveal computer-printed sheets of off-white paper. The first page concerned diabetes and how to eat right. Then an article about sleep apnea, and tree-nut allergies—*nice*—and under that, a binder clip held a stack of weathered paper together. The top sheet read, "Easy and Healthy 30-Minute Recipes."

I moved on to the kitchen and stared at the disarray. Chocolate molds lay adjacent to the oven, and a double boiler sat on the stove. Vanilla and mint extract bottles and caramels were grouped with other flavorings and chips on the large island. Mom was almost ready to make something yummy. *Perhaps we arrived at a good time.*

"What are you doing here, Marissa? You didn't tell me you were coming... Did you?" Mom said.

Or maybe it wasn't at a good time. "I didn't know we were coming either, but you called. And I figured we should stop by. Have you thought about going to see Dad?"

"There's nothing to do over there but sit. I'd rather be here at home."

"Yeah, I know that, but maybe Dad would appreciate you being there."

She let out a huge sigh. "Stuff to do. I have so much stuff to do!"

That had been Mom's standard excuse for years. "What stuff is so important that Dad has to wait, huh? If Will were in the hospital, I'd be there. Right now. Unless I had to be with the kids. And you don't have young kids."

Mom was ready with a quick response. "But my business is like my kids."

"That's understandable, but you have assistants who can do what you need them to do! Call them." These circular arguments with my parents were getting old. Maybe I needed to step away from the situation, but at the end of the day, I loved my folks and wanted to do what was right: help them with what they needed. "Listen, Mom, I don't care what you do. We can figure that out later. Dad should head to rehab in the next few days though. Do you think you can find him clothes and such?"

She sighed heavily once again and dusted her hands on her work jeans.

"Thank goodness it's summer," I continued. "He won't need too much. Once we find out how long he'll be staying we can bring more. But his toiletry bag would be good and underwear, undershirts, you know..."

Not giving Mom the chance to say no because she was the best person to put the things together, I walked out of the kitchen and into the family room to see what the boys and Luke were up to, wondering what sort of family I'd been born into and how in the heck I'd made it this long without going over the edge.

Luke had the kids set up over a game again, this time an old favorite, Operation, which made sense based on his chosen profession. I'd always enjoyed that game, but the *buzz* when someone missed jostled my brain. As I moved closer to the kids, the noise increased in volume. I placed my hand over the game and turned toward Luke.

"That went well." He'd known me for long enough to know I was joking.

"That good, eh? What happened? What did you need to ask her?"

"I wanted to know if she's going to see Dad. Nico can only stay so long. I can only do so much, and you—you'll need to start work soon, I'd imagine. It only makes sense for Mom to bring in her helpers and have them do her work here while she sees Dad. She won't have to stay at the rehab place all day, but he's going to be lonely."

"Uh, yeah, he is. She could put a pause on more orders too."

"Maybe I should suggest that to her..." I said. Then I thought better of it; Mom had never reacted well to people "telling her what to do," even if that wasn't the person's intent. "Actually, maybe I shouldn't. Anyway, I came to check on the kids. I know you're having fun, and I'll let you play babysitter today, but tomorrow, you're back to work. Or whatever they have you doing now." I pointed my finger at him, as if I meant business. Luke tried to interject, but I wagged the finger, shushing him. "I *will* keep you in the loop, I'll ask you for help, I'll even let you help, but right now, we need Dad getting ready to go to rehab. He'll be safe there. We shouldn't need too much help at that point."

"Are you sure?" he said. The game buzzer rang again.

"Yes, but I want to say thank you. My kids enjoy spending time with you. This would be more difficult trying to manage the situation if you weren't here."

Luke nodded and flashed a small smile.

"And on that note, I'm going back to see if Mom has Dad's bag ready, and then, I'll be headed to the hospital."

On the way to my parents' bedroom, I looked at older pictures hanging on the faded blue hallway wall and leaned close to the photos taken when I was young, maybe about three years old. One of the few pictures of me and Gabe before Nico was born caught my eye. Me on Dad's lap and Gabe on Mom's. We sat on the edge of the sandbox Dad had constructed for our first house: wood painted fire engine red with two seats and a huge space between the seats for us to play. Dad had scoured every store to find sand soft enough for us. I looked at Gabe and me, a little fuzzy in the picture. We were so young then. So were Mom and Dad. We all looked happy, but I couldn't remember if we were. Flickers of mom's moods and volatility, the gnawing in my stomach with not knowing what to expect after school, not sure what her day had been like. But this picture had been taken when it was clearly summer, and the warm weather and lack of schedule seemed to soften her. At least the photo said so.

I passed a few more pictures. Some with Mom, some without. Some that showed her smiling, others that highlighted her frown. Mom's complex personality seemed to shine from the grouping. I often tried not to behave like she did: off the cuff, without thinking. I didn't want my children to feel as though they couldn't come talk to me or didn't want to come home from school. What had made her like that? Did she behave that way with Dad?

When I got to my parents' bedroom, I pulled up short. Mom stood hunched over an overnight bag on the bed, mumbling to herself, her words muffled. She placed a couple of pairs of undershorts and an undershirt into the bag, then sat on the bed and looked down at the baseboard, it edges gray and dusty.

I tapped on the doorframe with my fingers and walked in. "Hey, Mom. What's wrong?"

"Nothing. I'm just tired."

"Well, I'm ready to go. The kids are going to stay here with Luke, and I'm headed back to the hospital. Is Dad's bag ready?"

"Oh. That's right. No, hold on a minute. I'll throw something together."

"Uh, I think you did already. Isn't this," I pointed to the small, slate-gray duffle, "the bag you put his things in?"

"Oh, yes. I'm not sure what to put in there, you know? But here." She thrust the bag at me.

A quick glance revealed the lack of razor, toothbrush, and deodorant. What the heck? "What about his toiletries?"

"They're over here." She walked into the bathroom and grabbed Dad's Dopp kit, handing it to me.

The nightstand next to Dad's bed held plenty of items Mom had passed over that I would have included in the overnight bag: the tattered prayer book, his beloved family photo, and his planner. The man had little to do during retirement, but he still placed every appointment, meetup, or milestone in that calendar.

"Do you want to go with me?" I asked.

"No, that's okay. I'll go another time."

A deep calming breath in and out loosened me up, waved away my irritation, and I didn't need to ask why she wasn't coming. The answer was obvious: she had things to do. Didn't we all?

CHAPTER 13: FRANK

A nebulous diagnosis of Parkinsonian-like symptoms kept me in the hospital for two days and change. Then I was transferred to a local rehab facility. The dates at the top of the newspaper delivered for the residents helped me track time. After almost two days at rehab—it was now Saturday morning, June 20—I was done with the whole place. Done. Mainly because I'd seen very little of Angela.

"So much to do," she'd said over the phone.

But with nothing but time on my hands, my thoughts turned toward the idea that she always had something to do *by design*. The business, three kids, life in general—they all drained her, and work helped with that. Provided her an excuse to stay away. Maybe she couldn't give whatever it was we, especially me, especially Marissa, wanted.

Years ago, after the initial honeymoon period had worn away for us, and we allowed our true colors to fly, mood changes here or there showed up: a little crabby one day, a little down on herself the next, and then a lashing out at me. And sometimes, an annoyed spark turned quickly into an inferno.

"What's wrong?" I'd say to her.

"I don't know," she'd reply.

She didn't know—until I dragged her to see a therapist after Gabe was born. They diagnosed her with a classic case of depression. Something that might be "fixed" with a little pill. So for a while, things moved in a more positive direction.

Then Angie decided she didn't want to be "dependent on a chemical" for her happiness, and she took herself off the medication.

Maybe I should have been more supportive of her decision, helped her figure out how to deal with stress better, but I didn't understand at the time. I barely understood now, years after the events and long after I'd thought about them. My job had kept me away, maybe too much. And now, I was away again, with leg issues and memory issues and this rehab place...

But at the moment, I had other things to worry about besides my wife. I glanced around the room: private bed and bathroom, television, window, courtyard view. How much for this drab, beige room? On top of that, I hadn't had a bowel movement since a few hard pebbles at the hospital on Monday.

That only meant one thing: it was time to get out. Standing was possible, and that would have to be enough. I pushed the button to summon the aide. With my eyes trained on the news, I waited.

Fifteen minutes later, which only confirmed why I needed to get the hell out of rehab, the aide stopped in.

"How can I help you, Mr. Raffaelo?"

"I want to speak to someone about being discharged."

Her eyes widened. She chuckled. "Oh, I don't think that'll be happening yet." She reached over to turn the news down. "You have occupational therapy and physical therapy to get through, plus this medicine list might be tough to handle at home by yourself."

"No, you're not *hearing* me. I want to speak with someone about being discharged." The gruffness in my voice, similar to my air force superiors, might have been unnecessary. I shouldn't take anything out on this poor aide, but I meant business. The food was awful. I wasn't seeing my wife. I hadn't shit in the last couple of days. I wanted my own bed, own meals, own house, own life. How in the hell did people stay in places like this long-term? Moreover, staying here couldn't possibly be good for my memory. One day after the other. Just like the next. Never-ending.

The aide wrote something on a paper she pulled from her pocket, mumbled a few words, and left the room. Who the hell knew who she'd be contacting, but I had been rude enough to make her listen. I sat back and turned up the volume on the news.

Sleep must have taken me and then, a woman tapped on my door and stuck her head in.

"May I come in, Mr. Raffaelo?" The woman turned the television off.

She was tall, and with me in a chair, she seemed even taller, but her face was kind. "I'm Lillian, the social worker. I hear you're hoping to leave us soon?"

"That's right. I'd leave right now if you'd let me." *Honesty might get me somewhere. Maybe.*

"Well, it says here, by the doctor's orders, that you're supposed to be with us at least two to three weeks. While the doctor isn't sure what's happening with your legs, we need to get them strengthened before we allow you to go home."

"*Weeks?* I thought this was going to be a short-term thing?"

Lillian touched my arm in a patronizing gesture. "Oh, Mr. Raffaelo, that *is* short-term. Many people stay here far longer than that. In fact, we have a place connected to this building," she gestured toward the doorway, which emphasized the empty hallway's institutional nature, "that's for people who stay for months, sometimes even longer."

Lillian could have smacked me, that's how surprised I was. *Shit.* "Oh." I wasn't planning on staying. They couldn't make me. Could they?

She went on. "So we need to look at how healthy you are and whether it *is* safe to send you home."

"Of course it's safe."

"You might think so. But do you have stairs in your home?"

The two sets in our trilevel home surfaced in my mind. "Yes."

"Then how do you suppose you're going to get up those stairs? You can't climb stairs yet, according to this chart." She held up a clipboard.

"Well, I can have my wife help me up. Or I can crawl."

Lillian smiled but shook her head and looked at her clipboard again. "I would be negligent and not doing my duty if I discharged a person who wasn't ready to go home. Right here, it says you can't make it to the bathroom, either—"

"I don't give a shit about that damn chart, Lillian."

The woman had the audacity to smile. "But *I* do, Mr. Raffaelo, and if you go home now, even in the next few days, you'll be going home AMA. Do you know what that means?"

"No."

"It means *against medical advice*. We write it down in the *chart*. And your doctors know then that you weren't ready. Just stubborn." She winked at me.

A wink? What... Hell yes, I was stubborn—the air force would be proud! God help me, these folks had seen nothing yet. Getting out of this plutonian place sailed to the top of my list. I didn't belong there. An old man shuffled down the hallway behind his walker, his slippers whooshing against the dingy floor. And then a woman in a wheelchair spun by, slowly, her wrinkled arms straining against the scraped wheels. I wasn't like them, even if I might forget a few things and stumble a few times. They were *old*.

Lillian's voice cut into my thoughts. "You're seventy-seven years old, Mr. Raffaelo. We need to make sure you're healthy before we send you home."

"What are you? A mind reader?" I mumbled, but she ignored me.

"And by the way, I contacted your daughter. Marissa, is it? She said she had a full schedule today but that she'd be calling you soon. Let's not make any rash decisions until you speak with her, okay?"

Rash? I'd never made a rash decision in my life, and I couldn't make a quick getaway. Agreeing to her terms seemed the only option. "Okay," I whispered and turned my head away.

Lillian smiled one more time, then left, pulling the door partially closed, and it seemed like a good time to get myself over to the armchair in the corner. The aide had dressed me in a polo and shorts with an elastic waist, and she'd even put shoes on me today, though I had no prior plans to move from the bed. The shoes would keep me from slipping on the shiny linoleum as I moved from bed to chair. I pushed up against the mattress into a sitting position, then swung my legs over the bed. To my right stood a night table, then the walker, and then the chair. If I could get myself to stand, each of those would support me until I was seated. "You can do it, legs." I pushed up again with my arms and leaned over, trying to grasp the table ends. The sharp, angled wood provided a perfect grip, and I stood there with shaky legs. *I'm up!* A shuffle of my feet to the right and then another, my hands moving one over the other along the table length, until I'd reached the walker. A burn surged in my thigh muscles, but one small stretch of my left hand found the metal edge. *Success!* My other hand moved to grasp the walker's right handle—

The burn took over my legs' entire length. My thighs split apart. My body gave way, and the world tilted. My right side hit the linoleum with a *thud*, and a shockwave coursed through me. I pushed the button hanging around my neck. Someone would come. Then, unbearable, searing pain. White light. Blackness...

And dreams. About the past. About Angie when she was young. About my time in the air force. My dreams were on fast-forward, flying as quickly as my aircraft, giving me small clips of life, things that had happened day to day. A conversation about Bellbrook High School's new golf coach with a friend at the golf course. Eating dinner at the Cloverbell Diner with the grandkids. A teeth cleaning with my dentist, now retired. The kids were all there in adult form and so were my parents, although they'd died many years before. The movement within the dream almost made me dizzy until I came to a stop in front of our house.

Angie sat there on the porch with a teacup in one hand and a novel in the other. Even in this other world I realized how long it had been since I'd seen her reading a book. She never got around to doing that anymore, and it was one of her favorite pastimes. In my dream, I stood there, taking the picture in, watching her sip her tea, open the book cover, read for a minute or so, and then close the book. She repeated these actions, over and over again. My dream self and my real self wondered why, but I didn't have a clue.

A slight push on my right shoulder, and a voice: "Mr. Raffaelo? Are you okay?" I opened my eyes. My body felt achy and chilled, despite the warm weather outside. Something woeful hung over me. Ambiguous yet maddening. More than being in this miserable place. More than my lack of a bowel movement. More than having fallen again. Something felt *not right*.

I couldn't place my finger on what it was.

CHAPTER 14: MARISSA

My phone had taken a place of loathing in my life, and I thought about shutting it off, but I knew better than that. Nico, Gabe, and I had been furiously texting regarding Dad. Sometimes the texts were irreverent and loopy, sometimes they relayed pertinent information. For that reason alone, it was good to have the phone. But when voicemails came along like the social worker's, informing me Dad wanted to leave... Those calls, I could do without. Thank goodness I was between patients. Already annoyed by having to work on a Saturday morning, my irritation would show on my face the minute I walked into an exam room if I wasn't careful. How in the hell did Dad think he could go home? If all signs point to illogical, it was probably illogical, right?

Earlier that morning, he and I had spoken about how he was doing. He'd detailed the bland food—standard, I said—his bowel movement issue, the smell, the sounds, everything. Then, he'd revealed the kicker: "And I've only seen your mom once for a short visit."

"What?" I straightened up in the office chair. "Let me guess. She says she has stuff to do."

"Yes, Marissa. She says that exactly. Which is why I want to go home. At least there I'll see her. Sometimes."

Dad had every right to be hurt by Mom's actions, but somehow, his response surprised me. He'd always made excuses for Mom, telling me he'd made mistakes over the years and that she'd been depressed for some time. He always had a reason tucked into his back pocket for her odd, often hurtful behavior. Many times, he'd say she was stressed, that having to fill all the candy orders overwhelmed her. But why do the work and get all stressed if it hurts your relationship with your family? As a child I didn't understand it, and I still didn't. Right now, she needed to be with Dad. Screw the business. Or at least be honest with him and admit she didn't want to be there.

"I'll talk to her, but I wanted to speak with you first, and you need to listen to me this time. Actually *listen.*" I settled into the chair, lifted my right leg across my left knee, and massaged my calf, which had been sore lately. "You cannot check out yet. Your legs aren't strong enough to go home. You'll be stuck in bed even more there because you don't have a recliner, and you don't have anyone who can help you get back and forth inside the house."

"No, I have to leave. Have you spent time here? It's clean and the aides are nice. I haven't been mistreated. But I can't stay here!"

I looked at my desk calendar a few days out. The next day was Father's Day, and nothing remarkable stood out for the following week... The summer was always a little slower because of vacations and such that patients took. Nico might have time to help too. I knew my dad. He was going to come home, "come hell or high water," as Mom used to say. Maybe I could put him off a little...

"Okay. I don't understand, but I do at the same time. Here's the thing. Mom isn't a medical person. She won't know what to do. Can you hang out there until Monday—"

"But I can't—"

"Two days, Dad." I pushed harder against my calf. Anything to find relief. "Through the weekend, and then you'll get to go home. And tomorrow, we'll all come visit for Father's Day. We'll shoot for Monday morning, which means you can start the week off the way you want."

A pause lingered before he answered. "You promise?"

"I promise."

A huge groan echoed over the line, and for a moment, I wasn't sure if he'd agree or not. If he didn't, there wasn't a thing I could do. If he did, I'd have to put something into action.

"All right. Can you at least bring her with you when you visit today?"

"Yes, that I can do."

And we'd left it at that, hadn't we? That he'd give it two days? So what had happened in those few hours to make him change his mind?

Lillian picked up my call on the first ring. "Your father's fine, Marissa, but we had an incident."

"An incident? When? Shouldn't you have said so in your voicemail?"

She sighed. "It happened but a few moments ago. That was an earlier voicemail, when I'd left your father's room. Apparently, after I left, he decided it was time to get up and move to the chair. I was just getting ready to call you." She filled me in on the details, including that while he'd broken nothing, he had a bruise developing along the length of his right thigh.

"And how did this happen? I thought he had a bed alarm."

"He did. He does but..."

"But what?"

"The batteries weren't working."

Oh really? "So how long did it take for someone to find him? And what you're telling me is that he fell because of your negligence?" Rude, yes, but also true. I didn't let her answer either question. "Someone will be over to speak to you and your manager soon."

Lillian sputtered at my words, and even though she couldn't see me, I shook my head. Something had to be done, and I knew the person who would keep his cool while doing it: Will.

He'd come into my life right when I'd needed him and seemed to do that still. A freshman in college, only eighteen years old, I was awkward and shy, a nerd to most, an outcast to some. But Will had seen something in me I hadn't before. He made me feel beautiful and smart and loved. All the things I wanted to feel at home.

Of course, I hadn't liked him at first. He and I had both rented lockers at the campus rec building, right next to each other. And apparently, we also frequented the building at the same time: 6:30 a.m. every Tuesday and Thursday. That first day I saw him, his tall and lanky self took up too much space. When he tossed a lock of hair out of his face, I figured the semester would be long. I expected him to walk with a skateboard under his arm, but I quickly found out he'd rather have a science textbook there instead.

That first Tuesday, he spoke one word: "Hi." I didn't even know his name then. The next time we met, on Thursday, he spoke two words: "Hi there." And by the third encounter, he had added one more word. "Hi there, Marissa."

"How do you know my name?" I asked. We didn't know each other from back home, and we didn't have any classes together.

His reply? An overt wink that caused a heat to creep up my neck and face. He walked away, leaving me there, discombobulated and jittery, a hum coursing through my body.

By Thursday, he was back, and this time with a four-word message. "I know your roommate." That's all he said as he rearranged his belongings, took out his gym bag, and slammed his locker door.

My roommate? Which one and how? The three of us spent little time together, but if he knew either of them well, I would have known *of* him at least. I went home that day, hoping to ask my roommates about the mysterious Will Moretta—I'd glimpsed the name on his ID—but as luck would have it, one was at orchestra practice, and the other had a soccer game an hour away. I didn't see them before I went to bed, and the next morning, they had both taken off for the weekend.

Day number five, and I stalled for time at my locker. I hadn't seen Will yet, but I wanted to. Where was he? Time marched on, and I had to get to my exercise class, and somehow, I didn't think of him again until I headed back to my locker. Tucked inside was a note on lined paper that said, "I was late. Forgive me." Five words. I threw my head back and laughed, skipping out of the building on cloud nine.

Who knew what would happen on day six, but a certain energy zipped through me, despite the zit on my cheek and the period that had arrived the night before. I spent more time in the bathroom that morning than ever, washing my face, placing each strand of hair strategically on my head. My bloated belly grumbled, but there was no way I'd not go to the rec center that day. I couldn't wait to get there.

Will wasn't late that day; he was leaning up against the lockers, a cell biology text in his hand and his overstuffed backpack by his feet. His one foot tapped a beat I couldn't hear over the din of the other students and faculty hoping to squeeze in fitness before classes. I stopped for a moment, dead in my tracks, just to look at him. What color were his eyes? And what about his earlobes? Did they connect or not? I couldn't say anything about him other than his presence; even the thought of him, gave me butterflies. He looked up then, his gaze meeting mine, and he smiled. I was a goner, and he hadn't even said anything that day. By the time I made it to my locker a few seconds later, he only spoke one sentence, and of course it had six words to it: "Will you go out with me?"

What could I say, no? He intrigued me. I rifled through my locker, shrugged, and walked away, knowing I wouldn't see him until the following Tuesday. When he and I met at the lockers that day, I gave him my simplest seven-word answer: "I would like that very much, Will." It wasn't pretty or profound, but like his words, they conveyed the message just as well.

Will and I had been together ever since, and those years made up some of the best years of my life. Years during which I learned how to be the woman I was and how to ask for help, though I was still working on that one. He'd taught me that lesson. To ask for help from the right people. This time, he was the right person. If anyone could smooth over this mess, it was Will.

CHAPTER 15: HER

All she ever wanted was her very own happily ever after. She'd looked for it everywhere: at home, in her business, in people she thought might give it to her and in those she suspected never could. Forget about making her own happily ever after; she didn't have the tools or the wherewithal to make it happen. Each time she sat in the stiff metal chair or on the armchair on the bed's edge, in front of what had become of her strong husband—a now frail-looking and sick man instead of the robust airman she once married—she wondered about their fate and that happily ever after. Was it his time, and would she be stuck here without him? What would she do then? She wasn't sure she could cope. He'd done so much for her, though she'd never been very good about saying thank you. She scanned his face, his closed eyes, his ashy skin, the smile lines. When had he gotten so old? Why had he fallen? Why did he keep falling? The questions swirled, suffocating her brain.

She sat as the people came and went, as her daughter helped with every situation, as that boy—Luke—moved in and out, same with Nico and Will, as they all lobbed question after question at her husband. Would they start in on her next? Had she had a hand in anything that happened? Who knew? She turned the memories over in her mind, trying to capture them all. She remembered making her chocolate and then being at the hospital and now this place...rehab. Home, hospital, rehab. Home. The in-between time details hovered, murky and out of reach.

She fidgeted in her seat, wanting to get up and leave, hoping to grab a cigarette, something to calm her nerves as she couldn't shake the feeling that this might be a beginning—her world would disintegrate, fall away like the edible silver and gold leaves she sometimes used to decorate her candy. Because if they asked her questions, her time would be up. They'd figure out she, too, was getting older, and she could no longer keep everything together. That the person who was sick wasn't lying in the bed but sitting in the chair. There was a reason she didn't come visit him. Couldn't they see that? Anxiety—over being caught, outed, as her son would say—seized her, and she turned inward.

Outwardly, her gaze moved to the window and the monochromatic sky painted there, and she glimpsed her happily ever after dissolve into the solemn nothingness.

CHAPTER 16: FRANK

Who should walk through my door to make my Saturday better but Will Moretta. The man commanded a presence. Always had. That phrase—"commanded a presence"—echoed in my head... I'd been watching too much of that damn Hallmark Channel Angie always had on the kitchen television. Those movies had started out boring years ago. Now? They'd ventured into mind-numbing.

Will didn't ask to come in, just entered and sat on the mattress edge. The scent of detergent wafted my way. Refreshed the antiseptic smell that had burrowed into my nose on the first day here in rehab, and I leaned forward in the recliner. The aides had placed me there after the rescue. It did not escape my notice that by choosing the bed instead of the small chair next to me, Will had given me space. The set of his jaw also did not escape my notice; he'd come here to say something. That meant only one thing: Marissa had sent him.

Would he start the conversation, or would I? Looking into his eyes, I wanted to have the upper hand and speak first because very little good would come of this situation. And airmen were no cowards. I could take whatever he'd throw at me. "So, Will Moretta, I'd ask what brings you here, but I think I know." Perhaps Saturday wouldn't be all that great after all.

"You're a smart man, Frank Raffaelo, so I don't doubt that you do." Will rubbed his fingers across his jaw, as if he were weighing his next words. "But why don't you tell me what you think I'm going to say?"

Was he toying with me? Did he really want me to say it? This was no time for playing games. "You're going to tell me that Marissa wants me to stay here in rehab and that what I did was my fault." The sting on the side of my thigh reminded me of my errant ways.

Will tapped a finger against his chin, then crossed his arms over his chest. "There's a first time for everything, I guess. Because that's not why I'm here. Well, not exactly," he said with a headshake.

Hold up. Had he actually come to help me? "When can I get out?"

Will leaned back on his elbows but looked me straight in the eye. "I'm going to level with you, Frank, because I think you need to understand something. Your legs need attention. We don't know what's wrong or why these falls are happening, but something's not right. Rehab *should* have been the best place for you, and Marissa did the right thing by seeing if you could be placed here."

"But? I can hear the but coming."

"But this isn't the right place for you. I just went several rounds with the manager, which effectively got me nowhere, and the director should be by," he glanced at his watch, "soon. I thought maybe you'd want to speak with them."

"Me? Why me? What would I say?"

Will cocked his head. "You realize—"

A knock sounded at the door, and the director we'd met the first day walked in. Worry lines crossed her face. "Mr. Raffaelo, I hope you're feeling better."

"Better than when I first got here or better after the fall I just had?"

Her eyes widened, and she nervously looked at Will, who had stood, arms crossed over his chest once more. Again, that presence. Great way to take up space in the room. He'd have easily made it in the military.

"Do you want to tell me what happened earlier?"

What was the director hoping for? Would Will step in? When I glanced at him, he raised his eyebrows in silent encouragement, much like I used to do to the kids when they were trying to hold their own against Angie in an argument. They rarely had a chance when she was in a mood, but—

The director cleared her throat. "If that's too much to ask, then let me suggest you give us another shot. Your chart indicates leg weakness, and we have the best OT and PT teams in the area. They can help you get where you need to be in short order."

Will moved forward. "With all due respect, you blew that shot. I spoke with the day manager. Not only were the bed alarm batteries not working, but apparently, no one bothered to answer the call button for sixteen minutes. *Sixteen.* Were you aware of that?"

Someone was supposed to come when I hit that button. "For emergencies," they'd said. Or bathroom breaks. "We'll be right there," they'd said. Guess not.

The director wrung her hands in front of her waist and then moved them behind her back. "I am aware it took longer than...expected to get to Mr. Raffaelo."

"*Longer than expected?* And what if he'd hit his head or had been bleeding profusely or had chest pain or any other number of emergencies that could have been dire, deathly even? What then?" Will turned to me. "Sorry, Frank." He turned back to the director. "What if something like that had happened? Do you have liability insurance?"

The director pursed her lips but said nothing.

"We won't be suing here, ma'am, but we will leave with him as soon as possible. In the meantime, I want eyes on him every hour, on the hour."

"But our staff—"

Will pointed out the door. "Mr. Raffaelo is literally three doors down from one of your nurses' stations. Have your staff put a timer on or whatever they need to remind themselves to get up, walk down here, and poke their head in for the remainder of the time he'll be here. That's perfectly acceptable, don't you think?"

"Actually, it's not."

"Then maybe I should mention that when I got here, I sat on the bed, which means it registered a body. When you came in the room, I got up. The bed alarm is going off in your nurses' station right now, and *no one's doing anything about it*, or it's still not working. Either option is simply unacceptable."

The woman grimaced and blew out a breath. "We'll do our best."

"You do that," Will said as the woman spun on her heel and exited the room.

"Wow." I adjusted my legs, hoping to get more comfortable. "You mean business, don't you? That behavior there—cunning—it reminded me of Marissa. You two make a great match, you know that?"

"I do. And don't forget what Marissa's job entails. Being an advocate for her patients, making sure they get what they need. She's the same with you, Frank. She wants what's best for you, whether you believe it or not. We're not here to discuss Marissa though. That last fall shouldn't have happened, and since we don't want another one, we're going to bring you home and hire help."

Help again? "Won't that be expensive?"

Will furrowed his brow. "What's going to be expensive is if you continue to have these falls and then we have to keep hiring people to help you. If we do this now and let you heal, it's quite possible that you'll be on your own in no time. Losing autonomy is difficult. I get that and so does your whole family, which is why we want to see you get back to the way you were. Do you trust me?"

That phrase echoed in my head. I'd said it once to Antonio, and he'd trusted me. Look where he'd gotten. Trust was something to be earned. But speaking of earned... "I want to be sure I can leave something for the kids, for Angie. If we go through all the money now..."

Will moved toward me and put a hand on my shoulder. He wasn't a demonstrative man with me, but the connection helped. "The money won't matter if you have another accident. You know why? Because if you fall and bust your head, you might not be on this earth anymore."

Such sharp words. "You been talking to Nico? No beating around the bush with you two."

Will glanced out the window at the cloudy June sky the color of steel. He moved his hand away. "We don't have time to beat around the bush. When you get home, *you need to stay put* unless someone, an adult someone, is helping. Me, Nico, Marissa, Luke, whoever we hire. Maybe Angie. Not Cam, not Eli." With each name, he jabbed his finger toward me. "That means no walking to the bathroom yourself or going to the refrigerator. No going to get the mail or the paper. You'll have a button or something like it, and you'll need to learn how to use it."

An achy tension began to build inside. "But—"

"No buts, Frank. I spoke with the doctors. While everything looks pretty good, your sugars aren't that stable. I don't know what you've been eating or not eating, but your sodium level is off too. By quite a bit."

"Sodium? What does that mean?"

"Sodium is necessary for many processes, Frank. Healthy muscles and nerves for starters. And if you didn't know it, your legs are muscles," Will gestured to his own thighs then moved his hands up his body toward his head, "which are directed by the nerves, the brain."

"All right, wiseass. I'm treating you like I'd treat my son. I hear you. But hear me too. I don't like this place. The room is small, the mattress is lumpy, it's loud, I can't practice my piano, I sit here all day, and I still haven't taken a shit. It's been days, I tell you. *Days.* How do you think I feel right now?"

Will laughed again. "So fun, isn't it, when the bowels go awry? Have you asked anyone for a laxative? Or prunes? Have they checked for an obstruction?"

"I've asked everyone. I can't remember what they did or didn't do, and they seem to think it will come. My belly is bloated. I'm uncomfortable. Either I poop or... I don't know what."

"Well then, next up is a poop." Will pulled out his phone and flipped it toward me. The notes section was open. "I'll talk to the docs again—writing it down now—and see what we can do while we get you ready to go. I doubt it's an impaction, but maybe they'll want to check. Fair warning though, Frank. It's a weekend, and it will be easier on everyone, *especially Marissa*, if you stay put until Monday morning. Just know that we're working to get you discharged. So will you do what you need to do? Use your call button and think before you act? Limit the impulsivity, please?"

"Monday? I need to stay here that long?"

"Worst-case scenario. Remember, Frank, the world doesn't revolve around you."

Arguing would do no good. Maybe a golf buddy could come over to help pass the time. Or the grandkids. Nico could come in and at least wheel me around the facility. Sitting and watching the news was getting old. Maybe a piano was here somewhere. Being away a little longer would give Angie time to catch up on her orders. "I understand."

Will stuck out his hand, and we shook. I wasn't sure what I'd gotten myself into, but I hoped that by the time I headed home, whenever that was, I'd leave here walking with an empty colon.

CHAPTER 17: MARISSA

The sound of the Bangles—singing about time and fast and fun—reverberated against the kitchen subway tiles, and I snorted, thinking of all the fun we'd been having. The phone calls and information juggling—what needed to get to which person, for what and why. I was grateful to Will, who'd taken on the rehab facility so I could head home after work, but I kept looking at my calendar and wondering what would happen next.

Mom couldn't deal with all the tasks the rehab professionals had been doing. Much less handle all the doctor information that might need to be taken care of. She couldn't even fathom the amount of phone calls I'd made or special trips over to the rehab facility or to the pharmacy. All the actions had been behind the scenes. And that had only been in the span of a few days. Who was going to help Dad and Mom?

Will laid a hand on my shoulder, and I jumped, turning toward him with a smile on my face. The set of his eyes told me he was concerned about something.

"We're all good, mostly. The rehab staff will check on him every hour, and your dad says he'll try to be less impulsive."

I placed my hands on his forearms, traced the muscles beneath his plum shirt, muscles kept strong from thrice weekly trips to the gym.

"Thank you. He listens to you, usually. Did he give you any reason to think he wouldn't this time?"

"No, but maybe Nico or Luke should have gone with me. Two men against one and all that. Quite frankly, your words alone should have been enough to keep him in line. Does he not realize how serious this might be?"

I shook my head. "You know Dad. We explain what's wrong, he says he understands, and then, either he doesn't, or he does what he wants. He shouldn't have fallen in his room, but honestly, rehab screwed up. So now what?"

Will removed my hands from his arms and leaned back against the kitchen counter. "Let's find that help. You can't take this on yourself, Mar. You just can't. Even if you could get PTO or FMLA, it's too much."

What he said made complete sense, but a feeling of obligation still perched on my shoulders.

"I know that look, Marissa. And no. Your father should be fine for the day, and we can probably find a person pretty quickly. Between your connections and Luke's? In the meantime..." Will leaned in, gently took my face in his hands, and tilted my face toward his. Our lips met, softly at first, and then with a bit more urgency. He deepened the kiss, nipping at my lip and pulling my entire body toward his, and a heat—

A scream sounded, and we froze. The kids were outside on the swings. They'd been kicking higher and higher, trying to "eject through the stratosphere" as Will had entered the kitchen. Were they—

I ran toward the sliding glass door. Both boys lay on the grass, rolling and giggling. My hand covered my heart, still beating an increased tempo. "They're fine. They're fine."

Will came up behind me and threaded his arms around my waist. "They have a knack for interrupting, don't they?"

The boys didn't last long on the grass and scrambled back onto the swings. Cam waited for Eli, and they pushed off together, each gaining height as their thin legs pumped steadily. They both threw back their heads and howled.

"They sure do. I used to love the swings, you know?" I said to Will. "And now, when I get on, the movement makes me so queasy and nauseous. Something about this whole situation with Dad makes me feel that way too."

Will tightened his grip on me and rested his chin on my head. "I'm sorry. I think the kids are the only ones not caught in this debacle with your dad," he said.

"That's only because we're working hard to keep their days normal. I'm not sure what's going to happen when he gets home, honestly. I guess we'll see." I stepped out of his embrace. "What are you doing for the rest of the day?"

"Not sure. We need to figure out what's wrong with those caterpillars and why they won't hatch. Maybe it's a bad batch, but you know, I'm with you—would love to see the transformation myself. For today, place me where I'm needed. Whatever works best for you."

Will rounded up the kids, bringing them into the kitchen, and we went over the afternoon agenda while we ate a snack. I felt like I was back at work, letting the staff know what was on the schedule and who had to be seen. My office called, but I let it go to voicemail. If it was important, they would call back right away. Or they'd send a text.

"Cam has an allergy checkup today, had to be rescheduled because of some family conflict or another. Maybe you could hang out with the boys and then take Cam? That will let me head over to see Mom or check in with Dad. Or both."

"Sure, that's fine. Anything else?"

"The appointment is at four-thirty. I have a lot to talk to Mom and Dad about, I think, so I'm not sure when I'll be back."

"So maybe I'll give them an extra-early dinner and then head out."

Eli raised his hand. "And after, we check the cocoon? Or before?"

Will's eyes widened, and he smiled. "Sounds like a plan."

•   •   •

With Dad staying put, my own plans involved visiting Mom first, figuring out what she thought about having a home health aide in the house. Not that she had a choice. I pulled onto my parents' street. Things had changed since I'd lived there: mature trees, now able to withstand the weight of playing children, stood in place of juvenile ones; updated and enlarged kitchens and bathrooms replaced cramped, vintage spaces from the nineties; ponds filled once-grassy backyards. A willow flycatcher flew across my field of vision and into a Norway maple in the neighbor's yard. Tree growth also brought more shelter for birds...another change.

Yet the people inside some houses—that was another story. My parents? They were still stubborn, stuck in their ways, full of tension. All the time. Even then, sitting in my idling car on the cracked asphalt driveway, the uneasiness extended from the house like menacing tentacles. Was it simply my reaction, or was there something to the notion?

The front door creaked as I opened it, and a light music filtered to my ears. Over that, a muted chatting. Mom was talking to someone. On the way to the kitchen, I recognized the familiar, warm voice.

"Nico?" I hadn't called him in, and there was no car out front.

"Hey, Marissa." He opened his arms, and even though we'd just seen one another the other day, I slipped inside, clasping my hands behind his back and pulling him toward me. My brothers had always given the best hugs, hands down. Looks like things hadn't changed at all.

One more squeeze and then I started asking questions. "What are you doing here?"

"Thought I'd take a break from lesson planning and come see if anyone needed any help. I'm pretty sure the last time this happened— the roof, wasn't it?—I was in the thick of my thesis. Figured it was time to step up, I guess. With Gabe not here...you might need it. We all might."

"Well, I appreciate you being here." I turned toward Mom. "Have you seen Dad today?"

She shook her head. "It's still early, and I haven't gone over yet."

"Okay, but what if Nico heads over to see him? He can take you if you want."

"No, I'll go over later. It's not far."

I breathed in and out through my nostrils, trying not to get angry at Mom. My statement hadn't been a suggestion, but she'd treated it as one, and I should have been prepared. It was her favorite tactic. But maybe if Nico headed over, Mom and I could have a heart to heart in the kitchen about what was to come.

"Where's your car, Nico? I didn't see it in the driveway."

"Luke dropped me off," a blush stole over his cheeks, "thought I could use one here, you want me to head over to see Dad?"

A run-on sentence? Something Nico rarely uttered unless nerves had taken over. I smiled far too wide for my comfort—Mom was looking away from us—but kept the peace, not calling attention to his mention of Luke. "Yeah. We'll try to get over there soon."

Nico left, and I rubbed my hands together. "All right, Mom, let's get to work. What do you need me to do so you can go see Dad?"

She surveyed the kitchen, then moved to the counter by the phone and gazed at the calendar. The large day-at-a-glance monstrosity always perched on the corner of that counter. She picked up a pencil, made a mark on it, and then turned to me. "It's...the twentieth. I'm caught up for now. What I need to do is print labels and such...then... I should check any online orders."

"You do online orders now? Who knew?"

"Not many. This is all getting to be a lot for me. I can't keep up. Been sending some orders to...to a business I know."

"So is it time to think about retiring?"

"I don't know...no... I like this. I find..." She trailed off, turned around, and checked the calendar again.

"I guess we need to print labels," she said and then ruffled her hands through her hair.

"I know. You just told me that."

"I did? Sorry. I'm worried...about your Dad, you know."

Stress could tax a brain, and even if Mom had an odd way of showing affection—meaning, she showed little—she loved Dad. Maybe getting her there, with him, and making her more comfortable with his limited mobility would help in the long run.

"Allrightythen. I have a great idea. Let's pack a lunch and bring it to Dad. He's been complaining about the food the last couple of days."

Mom paused as if she had to think about it. The urge to ask "What's there to think about?" rose within me, but I tamped it down. "Sandwiches are easiest. What does Dad eat?"

I scrounged around in the cupboards, looking for paper napkins and aluminum foil, figuring that if nothing else, we could throw together Sunbutter and jelly for Dad. I'd requested that Mom and Dad not keep nut butters in the house, just in case.

"Well... Let me check." Mom opened the refrigerator door, then moved the still sealed lunch-meat packages around. She looked at each package, then put it back in the drawer. It took her some time to come up with the choices housed within the drawer. "Turkey and ham are okay."

"They're okay? Or does he *like* them? Which one is it?"

"Well, we have them here, so I guess he likes them."

"And what about you? Is salami good for you?"

"That's fine."

I pulled out the cutting board and the unopened lunch meat, then took bread loves—rye for Dad, oatmeal for Mom—from the freezer.

"I can make my own," Mom said.

"I don't mind making it." The number of sandwiches I made in a few days had to outnumber those they ate in a month. If we didn't have leftovers, Will took two sandwiches for lunch each day, and the boys ate the same way he did. The day we had two teenagers in the house—watch out! Our grocery bills might rival the mortgage.

"It's okay. I'll do it."

Mom's snappish voice surprised me. She'd always been quick to anger, but over a sandwich? Of course, some days went that way for everyone, I supposed. "You stressed a bit?"

"Well, yes. Wouldn't you be? I'd rather your dad is at home."

"That's what we're working on, Mom. That's what we're working on."

CHAPTER 18: FRANK

Does this constitute enjoying myself? I bit into the sandwich Angie had brought with her. Apparently, Marissa had suggested Angie stop in with lunch; she arrived thirty minutes after Nico had, and we'd just now been able to sit and chat. The physical therapist had been here when Nico first arrived; she'd scooted him to the reception area for a few minutes. Seeing both Nico and Angie felt good. I'd been so lonely lately. No matter how chipper Megyn Kelly might be...

I swallowed another bite of the sandwich. Way better than the rubbery meat they called "chicken cordon bleu" at dinner the night before or the pasty oatmeal I had for breakfast. There wasn't much to this sandwich—turkey, cheese, mustard, and tomato—but it was the best I'd eaten in days.

The food wasn't the only problem though. Every day, people walked—or should I say shuffled—by my door. They trailed back and forth in small, painful steps, joints almost audibly creaking. A few hunched over their walkers. Others mumbled to themselves as they wheeled themselves by. *Slowly.* Their presence was a constant reminder of the ticking clock. I wasn't like them; I could still take care of myself.

Angie sat on the bed's edge, picking at her own meal, not saying much.

"You okay, Angie?" I said. A third bite of the sandwich, the tangy mustard tickling my taste buds, and a quick wipe of my mouth with a napkin.

"Yes, I'm fine. I don't like it here."

"You don't say... You try staying for a while! Now you know why I want to come home. And now they check me every goddamned hour. Can't get any peace around here."

She glanced up from her food. "*Can* you come home? Are they going to let you?"

I'd spoken to her about what I wanted to do—get out of here at any cost—and I thought that Marissa or Will had told her what happened, but maybe not. "Sure. I should be home soon."

Angie continued to pick at her sandwich, crumbs falling on her lap. Later, she'd complain about the mess.

I looked at Nico, who had his phone in one hand—as always, reading something—and a sandwich in the other. He looked older, more capable than he ever did when he still lived at home. *Be nice if he came by more often.* Despite our rocky past, I missed seeing him. And Gabe, but that situation couldn't be helped. "How's the job going? How many hours do you work in the summer?"

Nico lifted his head from his screen. "It's good. I enjoy the summer students, their outlooks, their ages, where they are in life. These kids *want* to be in school. So different from the high school kids who *have* to be in school."

"You were one of those high school kids once, you know."

"Don't I know it! I should apologize to *every* teacher I ever had, you know? Young and stupid, I was. Hot-tempered too. Just like you, I guess." He took a bite of his sandwich.

Me, hot-tempered? Yes. Young, stupid. Nah, not me. "Are you calling me—"

Nico swallowed, placed his sandwich on his napkin, and sliced his hand through the air. "We're not going there today, Dad. Wanted to see if I could help, figured you'd need a friendly face in this place. By the way, how are the bowels?"

"Still not good."

Angie piped up. "We have those pills at home, the ones that make you go. I can bring you those."

Nico shook his head. "Laxatives. Probably not allowed. Not part of the med list, unless the doctor puts him on something. We'd have to check before we give him something. Maybe someone could help with an enema, but again, we need to check on that first. Fruit will be good though. Did Marissa pack any?"

Angie reached into the container and rifled around. "Oh, here. She sent an apple, a cup of grapes, and this...this...purple fruit."

I looked at Angie. "That's a plum. That'll work. Could you please hand me one?"

She took a napkin, placed the plum in it, and extended her hand toward mine. The fruit felt perfectly ripe.

Nico reached into the lunch bag and extracted a white nectarine. Juice dribbled down his chin as he bit into it, and a grin spread across his face as the fruit's sweet scent filled the room. "There are worse places you could be than eating lunch with your favorite child, Dad."

"He's right. You could be where Antonio is," Angie said.

My heart thudded in my chest. "What? What are you talking about? He's been gone...for a long time."

"Dead," Angie said. "I just mean, at least you're alive."

Anger rushed in, and I grimaced. "That's an odd way to say you appreciate me."

Nico's gaze ping-ponged between Angie and me. He chewed his fruit, a thoughtful, expectant look on his face, but said nothing. He'd heard very little about Antonio over the years, and he probably knew better than to jump in.

Angie sniffed. "I didn't mean anything by it. But he's gone, and you're not. Have you thought of that?"

"Yes! Every goddamn day of my life, Angie, and especially on the day he died, the anniversary of which wasn't that long ago. Why are you bringing him up now?" Antonio as a subject was off-limits. And this was the most she'd said to me in a while...

She wrinkled her nose and wiped a crumb from her lip. "I... It's that I found an old newspaper clipping...the column in the newspaper...reporting his death—"

"And what about it? That was years ago, Angie. He needs to stay where he belongs. In the past."

"But why?" she asked.

Nico tipped his head encouragingly. "She has a point, Dad. Maybe it would help to get whatever bothers you about Antonio off your chest." He leaned forward and whispered. "He seems to be a touchy subject. Always has been."

My reflexes kicked in: a clenched jaw and tightness across the chest. "*Touchy* subject? There's nothing that *bothers* me. When I was away, he had an accident. I wasn't there to help him. End of story."

"An accident?" Angie said. "But that newspaper clipping—he drowned, right? What...why—"

"Listen. Some things are best left buried. Angie, you of all people should know that."

"What? Frank...that's nonsense—"

Nico wiped his mouth and balled his napkin around the nectarine pit. "Dad, I didn't mean to upset you. But what are you holding onto? What's that thing people say? Either get it off your chest or it will eat you away? Memories can hurt sometimes, sure, but if you—"

I slammed my hand against the bed, the vibration dampening too quickly for any satisfaction. "I'm not talking about Nico, and that's final!"

My son frowned. "Me, Dad? What about me? I thought we were talking about Antonio."

Nico, Antonio. Who knew? It didn't matter that Nico seemed happy. My love for both wasn't strong enough to save either of them.

CHAPTER 19: MARISSA

After seeing Mom off, I took care of a few tasks she'd appreciate—washing dishes in the sink, placing newspapers in the garage, and hauling trash bins to the curb. She'd always complained about those chores when we were young, cursing our inability to see what was right in front of our noses. Now that I had my own kids, I understood Mom's stance better.

On my way back in, I *observed* rather than *saw*. If we were going to hire someone to come in, we needed to give them a few details of what to expect, didn't we? In the living room, right next to Mom's butterfly lamp—*sure enough, Cam and Eli came by their fascination honestly*—the thick leather photo albums lined the bookshelf. I quickly thumbed the pages past family vacations and holidays, not wanting to spend time there. Too many negative feelings reached out from the page. One picture—why did someone take this one?—showed Mom, her eyes narrowed in anger, probably directed toward Gabe. Who knew what he'd done. Maybe something, maybe nothing. At that time in our lives, Mom's fury ignited like a fuse. Walking on eggshells became the norm for a little while.

Then, later pictures, photos of Mom and Dad alone. In Hawaii, at a work function, at a dessert reception Mom had catered—her first in fact. Her eyes each time—so angry, annoyed in every picture. Every single one. Where was the vibrancy that should have been there? The sparkle? Was her life too much for her? Were *we* too much for her?

Nothing in a photo album would be useful for potential health care aides, so I made my way into the dining room, my gaze landing on the large paper mounds that seemed to have multiplied from the last time I'd been there. What the hell were these papers? Dad had mentioned something about cleaning out files, which meant cleaning out and shredding, not piling up on a table somewhere. I laughed to myself and made a mental note to talk to Will about what we *shouldn't* do in the future.

The box I'd hunted through last time sat where it had before, so I picked it up and brought it to the window seat. Tucked right under the first sheaf of papers lay a book on memory care. The copyright date read 2013, too late to be useful for Grandma, who died in 2003, so... I flipped through the pages, amazed by the notes, scribbles, and underlines in Mom's handwriting. She'd always highlighted important parts of books and articles and tagged which pages she needed to go back to, her own personal annotating brand. Some habits, it seemed, were hard to break.

The papers themselves contained a journal article printout titled, "Experimental Aging Research: An International Journal Devoted to the Scientific Study of the Aging Process." It, too, had underlines and highlights, notes and squiggles. The third clip of papers held what looked like another scientific article called "Special Section— Behavioral symptoms of dementia: their measurement and intervention. Caregiver interventions for passive behaviors in dementia: links to the NDB model." I removed the clip and gasped: my parents had to have ordered this issue; they wouldn't have been granted access for *Aging & Mental Health* from her home computer, and it had been published in 2004. Maybe with her mother's passing, Mom had dementia on her mind. But if so, why had she kept this box? A thought reared its head: Dad was the one who verbalized fear of his own dementia. Did Mom know something we didn't about Dad?

I pulled out my phone to text Nico and Gabe in the group thread. It would be evening in Germany, but if Gabe could chat, he'd reply. And Nico would be, or should be, still with Mom and Dad. He answered right away in a private text to me.

Nico: *Dad's in the bathroom, and Mom stepped out. For what, I can't be sure.*

Me: *Hope he used his call button. And Mom? Don't get me started. But I'm here at their house, looking through papers.*

Nico: *Don't eat all the candy!*

Me: *I don't even know where she stores most of it.*

Nico: *Was there something you wanted? Don't take this the wrong way, but Dad had a blow-up, and the quiet is nice.*

Me: *Fine. Did you know they had a bunch of papers on memory and memory issues?*

Nico: *No. Where?*

Me: *In a box in the dining room. Mom marked them up like she always does.*

Nico: *Highlighter and pencil?*

Me: *LOL. Yes.*

Nico: *What exactly are you looking for? Did you just call to say you love me?*

A few music notes jumped on the screen, and then a Stevie Wonder gif appeared.

Me: *Stop! That's a good song, but not now. I started out wanting to get info to give to a home health aide, just in case. But now I'm wondering what all those papers are for and looking for answers to a question I'm not sure of. Answers to my question about you and Luke.*

Nico: *Sneaky. You won't find those answers there but nice try.*

Me: *I had to.*

Nico: *I know you did. And you deserve a conversation. Soon?*

Me: *If that's all you're offering, I'll take it.*

Nico brought up a good point: I didn't know what I was looking for, just following an odd feeling. Stress could be causing Mom and Dad to act strangely: the way Mom didn't answer my lunch question and avoided seeing Dad. And Dad—if he was perturbed by a memory issue... Were things changing here? Was something wrong that we weren't aware of?

I placed the box back in its place and decided to investigate the rest of the house quickly. It wouldn't take long to eat lunch; Mom would want to come back soon and do whatever she did in a day. A current to-do list might be in the kitchen on the calendar.

Snooping into Mom's things left a bad taste in my mouth for one minute, but I plunged ahead. Details of so much littered the calendar: everyone's birthdays on their respective days—her sisters, her kids, even her parents' birthdays, people who'd been long gone; appointments for both her and my dad; and the due date for taxes. Wedged at the back was a four by six paper stack held together with a simple butterfly binder clip: a phone list for family and friends, three appointment reminder cards, old receipts. I chuckled to myself and took a deep breath. Her calendar and the things she stored in it could have been mine, Gabe and Sarah's, maybe even Nico's. Then the next piece of paper caught my eye and burned a lasting image. In printed capital letters were her birthday and her name, first, middle, maiden, and last: Angela Maria Bianchi Raffaelo. She'd also written Dad's complete information and their address and phone number. Multiple times. Almost like a reminder.

My hand flew to my mouth, and an unease unfurled in my stomach. Was this information for something specific? Would I be feeling this trepidation if Dad hadn't said something about his own memory?

I pulled a bar stool out and sat down, placing my head in my hands. *Think, think, think. Of recent events. Things they've said. Think about Grandma, Mom, Grandpa...all of that.* Shit. Did *I* have a good enough memory?

After a moment or two, I scribbled a few notes on a piece of scrap paper. Mom's Dad had died in 1997, and my grandmother had declined in the years after that, as if having a husband to take care of kept Grandma healthy and robust. It wasn't until Grandma was at home by herself with the dog that she started to exhibit memory loss symptoms. Mom had told me about it when I'd come back from school to visit. How Grandma would repeat everything multiple times, how she ruminated on past stories, how she couldn't remember what she'd been told five minutes before. She overfed her dog because she couldn't remember if she'd put food out or not, and soon, the house exploded with paper piles, unwashed dishes, and dirty clothes. She couldn't find the checkbook, her purse, her glasses, her clothes, the keys. Items ended up in odd places, and eventually, one of Mom's sisters took their mother in for a diagnosis, which had been Alzheimer's. The disease *was in the family.* Why hadn't I concentrated on this fact before now? Why hadn't I looked for symptoms in my parents, both of them, before now? Why hadn't Dad thought to look at Mom and Mom look at Dad?

But accusing someone of having a problem based only on a few clues didn't seem like the right thing to do. How could I get more evidence? A quick text to Will informed him of my findings; maybe he'd have an idea.

Nico's incoming call broke into my thoughts.

"Hey, have we found a home health aide yet to help?"

Appreciative of Nico's use of "we," I disclosed the truth. "Haven't even started. Maybe I can get FMLA approved or something, but there's no way Mom can take care of him. And speaking of Mom," my heart rate picked up at the idea of voicing my thoughts, "I'm going to be watching her. Finding out what she can and can't handle. She's acting weird, and I'm, I don't know what to think."

"*Weird.* Is that some great medical term?"

"You know what I mean, asshat. Dad mentioned he might have dementia. I'm not sure if anyone has the problem, but a few things lately are making me wonder about Mom."

Nico drew in a breath. "That's harsh, Marissa. I mean, really harsh."

"It is. I know, but Grandma had Alzheimer's, remember? And so did one of Grandma's brothers."

"He did? How did I not know this?"

"Sometimes you're in your own little world, dear brother, and sometimes, you don't listen to me. That's why."

"Harsh again, Marissa. Harsh again. In fact, that's just *rude*. Why do you—" He hummed a few bars.

"Nico. Stop. It." That habit had to cease. Catchy song or not, I didn't want to sing it all day long.

He snorted. "At least it's another good one."

"*So* 2014, you know."

"Not really. Remember, my schedule *can* be flexible, if I want it to be, so if you need help, let me know. The question is, do I want to?" Happy-go-lucky Nico didn't sound so positive.

"What is it about you and Dad?" I asked. "Why does he push your buttons?"

"No clue. It's just..." Nico sighed. "He and I don't see eye to eye. You and I both know he doesn't approve of me and my life. Not that I need his approval—unlike you."

"Ha! Tell me about it. I suppose these deep thoughts need to wait for another day. Right now, we'll all need to pitch in. I'd love to say I can do it all, but I can't." So far, tasks had been handled, but a crushing fatigue lurked around every corner; it always did in these circumstances.

"Welcome to adulting, sis. I'm proud of you for acknowledging it."

"Hey now—"

"I'm not kidding. You've always taken too much on. So know this— we'll figure it out together. What do you think?"

"I think it's a shame this rehab place didn't work out."

"You and me both. Anyway, let's get on finding a person to help. Now, I'm going to finish up here with Mom and Dad as I have things to do and people to see. Or is it people to do and things to see?"

That Nico. He always knew how to close a conversation.

CHAPTER 20: FRANK

Owning up to my actions had never been my strong suit, but I had to the moment Marissa showed up late Saturday afternoon. She'd eventually find out what had happened. Too many days had passed on the inside of this hellhole. *Interminable* days in a prison cell. Days that melded into one another, all black. Days that had to end. In the back of my mind, I knew they would soon, but like Cam or Eli would say, *soon* couldn't come *soon enough*. But I wasn't ready for the erratic heartbeat and the sweat on my brow the minute my daughter poked her tired face through the doorjamb.

"Hey, Dad." Marissa moved silently into the room. She'd always had a light and graceful, almost fluid, movement to her. She'd have made a wonderful ballerina. Or a ninja. Right then, either option would have been preferable to her having become a medical professional.

"Come sit down." Each morning, I made my bed as best as I could or asked for help to pull the covers over the mattress. Usually housekeeping came in, too, and tidied the sheets, a small touch to help tamp down the anger inside; I wanted out of this place so badly.

Marissa sat in the armchair next to the bed and opened her purse. She took out her phone, messed with it for a few moments, and then slid it into her pocket. "Just wanted to set the phone to vibrate," she said. "These phones sound so loud in these small rooms."

Marissa had always hated the bell clanging, siren shrieking, or any other extraordinarily loud noise. She used to mutter that the sounds cluttered her brain. I always laughed at her until I came to rehab. The first moment my phone's ringtone reverberated off the walls, my mind jumped to four-year-old Marissa holding her hands over her ears. How many other things had I laughed at when it came to her?

"So," she started.

"So... I should tell you—because someone else will—that I did something I shouldn't have done."

"Oh, Dad, that doesn't sound good." She looked at me with a peaceful and nurturing expression.

I knew in that moment Marissa was both a great mother and an extraordinary nurse practitioner. She had the immediate reaction to soften, not harden. It must have been something she taught herself because that reflex certainly didn't come from either of her parents. Angie relaxing and softening...no. Those two words never came to mind when I thought of her. Maybe it would be okay to tell Marissa. "You know I haven't had a decent bowel movement the entire time I've been here, and at the hospital—rabbit turds on the first day. The discomfort became intense. Do you know what it feels like to need to poop?"

Marissa nodded and crossed her legs. "I had the same issues with each pregnancy and after each birth, so yes. I guess since *you* couldn't move, nothing else was moving either."

"That's right." A quick glance at the television. No sense to have it on now. I clicked the button on the remote, and the screen flashed off. Marissa seemed to mumble a quick "thank goodness," but I couldn't be sure. No noise on the television meant nothing to help cover up my admission. "No one would help me..."

"No one? Did they give you fruit? A fiber laxative? Any other—"

"Yes. We tried fresh fruit, canned fruit, and prunes. When I first got here, they said they'd come give me something stronger, and no one did. The doc even said he'd give me a prescription, but I'm certain they didn't, and the aide knew nothing about it."

"She can't prescribe, Dad."

"No, I meant she checked those damn charts and didn't see anything written up in terms of a laxative prescription."

"Oh. So what did you do?"

"I had your mom bring me an enema after lunch."

Marissa's hands flew to her cheeks, and she leaned forward in her chair. "And?"

"And I must have messed up. Because I bled a little. And the nurse got mad at me. I thought I better tell you before she did."

Marissa fell back against the chair and looked at the ceiling. "Of course she got mad at you! You could have perforated your bowels!" She closed her eyes, sighed, then pulled herself back up to sitting, directing a stony gaze my way. "Did you *really* think it was the best idea to give yourself an enema? Why didn't you ask for one?"

"No one was listening to me. I told you that."

"You're right. They weren't. But Dad, at least call *me* before you do something like that. Or Will or Luke or… Common sense, Dad! Had I done that when I was young, you'd be all over me."

She was right. I'd always expected a lot from Marissa, especially by way of common sense. As a woman, she'd have to prove herself brighter and smarter and better than any boy would have to. I just wanted to see her do as well as I knew she could.

"Oh crap." She looked at me then, and a full smile spread across her face. "Sorry for that awful pun, I didn't mean it. But have you? Did the botched enema at least produce results? Please tell me it did."

"Sadly, no."

"Okay, well, we'll do something about that pronto. And guess what? You're coming home sooner than you thought."

"What? What do you mean? I thought I was here until Monday."

"At the rate you're going—a fall, no batteries in the bed alarm, taking too long to come see what's happening, an enema for God's sake—I think they'll have you ready to go for us bright and early tomorrow morning."

"They will?"

"Oh, I'll make sure of it. Think of it as a Father's Day present. But you're still being checked out AMA, against medical advice. They want you here. And I do, too, but this isn't the right place. More importantly, you're a danger to yourself."

Danger to myself. Was I?

"So I'll get moving on my end, and we'll get you out as soon as possible tomorrow." She leaned in, lowered her voice. "Where did Mom got the enema, and how did she get it so quickly?" Marissa stood and stared at me.

Angie had so many items stockpiled around the house and car—pills, lotions, herbs, you name it, not to mention all the confectionery equipment and supplies. Acquiring an enema on short notice hadn't been a problem. I shifted my body, and my sphincter hollered at me, the drill instructor's sharp ring, reminding me of my actions. But Angie had made a mistake too, hadn't she? And— "What about Nico? Shouldn't he have said not to give me the enema?"

Marissa shrugged. "He's no professional, but... Where was he when Mom handed it over?"

I shook my head. "Out. I'm not sure. He finished up his lunch and then a text came in. He left shortly after, before your mom got back."

"Hmmm. Well, it's not like he was supposed to babysit or anything, but I'll see if he knows something. Maybe he got a text from Luke or something."

"Luke? Why would Luke text him? Aren't you all friends?" Back in the day, Gabe, Luke, Nico, and Marissa had been thick as thieves, as my mother liked to say. While I was glad to know he'd be back in the area, I thought he'd stayed in contact most with Marissa and Will, not Nico.

Marissa folded the light blanket at the edge of the bed then moved the trash can from one corner of the room to another. What wasn't she saying?

"Marissa—"

"Yes?" She glanced quickly my way.

"What aren't you telling me? Is something going on with Luke? Are you and he having an—"

She stopped in her tracks. "What? Why would you think that? Luke is a friend; always has been, always will be. And remember, I'm married. To *Will*." She straightened her spine, stiff with irritation that I'd put there.

"I know you're married to Will. And you have a heck of a guy there, do you know that?"

A smirk crossed her face, and I wondered who she was thinking of. Will? Luke? I didn't want to think of that. I had no evidence, but just the thought... Triangles never ended well.

She adjusted her bag across her body, then reached into it and grabbed her phone. "Yes, I do. And since I want to see my kids and that 'heck of a guy' at some point tonight, let's get this show on the road. Sit tight, and please, please don't do anything you're not supposed to! I'll be back as soon as I can, okay?"

"Okay."

Marissa crossed to the doorway, then turned and looked back over her shoulder. "Hey Dad? I wanted to let you know that I'll do what I can to help... Take time to get you situated at home and all that. I have a call into my boss about FMLA time, but that can only be short-term. We're going to find someone to help, okay?"

That topic again. "I'd rather it's you, Marissa."

She sighed. "I know, but...I have a job *and* a family. We'll find someone fantastic—I promise. And Mom has to help with all this as well. Let's hope she's up to the task!" Marissa turned and left, giving me one sidelong, worried glance before she exited the room, her phone buzzing in her hand.

CHAPTER 21: MARISSA

On my way back from the rehab director's office Saturday evening, after I'd put out a small fire via text for an overworked colleague taking a night shift at a partner clinic, I stepped into an alcove for a quick breather, texted Nico, Gabe, Luke, and Will with a recap of my conversation with Dad, and pulled up information on the butterfly life cycle and the kit we owned. My goal: to give definitive answers to the boys about what we might be doing wrong with the butterfly garden. One website suggested X, while another Y, but the idea to contact someone at the university worked its way into my brain. They had to know how to fix the problem, didn't they?

The phone vibrated in my hand, this time, a call from my boss. I'd spoken to my colleagues about taking FMLA time, and they were supportive and confident that the boss and HR would be too. Feeling a bit more relaxed at the thought, I answered the phone.

"Marissa?" my boss started. "Sorry for the weekend interruption and one so late. I wish I could grant you the time to take care of your family, and by law, I need to do that. But now's not a good time."

"It's not?" The news surprised me.

"No. We just had two staff members quit, and now, we're in an all-hands-on-deck moment. Looks like we might need to up your hours, not cut back. But I'll give you two days."

A wave of irritation washed over me, and my jaw clenched. Working part-time, tending to the boys, taking care of most of the housework, just the mental energy alone to deal with appointments, grocery shopping, finances, and more—and now, having to increase my hours?

"There's nothing I can say to sway you?" I asked. "I mean, lawsuits aren't my thing, you know that, but honestly... These are my parents we're talking about. And I—"

"No can do. Two days. Take it or leave it."

What would Dad say to me helping for only two days? Was there a chance he might move to another rehab facility instead? One that would have his best interests at heart, not allow him to be a danger to himself. And how was it that the weight on my shoulders seemed to compound so easily?

A huge sigh escaped as I looked over the discharge checklist and folded Dad's undershirts while he was with the activities assistant. His desire to be at home made sense—as an introvert, that feeling coursed through me often—but he didn't know what was to come when he stepped an unsteady foot inside that house. And if I couldn't be there to help, if Nico couldn't be there, then someone responsible would have to fit the bill. A text to Nico and Will—"Might need help finding someone to stay with Mom and Dad"—would remind us all to get back to the list we'd started. In the meantime, I'd help through Tuesday, if needed. But perhaps I'd try to persuade my boss too.

After settling Dad in for one more night—it was too late in the day to bother taking him home—making sure Mom was safe at home, and prodding Nico about his availability ("It might take a little finagling, but I'll do my best," he said), I made my way home for Saturday night relaxation with my family. Cam's checkup had gone well—nothing new to report—and everyone was up for a board game and ice cream cones followed by a discussion about where to go with the butterfly garden.

"I want it to work so bad," Eli whispered to me when I tucked him into bed, and I admitted the same to him.

•   •   •

Later that night, I ransacked my closet for easy outfits to take to my parents' house and looked over at Will. He sat propped against the bed pillows, halfway through the 1079-page *Infinite Jest*, a book I'd always wanted to read but never quite found time to start. I had to give it to Will. He was a man who conquered life goals the way a chess master conquered opponents.

"You think the kids will be okay while I'm gone?"

"Oh sure. They're used to you not being here part of the day, and they'll love the camp and being with my parents if you're gone more than we expect. Plus, I'll be here in the evenings, and we have tomorrow. We'll have fun. Don't think another thing about it. It's only a couple of days."

It hurt to think I wouldn't see my kids even for a short length of time. Unlike many parents who stepped away from their children for at least a weekend getaway, I hadn't been away, ever. "I know you'll be having more fun than I will be, that's for sure."

"I can't even imagine. All those hours of Fox News or the Hallmark movies. The infomercials! Maybe you can encourage them to shut off that ridiculous television while you're there." Will shook his head and laughed. "But you won't be pestered with questions about caterpillars and cocoons and butterflies!"

"Ha! You'll have to text me chrysalis pictures. I'm going to get to the bottom of our issues if it's the last thing I do. And yeah, my mom says she likes the noise. Sometimes I think they have it on so they don't have to speak to one another... Do you think we'll be that way? I mean, when we're old and retired?"

"No way. I like you. I always have." A full smile filled Will's face. Only eight words, all of them true.

"Right back at you." I threw an extra running bra into my bag. Would I have time to exercise? Who knew? But if I could get a break...

Will closed his book, took off his reading glasses, and looked right at me. "Honey, I want you to know that I think you're doing the right thing. Nico might be able to cancel a few classes and help, but you'll give your Dad and Mom peace of mind for a few days."

"Thank you. We still need to find someone to come in and take over, but you and I both know they have no idea what they're getting themselves into with having Dad come home. Nico doesn't either. Hell, I can only imagine what can go wrong over there. And those papers I texted you about... What is with those? I'd rather not have to clean up the pieces. Maybe this will be more proactive."

Will placed the book on the night table and his glasses on top of the book. His handsome face suddenly seemed youthful. More like when I'd first met him. "You're a good kid, Marissa. Clearly, despite anything you've told me about your childhood, your parents did something right. And by the way, your mom and dad are going to be fine because you'll make sure of it. You always do."

I shut my suitcase, climbed over the bed, and moved on top of him, brushing my lips to his. After several light kisses I'd be missing over the next few days, I whispered again, "Thank you."

Will knew me better than anyone. He'd homed in on my insecurities without me even saying anything at all. I'd never gotten validation or emotional support when I was at my parents' house, but if I needed it here, at my home, I'd always have it. *Always.* I rolled off Will, wrapped my arms around his waist, and settled my face against his neck. In moments, sleep took me away.

• • •

In the night's blackness, the movement of little feet next to my bed interrupted my sleep. I opened my eyes and blinked; Eli stood over me.

"What's wrong, honey?"

"Please don't go, Mommy. The caterpillars. I'm worried about them, and I'll miss you."

I pulled the covers off and opened the bed to him, showing him where to scoot his little body. He turned on his left side, facing away so we could spoon, him snuggled in tightly against my chest. A few sniffles, and then a tear dropped onto the arm that held him against me.

"It's okay, Eli. Really. The caterpillars will be fine. Daddy is very good at taking care of everyone, including the butterflies, and I'm going to figure out how we can make things work better with them." I stroked his hair. "And of course, you'll miss me. I'll miss *you*. But you're going to have fun. I bet you'll come up with so many things to do you won't even remember me."

"Oh, I'll remember you, Mommy."

He'd always been my little guy. The kid who cried when I dropped him off at daycare. The one who hung around my legs when all the other kids romped on the playground equipment. I squeezed him and tickled his little belly, tucking his head under my chin and kissing the top of the head.

"Eli, you'll have fun. I promise you that. I won't promise that you won't miss me a little, but you can text me or pick up the phone, and we can have you stop over to see me. And I'll call you every day, even though I'll only be gone for two days. How does that sound?"

"Okay, Mommy."

"Then let's get some sleep, all right?"

"Hmm...Mommy."

The topic would surface again—after all, this was Eli—but the crisis had passed for the moment, and he was already on the other side of sleep, hopefully dreaming of dancing rainbow-colored butterflies with gossamer wings. I smooched his temple and pulled him close, seeking the warmth of his small form. He seemed to feel safe and secure and loved. Hopefully, he would always feel that way.

•   •   •

Early the next morning, Luke stood outside the nurses' station at rehab, his back to me. His butt and hair gave him away. Back when we were young, he confided in me his insecurity about his flat back end. I'd never laughed, always assured him that with time and muscle, he'd gain a more rounded posterior. And he had. But I'd had enough practice to recognize that butt anywhere. In a silly moment, I snapped a picture and texted it to Nico, who texted right back.

Nico: *WTH?*

Me: *Who is this?*

Nico: *Luke. Why?*

Me: *Aha.*

Nico: *Aha what?*

Me: *Nothing. I'll tell him you said hi. *wink emoji**

Luke must have heard the scuffing of my feet over the rehab noise, which included community television Sunday services. He turned and smiled.

"Just checking to see that everything was good to go for today." His eyes sparkled with a hint of mischief under the fluorescent lights.

Something was off here. "Did Dad ask you to come?"

A sheepish look rolled over his face. "He did. I stopped in to see him, and he sent me to check on things. Gave me permission to ask and all that."

I snorted. "Geez. Do you think he doesn't trust me?"

Luke held up one finger. "Thanks for the information," he said to the nurse and then guided me with his hand on my elbow a few feet away to a sitting space. The garnet chairs, plush and soft, molded to my frame; these were far better than what was in Dad's room.

Luke leaned in toward me, a thoughtful look on his face. "I don't think it's that he doesn't trust you, Marissa. I think sometimes he doesn't want to bother you."

Bother me? No matter what had happened in the past or what would happen in the future, he was my dad. You only get one family, regardless of what you might or might not feel for the members of that family. "What do you mean by that?" I looked out the floor-to-ceiling window at the mild June day. There were worse places Dad could be.

Luke adjusted his body in the chair and leaned forward, keeping his voice low. "From what I can tell, at least when he talks to me, he always says how busy you are. With your job, the boys and their schedules, your volunteer work and Will's soccer. He's not sure how you get it all done."

"He told you about Will's soccer schedule?" Will played the game outdoors in the fall and indoors in the winter. Summer was reserved for time with the kids.

"Oh yeah. I know all about it. Their three-two loss at the end of last season, how Will's friend blew out his ACL. The whole shebang. Your dad tells me a lot."

Well. "He sure does. I think he might tell you more than he tells me."

"That's probably because of the Y chromosome I have and you don't. And, I talk to him a bit." Luke grinned.

I shook my head at Luke's admission. "I always thought he liked Nico and Gabe better than me. You know, that whole boy versus girl thing. Well, Gabe, anyway. Nico—they always knocked, still knock, heads. But how did I not know you talked to him so much? And *why* do you?" An aide strode by with a breakfast cart holding a bowl with the infamous oatmeal. Dad was right; the brown lump didn't look too appetizing.

"First off, I like him. I know, I know, he's got his quirks, shall we say. But he's not my dad. I don't have a history with him like you do, so I can take what he says and put it away easier, let it roll off my back. Furthermore, I don't have kids. I don't have family, really. I think I've told you before. Your family is my family. I'm sorry I'm poaching them."

I chuckled under my breath. He *was* poaching, but he was also right. Luke didn't have anyone else—his parents, while still alive, weren't supportive at all. If we turned our backs on him, he'd be close to alone. And that wasn't a nice thing to be in life. On the other hand, what Luke said made me sad. "It's okay. Sometimes they don't feel like family to me, so I'm glad they do to someone else."

Luke placed a hand on mine. "Marissa, I'm sorry you feel that way."

"Listen, that's a chat for another time, one that Nico might want to sit in on."

"I see what you did there."

I pulled my hand away. "I did nothing of the sort. And I can't stand when people say that. The astute will see it if someone does it, and the others, well, it'll go over their heads. You, Luke, are one of the smartest people I know. I can't pull anything over you."

"I'm flattered—

"The truth will *come out* eventually..."

Luke groaned. "You didn't."

"I did." I rubbed my hands together. "But say, speaking of Dad and Nico... Do you know how *that* conversation went years ago? Has Nico told you? Dad and Mom—let's just say they weren't as accepting of Nico as you might hope. Does that have you concerned at all?" My phone buzzed in my bag, and I took a quick glance. A text from Eli, checking to see how I was doing. My heart warmed.

"Actually, I have thought nothing about it at all. But maybe I should."

"That sounds promising."

"We're done here, Marissa. Doesn't your Dad need us?"

Like Nico, Luke always knew how to shut down a conversation.

•   •   •

Luke went ahead to Dad's room while I texted Eli back and then made a quick phone call to Mom. She picked up after she heard my voice on the answering machine and gave me trouble about coming to help pick Dad up. She eventually caved, ignoring my reminder that it was Father's Day and whispering, "If I can find the place," before hanging up.

Dad had been taken to the PT room for one early round of physical therapy while I waited for Mom in the rehab facility's modern lobby. My plan? To cut her off at the pass so I could ask why she hadn't wanted to come. I flipped through a magazine while waiting, waterfall tinkling in the background, until suddenly, feet came into view. Two sets. One belonged to Mom, the other Luke.

"Phew. I made it." Mom swept the hair off her forehead with one hand and clutched her old leather purse with the other. "I don't know why, but that turn to get into this place...makes me confused every time."

"It's a bit of a strange loop, that's for sure. Where'd you park?"

"Right out there." She turned and pointed to her silver Buick, which sat nicely lined up in the middle of the driveway—the driving zone, not a parking spot.

I looked at Luke and then out toward her car. "How long are you staying, Mom? If you're going to be here for a while, you should move your car."

"Why? I just got here."

My clinical spider sense tingled as I took in her face. No error recognition. A completely innocent countenance. Had a patient or patient's parent recounted this episode to me in my office, I'd have suggested keeping an eye out for further issues.

Luke took her by the arm and brought her toward the window. "That's not a parking spot, Angie. That's part of the throughway."

"Oh." She tried to laugh off her mistake. "I guess I better move my car then."

What. The. Hell?

CHAPTER 22: HER

That confusing parking lot. The small room, the antiseptic smells, the boxes mounted high enough so that the person in the bed could see the images on the screen from the bed and the chair. The closet-like bathrooms where the scent of urine always seemed to linger. He didn't belong there, and neither did she. He needed to come home; she needed him there.

She started to tell him as much when a lady came in to chat with him, to give reminders, she said. The woman spoke quickly, too quickly for her to hear everything. She listened to those reminders fly from the woman's mouth, catching only a few terms she knew, like sugars and blood and sodium. The rest of the words rattled in her brain, making her head a throbbing mess, so she stood and paced the room, patting her pockets. Glancing at the clock on her wrist, she excused herself for a moment, exited the room, and looked for the public bathroom. A small break was all she needed. A slice of time, all to herself. She hadn't had enough of those lately.

Moving slowly—this place was unfamiliar after all—she wandered toward the reception desk. Or so she thought. When she reached the wide atrium, nothing looked right. Where had the large planter gone? And the waterfall in the center? She'd used that to help her know how to get to the front doors.

"Can I help you, ma'am?" a young man asked.

Despite the shakiness in her hands, she answered, "No, thank you." For he could not. Maybe if she worked her way backward, she'd find what she was looking for. Pressing her purse to her chest, she turned and followed the hallway she'd just come down and then paused. A cigarette sounded good right about then. She dug around in the bottom of her purse but came up empty.

CHAPTER 23: FRANK

Rehab had turned me old and decrepit in a matter of days. The social worker and nurse forced me into a rickety wheelchair to get from my room to the lobby. They would have made me use it to get to the car, but I balked. Instead, they "allowed" me to walk with the walker to the car. The nurse had a frigid hand on me the entire time. Once I was tucked into the passenger seat—no driving for me, of course—Marissa placed a walker into the back seat. That damned walker! Knowing my daughter, she'd make me use it all the time, but who the hell wanted to do that?

Marissa played capable while I waited in the passenger seat: she made sure Angie had the medicines and discharge instructions with her before sending her home ahead of us with Luke, who'd offered to help. Then, she loaded all my personal items into the car, spoke one more time with the nurse and the social worker, and began the drive home. She'd brought her own car—the Subaru. It suited her. Had room for everything I'd collected.

Marissa's hands gripped the steering wheel. "Happy Father's Day to you, Dad!" Her lips twitched with a small smile. "You know, I'm going to have to get to the grocery store and the pharmacy today. You need good food and your meds to start the healing process."

I reached a hand to the crumb-covered dashboard as we rounded a curve. "I feel great. Thanks for coming to get me, by the way."

"You and I both know you'd have left even if I hadn't come. And I figured Mom might be too stressed out to handle this all by herself. It's a lot to take in if you're not familiar with all the medical jargon and processes."

"That's all we need. More stress for Angie." The words fell out before I could think better of it, but they were true.

Marissa started to say something and then stopped, following up only with a single, sideways glance. I didn't want an argument and kept my mouth shut and my gaze on the scenery outside the window. Eventually, we drove through the town's older section. Past the Methodist church and my favorite barbecue place, through the intersection that almost made us lose Gabe when he was sixteen, and over to the edge of the new strip mall. *Almost home.* My legs shook slightly at the excitement, but I couldn't *feel* the trembling completely— could see it, mostly. My limbs—had they lost their strength even more? Right then, I didn't care, just needed to be at home. In my room, my bed.

"You staying for lunch?" I asked Marissa.

A surprised look crossed her face. "Actually, I'm staying for a few days."

"You *are*? I thought maybe you didn't have time. And then what?"

"You're used to having someone bring you food and water and medicines. You're used to help in the bathroom. You're used to twenty-four-hour care, Dad. You won't get that here without me or someone else."

"Pfft. It's more about having someone around, and I have your mom."

She snorted and covered her mouth with her hand. "Not to be rude, but I don't think she'll be able to handle all this for you, Dad."

Truth. Or her version of it. Smack in the face the way Marissa always offered it. What were a few pills to take? The doctors had everything written, so all we had to do was stick to the timetable. Easy for an organized confectioner like Angie and an airman like me. Even if Angie was too busy, did Marissa think I was incapable of helping myself?

We pulled up to our neighborhood. Our home. "What are you saying, Marissa?" My daughter's implications warred with the relief I longed to feel.

"I'm saying this is going to be a long road. You have appointments to get to and medicines to take. And you can't even walk more than a few feet in front of you. With Mom's orders to fill and her euphemistic *stuff to do—*"

I grimaced. "She does that to you too?"

"Sure as shit does and always has. I haven't figured out what she has to do all the time. She has a good system, she *could* have assistants—if she'd call them—and she has downtime. She should be able to get her stuff done. The rest of us do."

My back bristled with the negativity. "Watch it. She's still your mom." Marissa shouldn't be talking about her mom that way, but she was right, though I wouldn't admit that to her.

Marissa didn't respond, just tapped her hands on the steering wheel as we reached the driveway.

What a sight! The grass blades, maybe four inches tall, needed cutting. The flower beds... I hadn't been gone that long, had I? And the weeds. I'd left that job for Angie. Hadn't she said she'd get to them? The neighbor boy could head over in the next few weeks, and I'd have to ask my neighbor to do the lawn for me. The week after that though—I'd be back for sure.

After stopping the car as close to the rear sidewalk as she could, Marissa looked at me. "Don't try to get out of the car. I'll come around and get the walker out, and then we'll get you to the door."

"But do I—"

"Yes, you do. Technically, you left the rehab place AMA, Dad. The only reason they didn't fight you is because of me, Will, and Luke *and* the threat of a lawsuit."

"But—"

"Not going to do this, Dad. I'll drive you right back to another rehab place." She put the key into the ignition.

Placing my hand on her arm, I said, "Okay, okay. I'll wait." Now wasn't the time to tell Marissa her behavior reminded me of Angie's.

CHAPTER 24: MARISSA

What a way to spend a Sunday, Father's Day no less. I'd gotten Dad out of the car and into the living room chair but then excused myself to get everything out of the trunk. A bad feeling about what was to take place slithered up my spine as I made my way back to the car, my gaze on the red-winged blackbird that skittered across the driveway. Maybe it was Mom's gaffe at the rehab facility or maybe Dad being himself in the car and me having to put my foot down, but I'd have my work cut out for me over the next few days. After lifting the trunk's lid, I texted Will.

Me: *Made it out of rehab and at Mom and Dad's. Wanted to say hi and let you know Luke is here. Nico might come by later. Maybe bring the kids if I think it's not too much for Dad? I'd love to spend Father's Day with you.*

A second or two later, a reply came in.

Will: *Thanks. Glad you made it. Say hi to Luke. One more word for you—caterpillars.*

Me: *Are you with the kids or doing research on them?*

Will: *Research. Not finding a whole lot. Kids are with my parents right now. Had an early start.*

Me: *Gotcha. I'll call you later.*

Will: *Okay. What are you wearing?*

The amount of junk Dad had accumulated at the rehab place distracted me. How many undershirts and handkerchiefs and washcloths and emery boards did one man need? How had they all gotten there?

Me: *Jeans and a shirt. Why?*

Will: *Oh, never mind. *wink emoji**

Pure Will. Here we were, texting about my parents, and had I let him, we'd have texted about other matters.

Luke walked out the back door just as I put my phone back in my pocket, and he wordlessly picked up random items off the driveway. He stopped, turned, looked at me, raised his eyebrows, and then walked back into the house. What did the raised eyebrows mean? He performed the same action two more times, tipping his head in the direction of the house on his last loop.

Was something going on in that house at that moment that I didn't want to know about? Or was he being Luke, toying with me the way my brothers would? Once again, I pulled out my phone and this time, texted Nico.

Me: *Going into the house. Will be surrounded by Mom, Dad, and Luke. God help me.*

I knew he'd reply in an instant. He never disappointed in that way.

Nico: *God help you? I'll be by later. With Luke there, I'd say you found yourself a cheerleader.*

He sent a stream of music emojis, and OMI's song popped into my head. How did he do it? How did he come up with a song on demand like that?

Me: *You need to market that ability, Nico.*

Nico: *Word.*

Me: *See you later. I'm sure Luke says hi.*

Before he could reply to my juvenile message, I tucked my phone away, picked up the last of Dad's belongings, locked the car, and moved toward the door. My feet moved slowly over the cracked asphalt, propelled only by a sense of duty. Not a good feeling to have. I wondered how long Luke would stay and if Will would bring the kids or not. And the kids... They'd be playing T-ball or kickball or painting T-shirts or maybe jumping off the diving board at the rec center pool soon, depending on what Will's parents could stomach. Finally, the thought of a tall, cold glass of lemonade appeared in my mind. I focused on an image of vibrant palm trees swaying in a gentle breeze as I slid open the back door and—

"What the heck, Mom? I thought you didn't smoke anymore."

She stood at the kitchen island, her eyes directed toward the ceiling, watching the wispy, gray smoke spiral upward. "I don't...but...I found these..." In the background, the chatter of Luke and Dad.

Waving my hands in the air, I coughed. "You've done enough damage to Dad's lungs and your own over the years. You said you didn't smoke in the house anymore. You said you don't smoke, period. Were you lying?"

"I've been stressed."

"Yeah, well, so have I, and you don't see me lighting up. Wait, hand me one of those." I tried to pull the pack out of her hand. "Give me one, please."

"Don't...don't you dare, Marissa." She shoved the pack into her shirt and put out the cigarette in the dirty, ceramic ashtray. "You don't, don't... do this, and now isn't the time to start." She picked up her glass, took a swig of water, and then looked at me with wide eyes. "It sounded like a good idea."

"You know how I feel about that, Mom. Smoking is *never* a good idea. I hate to say this, but if I see you doing it again, I won't bring the grandkids over here anymore. I *can't*. Cam already has an allergy. The last thing we need is for his lungs to—"

"Is that an—?"

"Ultimatum. Well, I guess it is. But it's the truth. Cam has enough problems, and I don't need to give him more. And it's not good for you. Or Dad."

Mom fell into the chair around the table. "Okay." Her voice was small and distant. I felt bad for yelling at her, but Dad didn't need a smoky haze when he was trying to get well, and neither did anyone else.

"Okay then." I moved a bag full of the week's newspapers from the chair to the corner recycling unit. "Is Dad planning on heading upstairs? I don't think he's strong enough to hang out in the chair in the living room for very long."

"I don't know. I haven't talked to him about it."

What? "Mom? I know this is going to be hard on you. It will be hard on all of us, but the only way for this to work is for all of us to pitch in. Communication will be huge. I haven't found anyone to help yet, so we'll need you." I took in the pencils on the table, the oil bottle on the counter, the mail pile on the island. "Is something wrong? What's going on?"

Mom looked at me, then turned away to stare out the kitchen window, which overlooked the back patio. "Nothing. Just tired, I guess."

With nothing more to say and so much to do, as Mom would say, I left to go join Dad and Luke, who'd been in the middle of a conversation, probably something about politics or an article in a money magazine. My conservative father shouldn't get along that well with a liberal like Luke, but Luke never came right out and declared his party affiliations. Something in the way he spoke made you think he was on your side, even if he opposed it.

"What was that all about?" my dad whispered.

I moved to the chair next to him. "She was smoking in the kitchen!" I looked at Luke. "Is that what your silent eyebrow message meant when you came out to the car?"

"Yes."

"Why didn't you just tell me? Or use the universal sign for smoking?" I held two fingers up to my lips and then pulled them away. "Or better yet, say something to her?"

Luke refused to look at me, guilt written all over his face. "It's *her* house. And I didn't want to tattle."

"Yeah, but you're a *doctor*. You could have put that hat on and gone with it. Plus, you care more about Dad than Mom, and tattling, as you like to call it, would help him—"

"Hey. That's not fair. I like your mom too."

"I know you do." *And maybe someone else in my family.* "Well," I slapped the chair's arm, "I could sit here all day, but Dad, you should get upstairs. You have to be tired, whether or not you realize it."

"I feel pretty good, and I'm hungry. Think I could get lunch?" His hazel eyes looked to mine, and a smile spread across his face.

"Guess I'm on duty as of right now. Not the best Father's Day meal, but sandwiches okay?" Nico had left a note saying he'd purchased a few deli items—"To make it easier on you," he'd written—and placed them in the refrigerator. "Let me tidy up a few things and get some of this put away, and then I'll get started. Luke, are you going to stay? I can make you a sandwich, and then you can earn your keep by sticking with Mom and Dad while I go to the store."

"Sounds like it's a deal." Luke leaned back in his chair, extended his legs, and crossed them at the ankles, like he was settling in for the afternoon. At that moment, I wondered how securely he'd settled into Nico's heart.

·   ·   ·

To say my folks didn't have food was an understatement. Mom had been there essentially by herself for almost a week, but the state of the pantry, freezer, and refrigerator appalled me, something I hadn't noticed when I made lunch the other day. Expired milk, past-dated sour cream, rotten potatoes, and moldy onions all went into the trash. Jars of crushed garlic—stored in the cabinet instead of the refrigerator—had long since gone bad, and the bread I found in the bread box could have been used for a science experiment. Where was the real food? The food they could actually eat?

The cabinets were stocked only with a few crackers and a jar of Sunbutter—thank goodness—and boxes of grocery store cookies. Dad's diabetes diagnosis came years ago. He knew the importance of nutritious foods. It didn't look like anything they had would be good for him.

I grabbed the grocery sack filled with the items Nico dropped off. "What have you been eating, Mom? There's not a lot here."

"I eat eggs."

"But every day? Eggs? What else?"

Mom gave me nothing but a blank look.

Throwing together sandwiches—one for Dad, one for Luke, nothing for Mom, "thank you," and one for me for later—took but a few minutes. After placing Dad's and Luke's plates on the kitchen table, I grabbed my phone and ran up to my room, punching in Will's numbers and hoping he picked up.

"Hey, it hasn't been long, but I think I'm ready to come home."

Will laughed, a sound I'd always been drawn to. He was probably leaning back on the couch in the family room or brainstorming ideas for another research project. He didn't sound distracted at all. *I wouldn't mind being with him right now.*

"And you should see the pills for Dad. Neurontin, sodium tablets, prescribed vitamins. They're not sure what the problem is, so I think they're reaching. I need to go through each one and confirm he needs it—not that I don't trust the pharm folks, but I've seen it before when the wrong med is given to the patient—then figure out a system for them. There's no way either of them can manage this many meds."

"Shouldn't your mom be able to keep track if they're labeled? Doesn't she keep track of her orders?"

"I thought she did, but the packets are overwhelming *me*, and we haven't even gone through them together yet. And if you'd seen Mom...sort of lost, almost...." I filled Will in on the smoking, the rotten food, and the parking debacle and reminded him about the papers I'd found with names and birth dates, not to mention the printouts.

"Maybe you should have been a detective."

"I am! I try to figure out what's wrong with people every day."

He chuckled. "True, and you do it very well. What's Luke doing?"

"Luke is going to babysit while I head to the grocery store and pharmacy."

Will laughed again. "Serves him right for meddling."

"You know it's not meddling. He *is* helping, and honestly, you'd do it for *me*, right? Maybe he's also doing it for Nico."

"That could be true." A chime sounded over the line. "And on that note, I need to go. That's an update from my parents—think I'll meet them for pool time. I love you."

In all our years together, there'd never been one instance when he hadn't said "I love you" before hanging up the phone. Even when he'd been annoyed. I looked at the phone in my hand and smiled.

CHAPTER 25: FRANK

Luke helped me into the kitchen, and I ate an early lunch at the old, mahogany table. Asking for help from anyone or accepting that help? Distasteful. But I had no choice. Marissa was in a rush to get to the store, and I couldn't blame her. Lunch back in the service sounded better than what was in my refrigerator. Thank God my hunger wasn't that strong. I hoped my appetite would pick up over the next couple of days. Maybe if I had a bowel movement...

"Can you put prunes or a laxative on the list?"

"That's right. You still haven't had a good poop." Marissa took a bite of her sandwich and jotted something down on the list next to her. "You know, I thought they would have had proper defecation under control at rehab. It's not like it doesn't happen all the time, you know."

"What kind of table talk is this?" Luke said with a smile. "What would Angie say?" he whispered.

"You try not pooping for a week and let's see what you talk about. That's all I think about these days." My lack of a bowel movement—the productive kind, as I'd had a few pebbles here and there—had superseded my worry about dementia. Like I could only deal with one crisis at a time. Maybe men were the simple creatures Angie talked about.

"That's for sure, Dad. I'll check the paperwork again, and when I'm at the pharmacy, I'll see what they recommend. I don't want to cause a problem with your pills. Speaking of which, I think you're due to take some."

She moved over to the kitchen counter, where she had stacked my pills next to the flour, sugar, and salt canisters.

Shit, I had a ton of them. I imagined the drill instructor, his you'll-do-this-because-you-have-to attitude. Bet he didn't realize his training would rise again this late in my life.

"Mom!" she called. "Are you going to give Dad his pills? It might be a good idea for me to show you the ins and outs of this since you'll be the one who is home most of the time."

Angie moved into the room and looked over Marissa's shoulder. "I guess I am... Yes." Her eyes widened. "Which does he need?"

Marissa spread out the cardboard folders on the counter and pointed. "These are the four he needs at lunch time. But it looks like he's been given a script for something at every meal and a few other times during the day. The top part here," she touched the label with her finger, "tells you when you need to give the meds to him."

Angie pulled the folder from Marissa's hands, squinted at the text giving the prescription name. She fumbled, tried again. Then flipped the cardboard over and huffed. "What...What am I supposed to give him and when?"

She could do this. "Angie, think of these meds like your business. The flavorings or something. You put a specific amount into your candies, right?"

Narrowing her eyes at me, Angie whispered, "If you know so much about this, why can't you take care of it yourself? You...you seem just fine, Frank, and I have—"

"I know, I know. You have *orders* to take care of. Good question though. Why can't I do this myself?"

Marissa glanced at Luke, as if waiting for him to jump in. He gestured with his hand for her to continue. "Honestly, that would be great if you could. But you have a script for Neurontin, which can cause drowsiness. And while you feel great today, I can guarantee by tomorrow that you're won't feel so alert. We want someone with a clear head to help you with these."

"And you think that's me?" Angie said.

What did she mean by that? "She might be right, honey. Remember that poster in the ambulance? The dementia one—"

"Oh hush, Frank. Just show me what you want me to do."

Well damn.

Marissa pointed to the name on each cardboard plank. "These names here are what you're looking for. I can write what each medicine means if it's easier. They're already grouped according to time. At eight in the morning, you take this pill, along with these three. And at noon or so, you'll take this set, and so on. Dad," she turned to me and tipped her chin up, "I'll show you how it works later. They've even put the Metformin in here. So anything he needs during the day—"

Angie dropped the cardboard and walked toward the cupboard near the stove. She rummaged through pill bottles, pulling each one out, looking at the container, and then putting it back. She frowned, lines etching her face. Whatever she was thinking was worrying her.

"Mom. What's wrong? What are you looking for?"

"The Metformin. It should be here."

A stack of what Marissa had pointed out was Metformin sat on the counter. At least enough for a week as far as I could tell. Marissa's gaze darted my way, Luke said nothing, and I shrugged.

"Uh, Angie. Marissa has the Metformin. It's with the other pills."

Angie's face ironed itself out, and she closed the cupboard. "Oh. Then let's go and see." She moved back next to Marissa like nothing out of the ordinary had happened. "Now what is this again?"

Marissa looked at me once more, her eyes dark. She then glanced at Luke. Both shared a moment before turning my way. While I could only speculate what they were thinking, I knew for sure what was going on in my own head: What in the hell had just happened?

.   .   .

The clock ticking on the mantle would drive me to drink if I had to hear it anymore. It spoke of time passing—my time—the minutes I'd wasted in my bed. The money I'd be wasting if we had to hire someone to help us. The waste of Antonio's life. The anniversary of his death had passed, so why was he still haunting me? Was this my time to die? Is that what my thoughts meant? Right on time for Father's Day. What a celebration.

I shifted in the recliner, where I'd been stuck while Marissa did the dinner dishes and then ushered Cam, Eli, and Will out the door. They'd chosen to stop by only to say hi. The boys were growing up fast. I didn't see Gabe's kids enough, and Nico, well, he probably wouldn't grace me with any grandchildren at this point. A few more would be welcome, but it wasn't my decision. I'd have loved to spend more time with them, but the truth was, I still didn't feel well. No big bowel movement yet, but maybe the fresh fruit and fiber Marissa gave me would produce results. Luke had gone home—said he had a "hot date"—and Angie? She must have been in the kitchen. If the ticking didn't do me in, the constant television chatter there would.

"Angie!" I called. "Can you please turn that television off?"

The volume increased then decreased, and then she strode into the room. "I'm working. I like having it on."

"What are you doing? Do you have time to sit with me for a bit? I just got home and I—"

Wiping her hands on the ever-present towel in her hands, she scowled. "I have a book club coming up next week, and they want special shapes. Something I'm not, something I...haven't done before. What do you need?"

What did I need? "I need *you*, Angie. My ass is screaming at me, and I ache all over. I want to see my wife for one evening, a Sunday at that. Can I do that?"

Angie sighed and sat next to me, placing her hand on my arm. "I'm sorry, Frank. You don't have to be so crude. It's... I have a lot to do."

"And what would make you *not* have all that work to do?"

"I don't know." She looked away, toward an old picture of the kids, one with all three, laughing in the shallow water of a creek. In that same photo, Angie sat on a nearby boulder, a thoughtful expression on her face.

"What were you thinking there, Angie? In that photo?"

"How would I remember?"

"All right then. That picture—it's always been a favorite. It captures your beauty. I thought maybe you'd remember what you were thinking about there. Thought maybe if you tell me something positive, I'll feel better about the predicament I'm in right now."

"Predicament? You...you did this to yourself, Frank. Doing things you shouldn't be doing...not thinking something through. Each time you fall it's because of an idiot decision."

"And does this make you angry? You *seem* angry about it."

She pursed her lips. "I guess so, and I'm tired too. Tired of trying to make everything right. And now...these pills."

"We're going to be fine, Angie. We'll figure out the pills, and we have money in the bank if we need to hire—"

"No, we don't."

A thunderbolt hit me in the chest as the ticking in the room stopped. "*What?*"

"We don't have money in the bank. It's gone."

"What are you talking about? Of course we have money. The investments—Dan would have called if there was a problem. What aren't you telling me?" When she wouldn't look at me, my voice grew louder. "Angie?"

"It's not *all* gone, Frank. I needed help at the bank...machine, so I asked someone."

"A person who works at the bank?"

"Yes...maybe? I got my money and thanked them and went about my day. But then, I couldn't find my card. I thought I'd misplaced it, like the other things that have gone missing around here. When the mail came with the letter from the bank, well—"

"What letter? And how much? How much is gone, Angie?"

She shook her head and closed her eyes. "I don't know. I'd have to look...I'm not sure."

"Angie?"

The number she revealed hit me like a missile, and my stomach turned over on itself as I caught my breath.

"And...I still can't find the card," she added.

Dammit. Gripping the chair arms with my hands and clenching my jaw so tightly it hurt, I asked in a trembling voice. "Did you call the bank, Angie? Did you *at least* call the bank?"

"I don't know, Frank. I don't remember. You won't tell the kids, will you?"

And get admonished by all three? Not a chance.

CHAPTER 26: MARISSA

Right before I turned in for the night, I checked in on Mom and Dad. The television flickered in the darkness of their stuffy bedroom, although both were peacefully sleeping. Would either of them wake up for Dad's 11 p.m. medication? The chime sounded, and my hopes dropped as quickly as my jaw; not one of them moved. *Shit, this can't be happening.*

I flicked the alarm off and gently shook Dad. "Hey. We need to give you meds, and you might as well go to the bathroom."

"O-kay." The word came out as nothing more than a mumble, almost a slur, but he tried to push himself upright against the mattress.

Gripping him under the arms, I moved him toward the edge of the bed and lifted him to the walker. One very slow step at a time, we made our way to the bathroom, where I gave him as much privacy as possible. On the way back to the bed, I snagged the 11 p.m. medication from the dresser, and once Dad was tucked in, offered the pills and the water.

He swallowed them, said, "Thanks," then pulled the covers up to his chin.

"Will you get up for the next round all on your own?" I whispered. "You need to take them at two in the morning."

"Sure. Set the alarm for me, will ya?"

Knowing he couldn't see my expression in the dark, I rolled my eyes. If he hadn't heard this first alarm, there was no way he'd hear the next bell. I dropped a quick kiss to his forehead and then walked toward my room. After setting my alarm for 2:03 a.m., I drifted off to sleep.

It's funny what happens when you're in an old bed in a former home, the things you think and dream. You wonder what's been running through your mind to cause such dreams and then realize that all the things you experienced in a day come back to you, rushing at you one after the other like an unstoppable waterfall. Unclear images of my family and me popped to the forefront of my mind that night. In my dream a carousel of memories spun.

Will as a young man, much like when I met him, flickered behind my eyes, only in black and white. Then college Will, who morphed into Gabe, then Nico, then Luke. The three taunted me until Mom, or a person I thought—felt?—was Mom came out and reprimanded them, expletives loud and clear in my mind. She placed a hand on my shoulder, then rubbed my arm, giving me the impression she understood. *But had Mom ever understood me?*

Back in the dream, a dark cloud passed over the sun, a crack sounded, and there, on the concrete, blood pooled around Dad's prone body, staining the concrete vermillion. He'd fallen again. Next to me, Mom, still monochromatic, screamed then sobbed, her shoulders shaking with each breath as she tried to get to him. Something held her back, but I couldn't see what, and she extended shaky fingers toward him as she clutched her chest with a tense fist. "I'm sorry," she whispered. "I'm so, so sorry."

Against the air conditioner's whir, a distant bleat broke through my sluggish brain's musings. Blinking in the diffuse yellow light of the butterfly nightlight, I tried to reorient myself as I threw on my bathrobe and trudged to my parents' room, where I leaned against the doorframe, the crimson stain still pulsing in my mind's eye. My glance darted around the darkened room, taking in the threadbare area rug and worn chair, the shoes that littered the floor near the end of the ancient, sagging mattress. We'd need to remove many of those items or Dad could fall in the middle of the night.

The beep of the alarm continued to reverberate against the walls, and still, Mom and Dad slept through the cacophony. The noise disrupted the peaceful night, but I waited. *One, one thousand, two, one thousand, three, one thousand, four, one thousand. Oh for the love of...* What if there were a fire? And again, what if I weren't here? Dad was supposed to do what he could, and Mom was supposed to be helping. She needed to wake up, dammit.

"Dad, your meds. You need to take them." This time, I pushed at his shoulder, then turned off the alarm and tapped Mom. "Hey, Mom. That's the alarm. Dad needs to get to the bathroom and take his meds."

Once again, Dad struggled to sit up as I stepped back from the bed. Mom lifted herself slightly and, eyes barely open, looked at Dad. "Frank, you need...to take your stuff." She didn't move to get the meds, just patted him on the arm.

What the...? In a few seconds, Mom would snore, and Dad might too. Any hope of an easy recovery for Dad fell to the wayside, and an urge to stomp my feet and pull my hair coursed through me. But adult Marissa knew that behavior would serve no purpose. Gently, I helped Dad to the bathroom and gave him his medications, all the while still ruminating on that dream. What was Mom sorry about? And Dad. *Ugh.* We needed to get a grip on whatever issue—besides impulsivity—was with him. Despite the complicated feelings for my parents, I wanted to see them happy and healthy, emphasis on healthy, and the only other worse feeling I would have had is if I'd dreamed that something had happened to Cam or Eli or Will.

As Dad finished up and washed his hands, I sent a short text to Will saying I loved them all—he wouldn't see it until morning—and took a moment to breathe. A glance into the mirror in my parent's bedroom at the purple half-moons under my eyes and my pale cheeks revealed more sleep would be useful, but it wasn't the only thing. I had to relinquish a good handful of duties. Get back to the basics. Like Cam and Eli, like Will. But how to do that with obligations to Mom and Dad?

And as I took a long look at Mom, chest slowly rising and falling, mouth open in the dark, clarity descended: my dad's recovery was important, but Mom's behavior would need to be addressed too.

CHAPTER 27: HER

It was comforting to have him here, in the bed next to her. He couldn't move as easily as he had before he left, but the warmth of his body made her feel at home. She'd missed him when he'd been away. She had prayed, repeatedly, for him to come back. She didn't know why it took so long for him to return from that place. Her daughter had tried to explain it all to her, but the information weighed her down. Too much to do and too much information in her head. *Too much, too much, too much* echoed, drowned everything else out.

She flicked on the box and settled in next to him, then adjusted the volume to a low lull, something that wouldn't bother him but that she could still enjoy. The movie looked good. It was something she'd seen before but didn't mind seeing again. It would drown out the worry about the money in the bank, about her orders, about the laundry, about the dusting, about Frank. Allow her to experience that happily ever after she always adored. Rewatching movies was like rereading a book, encountering familiar characters, favorite family members you hadn't seen or spoken to for so long.

The thought of characters reminded her she hadn't read a book in a while. She missed those books. In the morning, she'd have to go look at the bookshelves and choose a new story to read.

CHAPTER 28: FRANK

Angie was nowhere to be found in the dimly lit room the next morning, and I needed to use the bathroom—badly. I pressed my arms against the mattress and tried to lever my upper body. A couple of scoots and shimmies in the tangled sheets, and eventually, my lower body edged to the side of the mattress. And now, the walker... *Shit.* It was in the opposite corner, as far away as possible. Who had put it there? It couldn't have been Marissa. Had I done so in the night and forgotten about it? But how would I have gotten back to bed? Had I asked Angie to do so? Had this been a sign on the poster? Not remembering doing things and asking things and finding objects in odd places? *Oh God.*

The urge to use the toilet overtook my desire to understand if I had dementia. I had no choice—I'd have to call for help.

"Angie!" I yelled. Everyone had to be up already. *Everyone* being Angie and Marissa. The clock read 8:04 a.m. Marissa never slept late, and Angie rose at the crack of dawn so she could get moving on all the things she had to do. "Angie!" I called again, hopeful she'd hear me.

The seconds passed. Forty-five, forty-six, forty-seven—

Marissa rounded the corner, a concerned look on her face. Her gaze darted between me and the walker. "I'm not going to ask," she said. "But I'm not going to see this again either, Dad."

"This?" What did she mean?

"This." She pointed at the walker on the other side of the room. "You have a walker for a reason. *To. Help. You. Walk.* You cannot get to the bathroom without it. What the hell is it doing there?"

She peppered me with her ire all the while we shuffled to the bathroom. An accident with my daughter in the room—nurse practitioner or no nurse practitioner—held no appeal. I concentrated on holding my urine while she castigated me. The toilet bowl's cool porcelain met my ass, and I slouched in relief.

"Happy Monday to me, eh? I didn't put the walker there, *Marissa.* Or maybe I did but I don't remember."

"When I left you at two in the morning, the walker was on your side of the bed. And just now, it wasn't. I didn't move it. Either you did or Mom did. If you can't remember, I'm betting Mom is the culprit."

"Why would she do that?"

"Why does she do any of the fucked-up things she does?"

"Marissa!"

"I'm sorry, Dad. I didn't sleep well last night, and it's true. Why was she smoking the other day? Why didn't she come to see you in rehab more often? Why did the Metformin send her into a tailspin? Why? Why? Why? We can keep asking ourselves these questions and never get any answers. So why don't we ask *her*?"

"Oh no. She'll get mad at me."

"That, she will. So I guess the conversation stops here."

Marissa left me then. But I would have to get off the toilet, and I wasn't sure if she was coming back or if she'd gone to get Angie. I also wasn't sure which woman I wanted to come help me. Neither one seemed like a good choice.

Maybe I should have stayed at rehab.

Ten minutes later, still with no poop to show for my efforts but empty of urine, I tried to stand. The bathroom attached to our bedroom had never pleased me. Too small, too cramped, only one sink. But that day, the small space was a benefit. If I leaned over my knees, both the door handle and the windowsill would be within my reach. "On the count of three," I mumbled to myself, "one...two...three!" An enthusiastic rush left my brain but fizzled at my thighs, and I wobbled, causing my elbow to crash into the wood door.

"Frank? You in there? You...okay?" Angie's voice came from the edge of our bedroom.

Slumping back onto the toilet, I sighed. "Yes, Angie. I'm in here. Can you help?"

She opened the bathroom door with a frown on her face. "Marissa said you were up. How're you feeling?"

"No substantial poop yet. Does that answer your question?"

Angie stepped back and put a hand on her hip. "No need to be...testy, Frank. I'm sorry. Eat more fruit. It will come out when it's ready."

"So can you help me up? My legs... They aren't right, and I feel sluggish. Really sluggish." Brain fog, someone once said, and I hadn't understood it then. Now I did. "By the way, what are you doing right now? Can you show me that paperwork, er the letter, from the bank?" She'd been too upset, and it had been too late to do anything about it last night, but I wanted to make a call, brain fog or not. *Today*. Making sure our money was safe was important, maybe even more important than me and my health.

Angie wouldn't meet my eyes. "Let's finish up here, and I can put you out on the porch for a while. How does that sound?"

"And you'll bring the papers? I gotta call them today... The more information—"

"I know, Frank. I know."

Angie situated me at the table and chairs in the corner of the porch, promising to bring me a breakfast tray. "Fruit and eggs? And those papers? Please? I'm not sure how long I can stay awake."

"I'll be back."

And she was, with a breakfast tray of cereal and canned peaches.

"What's this?"

"It's...what I can do today. I didn't want to bother Marissa."

"And the papers?"

"I can't find them. But here's the bank's phone number." She placed the lined paper on the table, passed me the cordless phone. "Eat first though. The liquid is already in the bowl." Years ago, I'd made my opinion known on soggy cereal. Angie never let me forget it. But I appreciated the kindness. "Eat those peaches too. That's what Marissa told me." She nodded, a scowl on her face. "Now, I have to go."

"I know. You have a lot of orders to fill," I said, but Angie had already left, a trail of vanilla—maybe she was making cookies—in her wake.

The cereal hit the spot. The peaches, though sweeter than my usual preference and a reminder of mess-hall days, provided moisture to my parched throat. After pushing the tray to the side, I picked up the phone and called the bank.

A voice sounded on the line: "We're sorry. You have reached a number that has been disconnected or is no longer in service." *Dammit.*

"Angie?" I called and waited a few seconds. "Angie!" Where the hell was she, and where was Marissa? The front door was shut, as were the front windows. I looked around: no walker in site. Did Angie take it with her? We had enough furniture on the porch that perhaps—

Marissa poked her head over the porch's side. "I know that look, Dad. What are you doing?"

"Where were you?"

"In the garage. Do you need something?"

Being honest wasn't an option. "I'm looking for papers your mom told me about. Do you think you can head in there and take a quick look around? A letter from the bank? I want to see how the accounts are doing."

Marissa had always been astute, but financial matters didn't interest her. She'd take my question at face value. Or at least I hoped she would.

"Hold on. And by that, I mean, stay put. Do not go anywhere or try anything."

Marissa came back with a paper stack. "Sorry, Dad. I'm so tired, I didn't even look at these, but they were in the kitchen, and they might be what you need. I gotta get coffee, stat, or I'll be feeling like this all day. Check here, and holler if you need me. Or," she cocked her head in the phone's direction, "call me. You have my number. Mom's doing something downstairs."

Kids these days and their phones. I nodded and delved into the papers on my lap. Angie had always taken care of the paperwork. Our den, lined with file cabinets and bookshelves, held papers as far back as our wedding anniversary. This stack would need to be filed soon. Mortgage payment, credit card bill, grocery receipt, electric bill, memory supplement? What the—?

I pulled the paper from the stack and looked at it in the light. What was this? And who had ordered it? Had Angie been lying? Did she think I had dementia but didn't know how to tell me? Placing the paper on the right to save, I continued and found the January bank statement. Nothing looked amiss, so I called the number at the top of the stark white paper.

Joseph, our favorite longtime bank teller, answered. "What can I do for you, Mr. Raffaelo?"

I took a quick glance around to make sure Marissa wasn't lurking. No one needed to overhear this conversation. "I'm hoping you can help me with something. Something big," I whispered.

"I'm sorry, Frank, but it's hard to hear you. Can you speak up a little?"

"How's this? My wife told me she'd made a mistake." The details, still murky, maybe because of the meds, sounded strange as I outlined them for Joseph. If Angie could supply the actual paperwork she was talking about, I'd be able to tell Joseph the right story.

"Wait, what?" A crackle sounded on the line.

"Hold on. Sometimes this phone can be cranky." I scooted the chair to the right, moving only an inch. Then another. A third try and—"Shit!"

The chair tipped to the side, and time stopped. I seemed to hover in the instant, ass still on the seat, phone clasped in one hand, the other hand gripping the chair's arm.

"Frank?" Joseph said. "Can you hear me? Are you okay?"

His voice snapped me out of my daze. I leaned left, willing the chair to follow my lead. It complied, its feet sinking once more and *thunking* against the wood floor of the porch.

My hand trembled as I put the phone to my ear. "I'm here, Joseph. And things are okay." As I repeated what I'd told him, the thumping of my heart and the quaking in my hand slowed.

"Gotcha," Joseph said. "Why don't I look up your account, and we'll try to piece something together. But you say you think your wife was tricked? That someone stole your money?"

"Yes." Again, that nervous drumbeat from the night before, different from the scare I just had, moved through my body. I'd worked so hard for my money. Angie had too. We probably still had enough—most of our retirement assets were held by an investment company—but I could not stop the what-ifs from settling in my mind. "Well, if the person still has our card, they could siphon money away a little at a time."

"Okay, let's see..." Clicking sounded on the line as Joseph keyed in my information. "Hmmm. Can I put you on hold?"

"Do I have a choice?"

"Well, Frank, if you want me to do my job, I need to put you on hold."

"Good enough. But I hope you have good news for me. My life has been turned upside down lately. I could use good news." Good news? What was *good news*? That I wasn't losing my faculties. That my legs would work. That my money wasn't gone. What would I do if the money *was* gone? God dammit. That someone had stolen the money, could be *still* stealing the money, well that—

"Frank? I don't see that you've lost any money within the accounts you have here. How much did you say your wife thought the person took?"

I told him, and he whistled. "Yeah, I don't show that here. What I do show, and maybe this is where the confusion comes in, a transfer of that amount from your personal account to another account, which, hold on," a few more clicks and then, "yes, to Mrs. Raffaelo's business account. And I see a few minor withdrawals, pretty constant, same amount. But it looks like your money is safe."

Safe? "What about the card? Angie says the person took the card, which means she doesn't have it. And those withdrawals..." When was the last time I had gone to the bank? "What if that's someone taking my money?"

"Then let's make this easy and issue you a new card." More key clicks sounded on the line. "There. I've canceled your current ATM cards and issued you new ones, and I'm putting a note here to require an ID for any type of activity. When we're finished with this call, I'll double-check our records. If we need to open new accounts, we will. But as I said, I don't think there's anything to worry about here, Mr. Raffaelo."

"But what about a letter? She says she got a letter from the bank. Can you see that letter?"

"Sure. It's right here and, hold on a sec, yes. It looks like it was confirmation of the transfer to the business account. Is that a problem, transferring to her business account?"

"No, not really, though I'm not sure why it occurred. We keep those accounts separate."

"Then maybe it was an error. I'd ask your wife to check with her accountant or financial advisor because you don't want any tax repercussions. If the transfer *was* a mistake, we can easily transfer it back. Looks like maybe your wife got confused with this one." Joseph laughed. "Is there anything else I can help you with today?"

Help me understand my wife's confusion?

The call ended, and though a peaceful calm should have descended over me, it didn't. My focus moved to the opposite corner of the porch. To the walker that stood there. It had been there the whole time, and somehow, I had missed it.

CHAPTER 29: MARISSA

The hole in my stomach bellowed as I bit into a cracker and rummaged through the cabinets for Mom and Dad's familiar red coffee bag. Finding nothing, I leaned against the counter and closed my eyes. A day without caffeine was a day I didn't want to encounter, but somehow, I'd missed checking for coffee before going to the store the day before. My parents *always* had coffee in the house, at least as far back as I could remember. Grabbing a glass of water, I sat at the kitchen table, trying to figure out how to get caffeine into my body as easily as possible—

A wind gust rushed at me as the sliding door opened, and Luke entered, three coffees in hand.

"How did—"

"They gave me a key."

"My house, their house. Whose house don't you have a key to? But actually, I was going to say how did you know I needed coffee?"

"That would be Will. He called me this morning on his way into the office. He had to leave early, but he figured you might need a little pick-me-up. My first appointment isn't until noon today, so I agreed to come over."

"Well, in another universe, this could be awkward..."

"And if I weren't an old friend, it might be. He loves you. You love him. I'm the odd man out it seems."

"We love you too, Luke. Not in that way, of course. And if that's good enough for you, then drop the coffee and go. Or come in. You decide. To be honest, I don't care what you do. I just need the coffee. *Please*." A quick wink, and he'd know I was kidding.

Luke stepped into the kitchen, then placed the coffee on the counter. He opened the refrigerator, helping himself to the new milk container I'd bought the day before. He held up the carton, a silent question to me, and I nodded. Without words, he added a perfect splash of milk into my coffee.

The aroma of the brew as it wafted toward my nose sent me spiraling into contentment, and right then, I could have hugged Will for being so thoughtful, would have done anything he wanted. I whipped out my phone from my bathrobe and keyed in a quick text to him. *You are a lifesaver. And I love you. Thank you.*

He might not get the message right away—an early day meant who knows what was on the agenda. But he'd smile when he read the text.

"Thanks for the coffee. I needed it. You don't even know how much."

"You're right. I don't. It's coffee, not a miracle cure. So you're welcome, but be sure to thank your husband." He placed the milk back in the refrigerator and moved to stand next to me.

"I did already. What a sweet man."

"*Sweet*? No one wants to be called sweet," Luke said.

"Okay, at the risk of making you feel uncomfortable, what would you rather I call him? The best? The hottest? Utterly irresistible? I can't wait until I get home so he and I can get busy?"

Luke threw his head back and laughed. "You'd have to say a lot more than that to make me feel strange here, Marissa."

"You must be spending too much time with Nico then."

"Yeah, I have been spending time with him." His lips quirked up on the edges, but he looked away.

"Come on, Luke. What aren't you telling me? I mean, that hug— that sort of said it all, didn't it?" I took a sip of the hot coffee, savoring the earthy notes as they rolled over my tongue. *Give him time. Give him time.*

Luke nodded and pursed his lips. "It took me a long time to realize what an intricate and complicated character he is. When we were all young, I spent my time worrying about you. Like a sister, you know. Not that I was worried, per se. But you know what I mean."

Not wanting to give Luke a reason to quit talking, I sipped my coffee again, waiting for him to continue.

"And later, after I'd moved away, I had no real reason to see Nico, except that I did, usually when I'd come visit your parents. At first, I found it unremarkable that he seemed to be at the house when I visited, but soon... Well, I did some thinking and put two and two together."

Two and two together? So did I! "And what did you say to him?"

"I didn't say anything. And it wasn't that simple. I took a trip out west—remember the road trip that culminated in Wyoming?—and soul-searched about my life. You were included in that—"

"Me?"

"Yes, I'm pretty sure your parents would have loved to see us together, but that's for another story. Let's just say I discovered, or admitted to, really, a few things about myself."

"A few pretty big, important things, it seems."

Luke smiled and took a sip of his own coffee. "Indeed."

"So what if I have questions?"

A flush crept up his neck. "Like what?"

So many questions ran through my brain at that moment, mostly because I was happy. For him, for Nico. Luke had been an integral part of my teenage family. To have him possibly become an official member? A bonus. "Like, how long have you been dating?"

"About a year."

"A *year*? How did I not know this?" Had I been so caught up in my own life that I hadn't thought to check in? "And what drew you to him?"

He cocked his head. "Do you really want to know?" He held his gaze steady with mine.

"I do."

"His eyes."

"Didn't you say that about that girl you dated a while ago?"

"Did I?"

"Yeah. Well, how about this one, if you don't mind. When did you know that...that... What I'm trying to say is—"

"When did I know men were my thing and women weren't?"

"Well yeah. I mean, please don't think I'm this selfish or self-absorbed, but did you know back in high school? We used to be pretty close. If I think long enough about it, I might be offended that you didn't tell me. Though I realize this isn't about me." My lips quirked into a smile before I took another sip of my coffee.

Luke sat down and placed his hand on mine, then pulled it back. "Is that how you feel? Because I never meant to mislead any of you. You were, *are*, my friends, my family, but back then...I wasn't sure. Something was off. I didn't feel comfortable about *something*, but I didn't know what that something was, and honestly, having parents like mine didn't help. When I broke up with that girl, I thought maybe we were young or weren't right together. But then—"

"Then you realized that you and girls weren't right."

"It was a little more complicated than that, and it took a lot longer to figure things out, but yes."

Luke didn't seem ready for more questions, and it wasn't my place to ask. So I changed the subject as I opened the tin of Anginetti, Italian wedding cookies—my favorite—sitting on the counter. "Has he started singing to you yet?"

Luke furrowed his brow. "Nico? Singing?"

"Yeah. I can't remember when he started to do it, but almost every conversation we have, he interjects a song title or lyric. Makes me crazy! I get earworms all the time. I started texting him because I thought it would be better. *It's not.*" I tipped the open cookie tin in Luke's direction.

He took a cookie. "That's cute, but he hasn't done that to me. I'll be on the lookout. Have you had enough coffee yet to answer questions? I'm wondering how last night went."

"As doctor or friend?"

"As both." Luke popped an entire cookie in his mouth, the way Cam or Eli would.

What *could* I tell Luke, and what *should* I tell him? He was already wrapped up in this mess and seemed content to be that way. But somehow, wouldn't I be betraying my folks if I told him any more stories of their idiocy? I plunged ahead anyway. When I was finished, Luke sat back against the chair and stared out the door.

"Oh shit."

"Yeah. Which means someone has to be here until he's off those early morning meds."

"Or your mom has to step up."

"Or Mom has to step up."

"Do you think it will happen?" Luke said.

Neither the coffee nor I had an answer.

CHAPTER 30: FRANK

Summer—one of my favorite seasons. Maybe because I'd met Angie in the summer. Or maybe I just enjoyed the warm sun on my skin better than anything else, but everything about summer pleased me. The long days, the warm nights. Even the buzzing insects didn't get to me. Part of me treasured getting up early and brewing a pot of coffee. Sitting on the porch watching the sun wake up. I had always been an early riser. As the years piled up, the habit had gotten worse.

And there I found myself, on the porch on Tuesday morning—thanks to Marissa's help—legs stretched and fighting against the tingles of whatever was going on with me. I'd asked her to print out a few items about Alzheimer's and a Self-Administered Gerocognitive Exam (known as SAGE and suggested by the EMT), and I sat there, papers in one hand, coffee cup in the other. I placed the papers on the side table and poured a "slip of cream," as Marissa liked to say, into my cup. The ivory swirled across the coffee's top, dropped beneath, and barreled again to the surface. Like Nico used to do when he'd been a part of the diving team back in high school. The thought of Nico reminded me of Antonio. *Not today.* I pushed him to my mind's recesses as steam climbed from the mug and disappeared into the air, like the movements of a practiced air stuntman. Concentrating on my breathing, I opened the SAGE form.

A few moments later, a relieved breath escaped me. Every question on the paper—I could answer them. No problem. But I still filled the paperwork in and would bring it to my doctor to be scored to have the definitive answer to my question. It's not that I didn't trust Will or Marissa or Luke, or even Angie, who brushed off my memory concerns. But I needed proof. Evidence. Something I could point to and say, "Yes, I'm okay. My doctor told me so." So engrossed in filling out the form, I didn't notice Angie creep up behind me.

She slipped her hand onto my shoulder, taking a quick peek at the papers. "What's this?"

The sun hadn't quite risen yet. The porch's overhang kept us immersed in the dim morning light. "A test, Angie. An Alzheimer's test."

The warmth of Angie's hand lifted away from my shoulder. She turned back toward the door, which stood open, air conditioned coolness losing itself to the increasingly humid morning. Nico used to get in trouble all the time for leaving the door open and wasting energy—and money.

"Wait, honey. Where are you going?"

"I thought this discussion was over, Frank. Why do you think you have it... From one ride with those people? Your memory is fine. Can we please let this go? Sugar issues? You have those. Maybe if you were as worried about your feet and balance as you are about that memory you haven't lost, we'd be getting somewhere."

"That worries me too. And you're probably right. But I want to fill this paperwork out and bring it to my doctor. Get a baseline of who I am, you know, in case..."

In true Angie form, she placed her hands on her hips and looked at the ceiling, a slight sneer on her face. Then she glared at me. "In case of what? In case you...forget things? You're seventy-something, Frank. Forgetting things is...normal. And it might get worse. It most likely *will* get worse."

"Yeah, well. I'm doing this. And I think you should too." *Partly because I can't explain what happened with the bank.* But I knew better than to say *that* out loud.

Even in the muted lighting the horrified look on her face stood out. "Uh, no. I'm not...not filling out anything like that. I remember things. I write lists and cross things off. We all might be getting older, but...I haven't done anything to make you think I have any issues, have I?" The *I* screeched as her voice's volume increased. "My memory is *just fine!*"

Angie continued her litany of ways that helped her remember, and I tuned out. Why wasn't *she* letting it go? Was she touchy because of her mother? Maybe I needed to speak with Marissa about this. On the other hand, maybe I should drop the whole thing. Clearly the topic agitated Angie.

"Okay, honey. You're right. You're fine. Listen. I want to fill this out for *me*. What are you doing today? Want to go out to breakfast or something?"

"Frank, you can't go anywhere, you know that. And, well, I have orders."

"Do you want help? Or at least company? I feel slightly less foggy today, and I think I could help." Also, helping Angie meant I could spend more time with her. And if we were done early, we could order something for dinner or even ask if the grandkids wanted to come over.

"No, that's okay. It would take too long to show you what to do."

She huffed off then, hand pushing through her silver hair. An annoyed look on her face too. Apparently, I would need to find something else to do and someone else to do it with. Though it had been years since I'd spent time with Antonio, on some days, I really missed him.

•   •   •

A sharp noise startled me awake, and I wiped my mouth with the back of my hand. *Where...? How...?* Despite having fallen asleep on the porch,

I rested on top of the couch in the living room. My gaze caught the clock on the wall—11:43 a.m.—and then a note that sat next to the lamp on the side table. After shifting to a sitting position, I grabbed the note and flipped it open.

Dad—you were more than a little groggy when I checked in on you, thanks to the meds. So Mom and I moved you here. I'm out for most of the day, but I have a good lead on someone who can come in to help. Lunch is on the counter for you, and dinner is in the fridge. Nico said he'd try to come by. I'll be back by 8 p.m. Call or text if you need anything. Love, Marissa.

"More than a little groggy?" Is that what she called not remembering most of my morning? *Shit.* What if I really had dementia?

"Angie!" I didn't want to move, and even with the incessant background noise—that blasted television—she should hear me. *If I'm loud enough...* "Angie!"

Footsteps fell in the hallway, and then there she was, cornflower blue towel over her shoulder and breathing heavily as she crossed to the window and opened the drapes. "You okay? What's wrong?"

"Nothing. I just woke up, and I wanted to know where those papers that I had earlier went. The SAGE exam. They should come with me to the doctor in a couple weeks."

"What's a SAGE exam?" Angie didn't look up as she adjusted the fringed pillow on the chair in front of the window.

"The exam I wrote on...the papers that I printed, er, Marissa printed...the thing that I was going to show the doctor. It helps me understand if I have Alzheimer's."

Angie lifted her head with an impatient look on her face. "I already told you, Frank. You don't have it. Why *can't* you understand that?"

"Angie, you can't make that determination. You're not a doctor."

She turned and focused all her attention on me. "But *I* know. You're not...not doing anything like what my mom did."

Angie's sisters had taken on most of the work involving their mother, but in the short time Angie had spent with her mom before she died, she'd seen what Alzheimer's could do. The fear, confusion, anger that accompanies both patient and family members. After her mom's funeral, we'd had a huge discussion on the front porch about the disease and its repercussions. It had been one of the few times Angie had talked about what was happening in life. She had told me to tell her if she started doing anything like her mother had. I promised her then I would. So far, I had witnessed nothing out of the ordinary. *Except for—*

"Yeah, well, I still want to go see the doctor. It's better to be safe, if you ask me."

Angie let out a breath. "All right then. I know I can't talk you out of this one, so I won't bother trying." She picked up the towel and repositioned it over her shoulder. "I'm busy, though. Did you check the pile on the...the table in the foyer? Or maybe they're in the den."

"Good thoughts, hon. I'll check in both places. Can you grab my walker for me?" When she leaned in to hand the damn contraption to me, I kissed the top of her hair. Had we been in the kitchen, near the goods, I would have tried to swipe my finger through the melted chocolate she probably had sitting in a glass bowl on the counter. Like usual, she would have used her free hand to bat me away, adding, "You can lick the bowl, but I'm not done here." Tomorrow. Tomorrow I'd be in there again taking whatever sweetness I could.

Angie walked back to the kitchen, and I shifted my body to the right, glancing over my shoulder at her. I could just catch the furrow on her face as she concentrated on pouring the chocolate into her precious molds. She seemed busy, probably had a baby or wedding shower to cater.

"I'll find them," I said to no one in particular, unsure if Angie heard me or not. When I looked back one more time, she was leaning over the molds, using a clean white cloth to wipe away any stray drops of chocolate. Back in her little world.

"All right, body, can we do this?" The thought of calling Marissa crossed my mind, once, but I buried it. The credenza couldn't be more than thirty feet away. Despite my confusion earlier, I had confidence my legs could make it that far. I pushed up against the couch's arm, grabbed the walker, teetered forward and then back, and landed against the cushion. "Phew. Harder than it looks. Come on, Frank." Gripping the walker's arms, I pressed with great force and slowly lifted myself. A slight tingle in the right leg, and then, I was standing. Where was the applause? In the quiet of the room, I shuffled as slowly as those folks at rehab; it had never felt so good to be moving.

As it turns out, the papers were inside the credenza's third drawer, a place that Marissa had always used to file important items. What I hadn't realized, though, was how much *other* paperwork had worked its way into those drawers and the shelves surrounding them. Files held information from way back. Even in this digital age, we kept every paper scrap. Leaning against the furniture, I opened a folder and pulled out a receipt. The faded red lettering said, "ACE hardware, 1989." Really? I shook my head and moved onto the next file, full of old newspaper clippings. A story chronicling Sputnik being launched by the Russians. The man on the moon. Our engagement announcement. My father's obituary. My fingers trembled as I flipped to the next page. Old and weathered, worn on the edges from the many times I'd taken it out. The newspaper article about Antonio's death. A "suspected drowning" with "no evidence of foul play." No evidence of the boy who pushed him. No evidence of who Antonio really was either. The newspapers wouldn't print *that*, of course. No evidence of my guilt.

I'd had a long enough time to sit and wonder if I'd gotten to the scene earlier, would everything have turned out differently? Would I have been able to save him? Should I have ratted out the perpetrator? Even in the twilight, I'd seen the look on that awful kid's face. If he was so willing to harass and kill my brother, a sinner in his eyes, he'd likely have turned on me too. And what would my parents have done then?

My fingers shook from the memories as I traced over the words that said nothing but hurt anyway. Shame, remorse, anger. They hurtled through me. Guilt once again quickly followed. I couldn't save anyone then, but if I went to the doctor, owned up to my symptoms, I could save the kids and Angie a little heartache. A burning started in my eyes, and I blinked then tucked the newspaper back into its place.

The folder stuck to the one behind it as I pushed it in, and I tugged the new one out, being careful to shift my weight. Not good enough. The printed papers inside the folder fell onto the floor. "Dammit!" Picking them up would be too difficult, so I stood there, staring at the top sheet from Mayo Clinic. It read, "Memory Loss: 7 tips to improve your memory." Next to it lay another paper, an advertisement for...Prevagen. The only other words I could read were "memory supplement." *What the hell?*

Angie must have thought I had a problem, so why hadn't she said anything to me? No one else would have had the time or opportunity to print these. Not the kids, not the grandkids. Angie had to have done this. It didn't matter to me she was busy, I wanted an answer, and I wanted it now.

I threw papers I still held onto the pile on the floor, closed the drawers, and grabbed the arms of the walker. A quick shift of my right foot then a shuffle of the left, and the rhythm took over. But as I approached the stairs leading to the basement on my right, that nasty tingle began again. *Shift, shuffle.* Angie was still banging around in the kitchen—the smack of what sounded like cookie dough slamming up against the mixer's bowl rang out. A sound I'd become familiar with over the years, and my mouth watered. *Shift, shuffle.* Sweets should be off limits because of my diabetes. But Angie was so good at making candy and baked goods. A small nibble here and there wouldn't hurt, *Shift, shuf—*

My left leg lurched and tried to move forward, but my foot never connected. That recognizable twinge ran up both legs, and I tried to command my left to follow the right. But my limbs were not listening to my brain. My body pitched to the right, hit the wall, and tumbled down the stairs to the basement floor. As I landed on the cold linoleum, my head knocked against the plaster wall.

A murkiness crept into my vision as I opened my mouth to speak. I urged my brain to cooperate at least in that capacity. Would Angie be able to hear my weak voice over the mixer's ruckus? I lay there for a while—minutes or hours, I couldn't be sure—before I let the darkness take me.

CHAPTER 31: MARISSA

The call came in at 7:55 p.m., a few minutes after I'd put the kids to bed. I had planned to head back over to Mom and Dad's for one more night, but I wanted to check on the cocoon. Doubts about this butterfly project loomed large: the caterpillar had seemed healthy. The cocoon? Not so much. Just the thought of having to show Eli and Cam how fruitless our efforts were brought my mood down, and I was tempted not to answer the phone. Regardless, I slid the green button to the right and said hello.

"Did you know Dad is in the ER?" Nico's rushed words greeted me.

I gripped the phone tighter in my fingers and sat up against the back of our old plaid couch, steadying myself. My heart galloped within my chest. "What? I was heading over to their house soon. What the hell happened?" A sweater of guilt slipped over my shoulders. *If I hadn't left them. If I'd had someone with them. If I'd checked in...*

"I'm not exactly sure. All I know is that he fell. Not sure how, but Mom found him at the bottom of the basement stairs."

Holy shit. My hand flew to my chest, my mind envisioning the whole debacle, the clinician in me assessing, without evidence, what he might have broken. "Did he fall all the way down? Please tell me he didn't. And how is he?"

"I don't know what happened. Do you want to head over, or do you want me to?"

The need to see that Dad was okay and being taken care of properly washed over me. Plus, what would the doctors think with two falls within such a short span of time? My feet kicked away the light blanket that covered them, and I rose from the couch. "Let me talk to Will. I'll meet you there as soon as I'm able."

After Nico's last word—a song I couldn't identify—I grabbed a light sweater, pulled my hair back in a ponytail, and went in search of Will, certain I'd find him passed out on the couch in the den, sports on the television. He seemed to fall asleep most nights without meaning to, regardless of the time, despite my nagging to come to bed.

I rushed into the family room and none so gently pushed at Will, who slumped against the couch arm. How could that position even be remotely comfortable? His long frame was twisted, and his face sported hatch marks from the fabric.

"Honey, I need to go." I looked around the room for my shoes, which never seemed to be where I left them. "My dad's in the hospital."

Will rubbed his eyes like a kid. "What? What happened?" He tried to straighten himself up, and his bones creaked loudly. He was too young to be sounding that way, especially at this early hour.

"He fell again. I don't know any more details, but I have to go." I spotted my shoes next to the back door and after slipping my feet inside, thought about what else I needed. Phone, purse, a book maybe? My hands shook, and I took a deep breath. *Don't worry unless you have to. But for this to happen so close to the other fall...*

"Okay. The kids are in bed?"

"Yep, though I doubt they're asleep yet. I'll find a minute to text you later to let you know what's happening, so keep your phone handy. I know it might not wake you up, but at least when you get up in the morning, you'll have a report."

Will blinked his eyes rapidly and stretched his arms over his head. "Sure, okay. You want me to come? I'm sure we could see about getting the neighbor over..."

"Nah. Let me see what the situation is before we do that or make plans for tomorrow. I wasn't going to be here tonight, anyway, and if you're not here, it'll worry the boys. I'll keep you posted."

Leaning in, I kissed him on the mouth, savoring his warm lips. Had he been more awake, he'd have pulled me onto his lap. I looked back once on my way to the garage as he slumped over again. He'd still be there the next morning, and I wouldn't have it any other way.

•　　•　　•

The scene at the ER was calmer than I expected. After winding my way past the reception area and through triage, I found Mom sitting next to Dad in a bay. He lay in the bed, IVs and monitors hooked up to him. The news scrolled across the television screen mounted in the corner of the room. Dad didn't look too bad—rather pale face, tired eyes, and the beginning of a rose-colored goose egg on his forehead. Mom didn't look upset. Aside from that lump on Dad's head, I'd have called this a case of déjà vu.

Nico cut me off before I said anything. He placed a hand on my shoulder and escorted me around the curtain, into the hallway. "One thing, and I'm not trying to be awful or unsympathetic, but I want you to be gentle. I don't want you to get mad or be a basket case about it." Nico paused. He hummed a few bars of the always popular Green Day song, probably to lighten the serious situation, take some of the weight away. When I didn't respond he continued. "Apparently, Mom messed up."

The theatrics. "Oh good God. Come on, I know how to be gentle. And thanks. I'll be singing that song all night now."

"You're welcome. It's how I deal with stress—" Nico took me by the shoulders and leaned in. "Remember, *be gentle* with her. With them," he whispered into my ear. "They're both still alive and mostly healthy."

"This time."

A smirk crossed his face. "Touché. At least let me beg off and go get coffee. I seem to do that well, don't you think? It could be a long night."

He hummed the chorus of that damn Green Day song, then sauntered down the hall, pulled out his phone, and messed with the screen, probably texting Luke.

As I yanked the curtain back, I pushed thoughts of Luke and my brother out of my mind. For now. "Hey, Mom. Dad." I closed the curtain.

Dad rotated his head against the pillow and smiled, his lips forming the U slowly. Mom, sitting upright and rigid, kept silent, but her shoulders relaxed slightly.

"What happened?" Nothing like getting right to the subject.

"He fell," Mom said.

"Hmm. I can see that. What I mean is, *why* did he fall?" I looked at Dad then. "You promised me you'd be more thoughtful, Dad. What happened?"

"I don't know," Dad said at the same time Mom said, "I wasn't there."

I settled myself on a hard plastic chair. Too much time here and my tailbone would be screaming. "Let's back up. What do you mean you weren't there, Mom? Were you in the house? When I went out, you said you'd be home all day. Dad wasn't supposed to be left unsupervised."

"I *was* there all day."

"Okay then. You were at the house, but you didn't see him fall?" She nodded. "And what time did he fall? How long after dinner?" I checked my watch—8:23 p.m. How surprising that he wasn't in bed. That medication— Wait. "Did you remember to give him his meds today, Mom? Is that it? Did after-dinner pills make you sleepy?"

Mom looked at Dad, and Dad looked at Mom. Both faces flashed *guilty*. What hadn't Nico told me?

"He didn't fall after dinner," Mom said in a matter-of-fact manner. "He fell earlier in the day...but before dinner."

What the fuck? Knowing better than to let that expletive loose, I took a deep breath and let it out slowly. "Then why am I just now getting a phone call that Dad is in the hospital?"

"Because we didn't get *here* until after dinner."

"And that is because..." What had happened in those intervening hours?

"What do you mean?" Mom said.

"First, I thought Nico was going to stop by, not that this is his fault. Second, why didn't you bring Dad to the hospital earlier? If he fell, you should have brought him in right away."

"Well... I was busy with orders...and then, when I went to the basement...there he was."

Oh my God. Everything about this situation felt like fire on my nerves. "What? You found him at the bottom of the stairs? You didn't hear him fall?"

"No. I...left him on the big seat in the living room."

I glared at Dad. "She left you on the"—*big seat?*—"couch, and you decided to get up?" I softened my voice so he'd remember I cared because who knew what words might come out of my mouth. "Dad, we talked about this. You couldn't walk at rehab, and it *hasn't been that long.* You were supposed to ask for help. What could be so important that you had to get up? And honestly, how did you do it?"

He shook his head, revealing nothing.

Mom piped up. "My...my orders. I heard nothing because the mixer was on."

My blood boiled, ratcheting up my blood pressure, but concern flared too. "I hear you, Mom, but I'm still confused by the timeline. Once you found him, what did you *do*?" The monitor's beep kept time for Mom's silence, which stretched a little too long.

"I shook him and asked him if he was okay."

Holy— Shake someone who fell? Not knowing if you've messed with their nervous system or anything else? Of course, she wouldn't know that.

She continued, "He said he'd be fine, that he needed to rest. I gave him a...blanket and pillow and...went back to the orders."

Anger barreled through me, and I stood and paced the small area. "Are you *kidding* me? Your husband was on the ground, hurt, and you didn't think to call 911?" *Breathe. Try to keep calm. You don't want her to clam up.* "And then what?" I felt like a detective, trying to parse information from a reluctant suspect.

"Then I went to get the mail because I'd forgotten to get it. Usually I do it after lunch...and I saw our neighbor...you know at the front."

"And?"

"And he asked how things were going...told him your Dad had fallen. He came into the house to see how he was doing."

I stopped moving and glared at my mother. "So the neighbor called 911?"

"Yes."

"And you didn't bother to call your kids right away because you didn't want to bother us, right?"

"Exactly." Mom nodded. "But Nico showed up as the white van was leaving."

What the hell had Mom been thinking? What had happened to good old-fashioned common sense and judgment? My mother had walked away from a man who needed a "white van"—her husband no less. What did that mean? How could that lapse in judgment even happen? Furthermore, had the intake nurse heard this story, and would anyone call the Department of Aging? Was this ludicrousness something they might be concerned about?

"Mom. Why didn't you call 911? Right away, I mean?"

Her brow furrowed. "We *did* call 911. Our neighbor did. I told you that."

"Yes, but far later than you should have. Mom, this is serious. Dad is sitting here chatting with us, but a tumble down the stairs... It could have been deadly. Do you understand?"

"Oh."

I might never truly comprehend the logic behind this story. At this point, we were right back in the same spot we'd been when we checked out of rehab. A never-ending cycle of fall, ER, fall, ER, repeat, repeat, repeat. What would they say this time? Speaking of which, where in the hell was that doctor?

Against a backdrop of noises—foot scuffles, door whispers, Dad's monitors, someone's ringtone—I looked at my parents. While I'd never gotten along fully with my family, I still loved them, and I didn't want to see anything happen to them. A Rockwell family portrait had always been something I'd strived for, but...that seemed impossible. I had been so preoccupied by and troubled by Dad and his health, and now? All the puzzle pieces slid into place in my brain. I'd pushed the situation away long enough; Dad wasn't the only one we needed to be concerned with. But he would require proof before he believed me.

My head dropped into my hands, and a chill stole over my skin as sorrow filled me to the depths of my entire being. Tomorrow I would have one item on my list: find a caregiver who could help Dad *and* monitor Mom and her disturbing behavior.

CHAPTER 32: HER

She sat down at the silver machine, running the fingers of her right hand over the smooth top of the clicker. She pressed on the button, bringing the screen to life, an action that somehow surprised her. Someone must have forgotten to turn it off the last time. Had she done that? She hadn't been on this thing, had she? But *he* had. Something about research that he needed to do. Whatever the research had been, it had kept him up late that night. She'd fallen asleep waiting for him and woken up in the night, later, with a funny feeling in her neck. Had he tried to wake her when he came to bed? And what had been so damn intriguing?

A stack of papers winked at her. "SAGE: A Test to detect signs of Alzheimer's and dementia." She thought about throwing out the papers but thought again and looked at the questions.

She scanned the first section, which asked name, schooling, race, and medical background, before moving on to the next question. The date. Dates had always been trouble for her. That's why she had her calendar—to make sure her shipments had gotten out on time. But she knew what day it was. The next couple of questions involved identification of pictures. A rectangle with dots? Flattened...dice? What were those called? Nico liked to line them up on the floor, then flick them with his finger and watch them fall. The *clickety-clack* of one as it hit the one in front of it echoed in her mind, and she massaged her forehead. If she moved on to the next question, perhaps the answer would come.

But the next question had three directions listed: 1. Draw a large face of a clock and put the numbers in the correct places; 2. Position the hands for ten minutes before 11 o'clock; and 3. Label *L* for the long hand and *S* for the short hand on the clock.

Would she be able to do it? She reached for a pen, her hands trembling, fingers fumbling, then grasped it in her fingers. The whole pen shook as it hovered over the paper. And instead of drawing the clock, she put the pen back in its holder and the papers back where she found them. The woman did not need to see how she'd do on this test.

CHAPTER 33: FRANK

The sweet aroma of baked goods combined with the spicy scent of onions as Dee, the health care aide Marissa had hired, helped me enter the kitchen and into a seat at the table before leaving to take care of paperwork. The doctors had found no reason for my fall besides "impulsivity" as Marissa worded it. Though I had a bump on my head and large, purple and red bruises across my back, after one night in the hospital, they'd sent me home with strict instructions: "Hire an aide, listen to the aide, listen to your kids, and get better." Two days and multiple promises to Marissa, Nico, and Gabe later, and here we were.

Angie stood at the stove with her back to me, an old wooden spoon in her hand. For a moment, my mind wandered to the day we met inside her parents' kitchen, after a day of mowing her father's lawn (me) and sunbathing (her). She'd been long and lean then, a force to be reckoned with. Though time had passed, the woman before me still cut quite the figure, the sun's rays glinting off the silver threads of her hair. Now, she muttered to herself like she usually did, the words muffled against the talk show host voice that filtered through the television speakers. Angie required noise when she worked. Lately, it seemed like the television or radio was always on in the background. I leaned over and pressed the OFF button on the remote. She spun around, her face lined with annoyance.

"Frank! Why did you do that? I was listening to that." She turned back to stir whatever was on the stove.

"It's hard to hear. Sometimes I need quiet, and I want to talk to you." *About the bank incident, the SAGE papers, life...*

Much to my surprise, Angie placed the spoon on the rest and dusted her hands off on her faded floral apron. She leaned against the countertop's edge. "About what? You're worried about...what's going on?"

Dropping my head back against the chair, I hesitated. Why was she giving me this attention now? What had changed? "Worried? Maybe not. But concerned? Yes. I can be stubborn in my ways. I get that, and I hear what you're all saying about being impulsive. Thankfully, I've been healthy, but if something happens to me, what happens to you? The kids?"

"Oh, come on, Frank." She took a step away.

I tugged on her arm, pulling her toward the table, encouraging her to sit across from me, and I extended my hand and grabbed her fingers. The warmth flowed from her palm to mine, then up my arm, but it waned before going any farther. "I worry. I always have. About you, and Nico especially. Gabe has Sarah and the kids and Marissa, the same. Will couldn't be better for her. But Nico—"

"How did this go from...talking about you to talking about Nico? Maybe your brain *does* need as much attention as your legs." She frowned.

"I'm concerned about him—you know that. Concerned for all of them. You."

"Worry, concern, and...butting heads are different things, Frank. You're both...up against each other a lot and too smart for your own good. Two...peas and all that."

Two peas? Not sure about that. Nico reminded me more of Antonio, who'd been a few years younger and so much wiser. Braver. Generous. Kind. Misunderstood. But Angie hadn't met Antonio, and my ability to dwell on those days, much less talk about them, would never come.

"Frank?"

I shook my head again.

"Where'd you go? You...you weren't listening there. I don't know what's wrong with your legs, but you...don't have dementia." Angie held up a finger. "What day is it?"

"Friday, June twenty-sixth."

She nodded. "Year. What year is it? Who is the president?"

"It's 2015, and Barack Obama is the president. He's the forty-fourth, you know."

"I believe you. And...your brother's name."

My heart stuttered in my chest. *Say it and move on.* But my mouth didn't cooperate.

Angie raised her eyebrows. "Your brother's name?"

"Antonio Lorenzo Raffaelo," I finally said, but my voice cracked. A single image of my brother the last time I'd spoken to him flashed in my mind. The sunset behind him, his look of pure joy shining from his face as he tossed the fishing line into the lake. "See you in a bit," he'd said.

Angie stood. "See? You're fine. You answered all the questions."

"And what about *you*, Angie? I found those papers in the credenza. The ones about dementia and Alzheimer's, a bunch of printouts with information. Why were they there?"

She paled, then narrowed her eyes. "I don't know. *I* didn't put them there."

"Are you sure?"

"Yes, I'm sure! What the hell, Frank? I don't...I don't have time for this."

If Angie spoke the truth, that wouldn't explain the bank fiasco. With all that had gone on recently, I hadn't told her about my conversation with Joseph. She needed to know. "Okay, but there's another thing. I talked to the bank and I—"

"Frank." Angie's lips thinned, and she sighed. "This is odd. It's good you spoke to the bank, but...I have so much to do, and I can't get everything done. I can't. You're being ridiculous, you know that?"

Ridiculous? Well, shit. We'd had a good marriage, mostly. Not too many altercations over the years once I'd learned how to stay in line, but her brush off here... It hurt, more than I thought it would. But the queen had spoken, and I only had one more thing to say. "Speaking of getting everything done, Marissa texted, and she and the kids are coming for dinner. Will too. You need to plan for four more."

Angie glared at me as I sent a quick message to Dee, who preferred texts. She couldn't get me out of there quick enough.

CHAPTER 34: MARISSA

Work had been more arduous for those of us still in the clinic covering patients for the two on maternity leave, and the stifling summer heat, usually welcomed by me, bristled this year. So the last place I wanted to be after a full work day was with my parents. A harsh statement, yes. A true statement, also yes.

As I pulled the car up the driveway and put it in park next to Nico's vehicle, the house stared back at me. It had room for all of us—Nico, Gabe and Sarah and the kids, and me and Will and Cam and Eli. But prior to Dad's health crises, we were rarely there all at one time. It wasn't as if we all lived that far away, well, except for Gabe and his family. With Nico in Springboro and my family in Kettering, we should have been holding family dinners or extended holidays more often. But something about the place itself made my blood pressure rise and my shoulders ache, and that was enough to keep me from gracing my parents' home as much as I should have. Did Mom and Dad ever realize the tension that seeped from their home? The hope that I wasn't following in my parents' footsteps hit me in the solar plexus; I'd talk to Will about it later.

As usual, the kids scampered up the sidewalk without a care in the world, and this time, they didn't wait for me. Just rapped a quick knock on the door and then motored into the house. What would Mom think?

It didn't matter because I was on a mission: to check in with Dee, a rare find whose previous long-term clients had recently passed away. At the time of Dee's hiring, I'd spoken to her about what we needed. As much as I didn't want to pull an outsider into our drama, Mom had me nervous. The idea that she did not and had not thought to call 911 ate away at my insides. A simple, momentary lack of judgment or something more sinister? And I could not ignore the "white van" comment. How many more of those had I missed? In my head, there was only one way to find out: watch her. And who better to do that than the person who'd be in the house the most? Dee.

The day of Dee's interview, I'd reviewed the proposition I had for her: help Dad as needed but observe Mom too.

"What, pray tell, are you thinking of, Marissa?" Dee had asked. She had come from down South years ago, she'd said, and sometimes, those Southern expressions crept into her conversation.

The few examples I had of when Mom made strange decisions spilled forth, and when the story reached the part about not calling 911, Dee gasped. "*Listen*, that's not right, quite worrisome too. Hence your decision to talk to me, I reckon."

"Indeed. My boss needs me at work, and since you'd be here, I thought maybe you could watch and take notes. Keep a notebook or journal of what Mom does when you're around her that might seem odd or a little shifty to you. Heck, use your phone if you have to. It should be the least invasive and gain the most information."

Dee rubbed a hand over her cropped hair. "Oooh-wee. And if she finds out? She's going to be madder than a wet hen! You know that, right?"

"I do, which is why we haven't told Dad yet. He might stay mum—he doesn't like to stir up anger—but he might not." Asking Dee to keep a secret felt dishonest, and while the idea didn't totally sit well with me, I also felt locked in, as if we had no other choice. "If Mom has any issues with her memory, she'll deny everything, Dee—that's what she usually does. Dad's been barking at her for years to get that cough checked. And the pain that sometimes bothers her in her left leg? He's asked about that. Heck, I've asked about that. All she says is that her doctor is aware of it. Who knows if that's the truth."

Part of the reason we'd chosen Dee to help over the other people we'd interviewed was her compassion, fairness, ability to be logical and reasonable, according to her glowing recommendations. She hadn't yet established true loyalty in this household, so—

"I'll do it. I was just thinking of something Angie said when she let me in... I can't remember now, but it was enough for me to stop in my tracks, think that things might be a little cattywampus. Maybe if I think a bit more, it'll come to me. And I'll place it in the notebook."

"*Cattywampus*? I can't say that I've heard that one. Will I become well-versed in Southern expressions the longer you stay around?"

"You might, Marissa. You just might."

Now, I removed my shoes in the foyer, then listened for the commotion that was sure to be brewing with two little boys in the house. Chattering in the kitchen, Dad's voice in the back room, giggles from the boys, probably because Nico was tickling them. Taking my chances, I moved to the kitchen and met Dee as she was headed out of it.

"Dee! How are you? How is everything going?"

She widened her eyes and nodded in the direction of the living room, which I took to mean "follow me." Once there, we settled on a set of chairs far enough from the kitchen that Mom wouldn't be able to hear us. Of course, the giggling kids, droning television, and scraping of metal against metal provided perfect cover.

"What's wrong? Is Dad being, shall we say, obstinate?"

"You know your father well," Dee said and smiled. "I've never in my life come across a man so stubborn, so intent on doing things himself. I'm not sure if he's impulsive, tenacious, or in plain denial of his abilities!"

Finally, someone who saw what I did. I placed a hand on Dee's forearm and leaned in. "You pegged him, and there's no simple answer. But is he doing okay?"

She nodded, her bright smile assuring me she had his best interests at heart. "He is. I have my work cut out for me, which is far better than me sitting around looking at my phone all day. I like to stay busy."

The first part of her response caught my attention—did she have time to play stealthy with my mom?—but if she wanted to stay busy...

"All I can say is that I have information for you. If Angie or Frank found the notebook, they'd be furious, so I keep it in my room. On me, sometimes, but it's in the bureau's top right drawer. Before you leave, check it out. I think you're on to something."

A voice from the back room hollered, "Mom!" *Cam.* Time was sparse. "And do you think that safety is an issue? Could something happen to one of them?"

"As long as I'm here, I'll do my best to not let anything happen. But you and I both know that time might be of the essence. Now," she shooed me away with a hand wave, "you go be with those precious kids of yours. We'll sort this out eventually."

CHAPTER 35: FRANK

When Marissa first walked in the room, two ideas sprang up front and center: I hadn't seen her with Will lately, and she tried to do too much. These days, despite the smile she had for us, her face sported the shadows of fatigue. She'd always been so busy, the sort of teenager who filled her schedule with National Honor Society and science club and a part-time job and newspaper. And as she moved into womanhood, she'd dragged that same mantle with her. Job. Local theater board member. Weekend monthly volunteer at the soup kitchen. Which meant she didn't have the energy a younger person would have for anything, including her mothering duties. I should know. Twenty-seven—when I got married—was a lot older than most people back in the day. As I took in the sight of my daughter, something pulled in my chest. My love for her was great; I probably should have told her so more often. Maybe then she'd listen to me when I said to take care of herself.

Marissa came around the corner, and those tired eyes filled with mirth for a split second when they landed on Nico and the boys, squashed into a pile. "Hey, Nico. You look busy," she said.

"Mommy!" Eli called as he stuck his head out from under his brother. "You didn't tell us Uncle Nico would be here."

"I didn't know until we got in the driveway. I'm surprised you didn't notice his car!"

Her words fell on deaf ears as the boys, all three of them, fell into a spasm of laughter. Marissa smiled and then sat in the chair opposite me, leaned her head back, and closed her eyes.

"Everything okay?" I asked.

"Yep, another long day. I think I need a vacation, you know?"

"You and I both."

She opened her eyes. "Dad, I know this has been hard on you, and I'm sorry you've fallen and that you have to rely on Dee, who's great, by the way, but you're retired. Can I wallow for one minute? I'm exhausted." She closed her eyes again and took in a few deep breaths.

Knowing better than to push, I focused on the kids, who'd taken out their favorite item: the yoga ball. Angie still stood at the stove stirring whatever she'd started before. Based on the tangy aroma and the extra guests we'd have at dinner, she was preparing a huge pot of Italian-style sweet corn and pepper soup. An odd choice for a kid to like, but with hearty Italian genes from Marissa *and* Will, somehow it didn't surprise me that the chowder stood as the boys' favorite. I could live without it, but when the grandkids were around, my preferences didn't matter. And maybe that was okay.

Angela's voice interrupted my thoughts. "Hey, Frank? I thought we had cream in the refrigerator. It's not there."

"Heavy cream? You mean the kind I put in my coffee?"

"Yes. I need it for the soup."

"I might have used the last of it this morning." Coffee without cream was no friend of mine.

She huffed. "We had another full container in there yesterday. I needed that cream, Frank."

"The amount I used for my coffee wasn't a lot, Ang. And the other container—Dee checked the date on it. It was *old*."

The air prickled with something. Even the grandkids looked up at the sharpness in my voice. But we didn't know this morning that we'd have more people around the table at dinnertime. With the way Angela was so busy these days—baking, cooking, packing up orders left and right—I figured I'd be eating Sunbutter and jelly at the breakfast bar. By myself. Or with Dee.

Angie wiped her fingers against the ubiquitous kitchen towel and leaned away from the stove. "Then someone needs to go to the store and...get me a container. The soup won't be the same."

My body had no intention of moving for the likes of soup I didn't even want, and Dee would have something to say about me going to the store. "Can you use something else?"

Angie's eyes opened wide for a moment and then narrowed. "No. The recipe calls for cream, and that's what I'd like to use." She turned her back, and a flash of lemon-yellow appeared as she threw the kitchen towel over her shoulder. End of discussion.

No "please," no sincere request for help. Simply a demand, which implied my fault for using up the damn cream. I wouldn't take the blame on this one. Other more important sources of guilt resided inside me.

"Next time you begin a recipe, Angie, make sure you have all the ingredients you need." Not waiting for a reply, I nodded to Marissa, who jumped up and helped me with the walker. "Let's go," I said. My mind jumped to the legacy article in that magazine and what I'd leave behind when I passed. *Lifelong grocery shopper.* My epitaph would read: "He was always willing to go to the store." *What kind of shit legacy is that?* And "willing" wasn't necessarily the right word to use there.

Dee met us with the keys and a quick, "You okay to go?" and she helped settle me in the car as Marissa ran back to say goodbye to the kids. Marissa would be glad to drive—she'd harped on me enough about how the limited mobility in my neck and shoulders meant I shouldn't be driving anymore. My standard response? "Nothing severe, just a normal consequence of aging." Maybe being in the car with Marissa wasn't any better than being at home when Angie was in a mood, but I'd missed my chance in asking Nico to go.

Marissa slipped quietly into the driver's seat. When I looked back at the house as she pulled away, one word marched through my mind: *autonomy.*

CHAPTER 36: MARISSA

The silence hung heavy in the car, swirling and suffocating me on the ride over to Bloom Market. Thoughts of Dee's notebook and what she'd observed looped in my mind, followed by the boy's butterflies. Oh to have wings right now, gain speed with the wind, find a new pathway, and glide for a while. Away from Mom's behavior—bitchy, there was no other word for it—which impacted Dad the most now that we were all out of the house. Maybe he was used to it, but it still bothered me. He looked out the car window as we passed row after row of corn standing tall in the breeze. We neared the turnoff for the store, and Dad turned toward me, guilt plaguing his voice.

"I'm sorry about that back there. Sometimes I think your mother likes to stir up drama. Maybe that's where you get it from."

My entire gut clenched inward, and heat rushed to my cheeks. "What? What the hell are you talking about? If you haven't noticed, I'm trying to help you, you know, with whatever is going on right now. Spent a few days with you, hired Dee. The drama is all yours, Dad. When you do things impulsively."

"Impulsively?" His lips thinned as he paused. "You mean like inviting Luke over for dinner?"

"Oh, did you? It will be good to see him again in a natural setting."

"Oh *really*?"

That was a leap I didn't anticipate. And what in the hell precipitated it? "What's that supposed to mean? Luke's a friend of ours. You know that."

"Yeah, and he's back. Why do you think he came back? It's not for his parents, that's for sure. Those no-good sons a bitches. They did nothing for that young man."

The light turned yellow, and I slowed. "Tell me how you really feel, Dad. Though I agree with you. And I told you months ago about the interview he had at the hospital. He came back for the job. You know this, so why are you bringing it up now?" It wasn't my place to insert any of my personal commentary on being back for Nico. Luke and Nico could do that all themselves. Maybe at dinner...

Dad tapped his finger on the dashboard, a habit that churned up car dust and reminded me how unclean the vehicle was, another task on my long list of things I hadn't gotten to. "The job or *you*?"

My ire rose, and I held back a few obscenities. "Talk about stirring up drama, Dad. You got that covered. You know as well as I do that Luke and I had nothing... Okay, maybe I had a small crush on him when I was younger. But that went by the wayside the minute Will walked into my life, if not before."

"Do you think it could have worked out? If you and he..." He pointed at the light, which had turned green.

"We what?" This time, I tapped a dance against the steering wheel with my fingers. "What are you trying to say? This convoluted conversation—I can't keep up. We were talking about Mom, and now we're talking about Luke and an imaginary relationship you want me to have with him." My voice sounded weary in the small space. "Can we just go to the store? I'm so, so tired."

"Yeah, you told me that already. So I suppose."

The cavalier tone to his words struck my heart. Just once, couldn't I land at the top of his priority list? My eternal hope for a more loving relationship with my father withered and retreated right there on Randall Road. Loving someone was never easy. Getting past deep relationships was never easy. But even when you healed and moved on, memories lingered. Feelings lingered. I was lucky—my deep relationship was with Will and only Will.

"I..." Dad said as we turned into the lot. "I've been thinking. Had a lot of time to do that lately, you know. And you know your mom and I like Luke. We like Will, too, and he's your husband. Remember that."

"I will, and I do." Could he hear the annoyance in my voice? I'd never given them any reason to doubt my marriage's sincerity. And, was *my* marriage even their business?

"Well, maybe he's trying to win you over or something."

"Maybe he's trying to win someone over, but it sure isn't me." *Shit.* Would Dad catch on? "But if you think that, then why do you let him come over so often?"

"You know your mother. She has to play the part of the gracious host. In her mind, he's a friend, an old friend; I hope he's not anything more."

A large, exasperated breath left my mouth, and my attention landed on an enormous bird circling in the sky above the parking lot, possibly looking for prey. A turkey vulture. It looked confident, strong, ready to swoop in and steal its next meal. Would it be a squirrel? A mouse? A shiver ran through me at the thought, and I shook my head, focusing instead back on Dad. At least he had told me the truth. But one thing didn't compute. "And is Mom thinking about this too? What is that all about?" Confusion jammed my brain. What, really, did this conversation concern?

"Cut her some slack, Marissa. She's still your mom, and she cares for you."

"Whatever, Dad. She *is* my mom, but you know what? She's got a funny way of showing me she cares sometimes." *And again, why bring this up?* "But what aren't you telling me?" Had one of them had an affair? And if so, what did it matter now? Or was he telling me to cut her slack because he knew—had definitive proof—about her health? Was he holding something back?

"Nothing...it's that...I've been where you are. Busier than I should be, giving more to work than family—"

"Whoa. Back up a minute." My mind screeched to a halt, but my foot gently applied pressure to the brake as I turned into the parking space. "Hold that thought." Glancing behind me, I aligned the car perfectly and placed the car in park as his words skimmed the outer edges of my brain. My hands shook against the steering wheel, and I turned toward Dad. "*Giving more to work than family*? Are you kidding me? Are you judging me as a mother? Because I work part-time to take care of the kids, to give them what they need and deserve, and it works for us. I don't see Will or Cam or Eli complaining. Do you?"

"That's not...never mind."

"Don't never mind me. Answer the questions, please. I'd like to know, since that's what you're insinuating. I love my husband, and I love my children. I give one hundred percent to them, and I always will, even if it takes everything in me. Furthermore, I don't understand what you're trying to say. Or why you're all worried about me. And by the way, while you might not care about *my* feelings at all—and again, there's nothing between Luke and me—did you think about Will? What would he think about having Luke over for dinner if there *were* something between Luke and me? Hmmm?" A thumping pulse echoed in my head. I'd have been better off staying at my parents' house. Better yet, not coming over at all.

"I...didn't think. I get it, but... Forget about it. Forget we had this conversation. I know there's nothing going on with you and Luke. And don't be so hard on your mother, okay?" Dad's face revealed nothing.

I pulled the keys out of the ignition and glared at him, but we both sat, speechless. Where to go with this ridiculous situation? Unsure of myself, I opened the car door, letting in the hot, sticky air. Anything to escape this confining conversation.

"I thought you needed to know," Dad said before I hauled myself out of the car.

"To know what? You didn't exactly say. That I'm a shitty mother? Or that Mom's a shitty mother?"

Dad placed a hand on my forearm, stopping me. "*Marissa*, I didn't say either of those things, and you're walking a thin line here. Your mom did the best she could. Like you do. I'm just saying that your mom loves you. She worries about you and always has, whether you knew it or not. And I do too."

Too little too late. "Okay."

"And sometimes we don't have the whole story. Let's get the cream. She'll have both our heads if we don't come back soon."

And *that* was the most coherent thing Dad had said since we had gotten in the car. Shit, maybe he *did* have dementia—I had not a single clue what he was talking about with this convoluted conversation, and I didn't have the energy to pursue whatever *it* was. But he'd put me on alert. If the man was trying to tell me something about Mom, it meant he felt guilty. I just didn't know *why* he felt guilty. And if he thought that going to buy heavy whipping cream for my mother would absolve him of whatever he'd done—or hadn't—then he was more far gone than I realized.

CHAPTER 37: FRANK

I told Marissa to go into the store by herself so I could sit with my thoughts. She had the audacity to laugh—"Dad, you're in no shape to go in there, and I figured you'd sit tight for a few minutes"—but apologized afterward. It wouldn't take long to find the cream, and then...then we'd head back. A couple of stifling minutes with her in the car would be uncomfortable, just like minutes with that drill instructor, but I had no intention of circling around to the conversation we had on the way over. I wasn't even sure how we got there in the first place. Marissa had never given us a sign that she and Luke were an item, so what had spurred me to think that? Was it my brain? Something I'd seen? Something Angie had said? Before I could forget to ask, I called Angie.

She picked up on the first ring. "Can't you find it?" A snap to her voice, an edge that came sometimes when guests came over.

"Hello to you too." The ups and downs with this woman sometimes baffled me. "Marissa is getting the cream. We had a discussion here in the car, and now I'm curious. Do you think Luke might want her back? I haven't—"

"Frank, it doesn't matter."

"Doesn't it?"

"Not really. I just need the cream."

"And do you need anything else?"

"No. I need to get back to—"

"Angie? Are you okay? Everything okay there? Your voice sounds off. Is it too stressful to have everyone over? We could put it off." Or maybe, maybe she wasn't feeling well. Maybe too much was happening, and she didn't want to say it.

Angie sighed, years of practice in the sound. "I'm fine...busy. I have a lot to do."

She always did, so I ended the call and stared out the windshield. What if that was it? What if she needed me but didn't know how to ask? Life had been so full lately. I'd taken up a good chunk of time too. Maybe... I could have been a better husband. Better husband, better father. Better *brother*.

I called Angie back as the heat rose inside the car. "We're almost done here. But I'm sorry."

"*Really*? Sorry for what?" she said.

"I could have been a better husband."

"Frank? What the...? You don't have dementia, dammit. Stop acting like your life is going to end tomorrow. It won't."

And there it was again, the Angie whose rage flamed at the oddest of times. Depression, if she still flirted with that, could explain some of it, but it didn't explain it all. Back to walking on eggshells. My mind dwelled on that little pill she used to take, if she'd start again or find another one to help take the edge off. She might have not preferred that pill, but Angie never realized that our happiness—mine and the kids'— seemed to depend on that medication.

"It's fine, Angie. I'm fine. It's hot, but Marissa will be out soon." I wiped my forehead with my hand. "I've had time to think in the car, and I don't think I've been there for you like I should have been. And I'm sorry. I want to be there for you now. What do you need?"

The clang of metal against metal drew my mind to the scene outside the car window. A few vehicles over, a young kid had slammed his cart into another one, which forced it into oncoming store traffic. The frazzled mother, red cheeks and eyes blazing, most likely concerned for her son's safety, yelled at him.

That look? I'd seen it in Angie too many times. Overworked and overwhelmed. Had I recognized it then? Seventy-seven long years had granted me more insight than I probably deserved. As I stared at the kid and his mother, recognition dawned. Maybe Marissa was right. Maybe Angie could have done better too. Been accountable for herself and what she was going through.

"Angie?" I said. "You still there?"

"I love you, Frank, but sometimes, you...confuse me, make me angry. But I have a batch of...a batch that needs to be attended to after this soup. So bring me the cream, will you?"

"Sure." I ended the call again, images of her confections in my mind along with a memory of the day she asked if she could take a baking class. The kids had been little then, and I'd had long hours at work. Who knew what I was thinking? I'd wanted to see Angie happy, but I also wanted dinner on the table, the house clean, and the kids taken care of. So I'd said no. Chauvinistic? Probably. Angie didn't argue, but she never forgave me, as evidenced by her eventually doing it anyway. From time to time, still, she threw that episode in my face.

An incoming text interrupted my thoughts. I looked down at the phone in my lap. It was from Will.

Will: *Heard you think Luke has a thing for my wife.*

Marissa had worked fast, faster than I would have expected, if I'd expected that she'd tell him about our conversation. Faster than I deserved. I wrote back quickly, before she returned.

Frank: *Come for dinner at 6?*

Will: *I see what you did there, but sure. Marissa already let me know.*

Frank: *Good see you then.*

That didn't go too badly. Will had to know that I loved him like a son, didn't he? No amount of Luke Butterfield could take the place of Will Moretta. Both great men, just different.

Will: *By the way, Luke's coming too. Maybe you can fill him in on your theory.*

Oh shit.

CHAPTER 38: MARISSA

After a silent car ride home, I walked into the kitchen from the garage and placed the cream on the counter. My plan involved finding that notebook in Dee's bureau. But out of nowhere, a hand caught my arm and pulled me toward the back door.

"Marissa," my husband said. "We need to talk."

It had been a long time since he and I had spoken about anything that didn't have to do with children's shoes or our jobs or insects or the groceries or who might take out the garbage. "What are you doing here already?" I glanced at my watch. "And how did you get here so quickly? What happened to those late afternoon experiments you supposedly had?"

The look in Will's eyes told me it might be something important—the kids?—and he escorted me onto the back porch, pushing me gently into the chair.

"Let the new researcher take over for a bit. Listen, a voicemail came in at work, but I checked it when I got here. It was meant for you."

"Not again." Our cell numbers were one numeral apart, and during any given week, no less than two people misdialed one of us. Last time, my gynecologist left a message about an upcoming appointment on Will's voicemail; the time before that, our insurance company was trying to get a hold of Will—as guarantor, of course—but they reached me instead. I rolled my eyes as my gaze settled on the emerald green grass rippling in the hot summer wind. A perfect picture of quintessential southwestern Ohio summer days. If I stared long enough, one of the kids' beloved butterflies would pass by.

"Uh, honey..." Will's voice lacked its usual confidence, and I looked at him. "The call was HR, from your company. And while they should *not* have left a message, they did. You better call them. They're not happy."

"About what?"

"About the time you've taken off. That your boss told you he needed you. Whoever made that phone call? They were pretty pissed."

"Shit." I passed a hand across my eyes as I closed them. "Did you delete it?"

"Of course not. Here." Will thrust his phone into my hand.

A few swipes and then the recording. Phone to my ear, I sat, listening, while Will waited. A sparrow landed on the porch railing and joined in Will's assessment of me. How unnerving. Will wasn't kidding. The woman's clipped tone revealed all the things she *didn't* say with her words.

Will stared at me. "What do you think?"

An icy feeling gripped my shoulders. "They can't take my job away, can they?"

He relaxed against the chair. "I would think not. My guess is there's been a mix-up in communication or something. My first reaction was to get angry. I've seen you fill out your timesheets and call your boss. You've been there when you're supposed to be. You're allowed to take vacation days, FMLA."

"Dammit. This is not what I need right now," I said and blew out a hard breath. "Honestly, have you ever felt that life is throwing things at you like those tennis ball contraptions? They keep shooting the ball forward, one after another, whether you hit them or not. That! That's how I feel. This HR thing might not be a major obstacle, but it's a nuisance. It's time out of the day I don't want to take to figure out something I don't think I should have to figure out. But I'll keep thinking that it's simply an annoyance because dwelling on the alternative, that I'm about to get canned, is even worse. We still have a mortgage and school loans and the car. God, Will, we haven't even started on more clothes and braces and—"

"Honey?" He took my hand in his and stroked circles on the back of it. "You have a lot on your plate," he stopped and smirked, "make that an *enormous* amount on your plate, but I'm here to help, and Nico's pitched in far more than I thought he would. Shit, even Gabe sent dinner from afar the other day for your parents. Remember all the good things, even one little thing. Focus on that, and you'll be okay."

"Will I though? Will we? If I lose my job—"

"I can't say for certain, but I think that's unlikely. Call them back, see what they have to say, and then we'll worry about possible outcomes. But here and now, can you tell me where this anxiety is coming from?" Will frowned and squeezed my hand. "What's really going on? Is there something other than your parents and everything else?"

"Maybe." *Probably yes.* "I've been putting something off. Come with me."

We moved to the foyer, where I grabbed my bag, and then I tugged Will to the back bathroom. "Stay right here for a minute, will you?"

After I shut the door, I leaned against it, gathering courage, then riffled through my bag for the tests I'd bought the last time Dad sent me to the pharmacy. A two-pack. A double-dose of confirmation that we'd be entering uncharted waters, if they turned up positive. Entering a stage I wasn't sure about, going from mom of two to mom of three. What were the chances? Slim, maybe, but my fatigue, my noise sensitivity, my nausea, not to mention the missed period—all signs pointed to something I had desperately been trying to explain as being overworked and overtired.

With trembling fingers, I opened the package and followed the directions. Three minutes was all it would take to know if the servings on my plate would multiply. After flushing, I washed my hands, and just like the other two times I'd peed on a stick, the pink line didn't even pretend to be shy. The light thumping that had begun inside my chest boomed.

"You okay in there?" Will whispered through the door.

Blowing out a breath, I adjusted my shirt and shook my head, then grabbed the stick. I opened the door and shoved the test toward Will as hot tears trailed down my cheeks. "*This.* This is where the anxiety is coming from," I whispered.

He stared at the stick, then let his gaze drift up to meet mine.

I wiped the tears away. "I'm sorry to say this, but I'm not sure I can be happy about this. Everything... It all feels overwhelming right now, you know? Hold on, overwhelming doesn't even cut it. To bring another life into the one that already seems so fragile. It's that..."

Will wrapped his arms around me and kissed the top of my head. We stood there for a long time before he whispered, "For what it's worth, I'd have ten babies with you if you wanted to, and we'd be able to handle them all. We always have room for more love." He pulled away and looked me in the eyes. "But I also hear what you're saying. This will affect you the most, and I get that. Let's give it a few days, maybe a week, and see how you feel then. Okay?"

His words helped push against the tightness in my chest, loosened everything up, at least a smidge. How in the hell had I gotten so lucky?

CHAPTER 39: HER

Looking around the room at her guests flustered her. Having too many people in such a tight space, although really, the space wasn't that small. When they'd had the kitchen worked on, they took out the wall and made the room bigger to form a kitchen/family room combination. For times like these, when she could have anywhere from a handful of family members to a larger dining party.

A few moments ago, she'd been looking forward to a visit from her grandkids. Their toothy grins, the light thumps of their feet again the tile floor. Their jabber. But so many people were here. She put her hand to her temple and pushed against the ache forming there. The guests would have to go soon. At least into another room. The throbbing behind her eyes, the fuzziness of it all, told her so.

"Everyone," she calmly spoke as she laid a towel over her shoulder. "Can everyone leave this room?" The pain in her head might have spilled into her words, but it didn't matter. She wanted them out. No more talk about the hospital, Frank's "issue," the blooming daylilies, or the winged things that her grandsons so liked. A move toward the peace and quiet she longed for. She had the cream, so she could serve the meal, do the dishes, and... She hadn't checked her orders yet, but at least a couple of boxes of chocolate-covered something required packing and shipping to...to Wisconsin.

She turned her back on her family, who flowed around the corner and into the living room, the chatter of voices left in their wake. The noise reached her ears, but unlike all those other times she had sent her family away, she couldn't make out all the words. A white noise filled her head instead.

CHAPTER 40: FRANK

Marissa had taken the cream into the house, and I stayed on the front porch in the wicker love seat, where she had placed me. If I wasn't welcome in the kitchen, I wouldn't be going in. Someone would come get me when it was time for dinner. The newspaper lay on the side table, and I opened it to the obituaries. A fascination with the dying had always preoccupied my mind; something about the individual lives, their details. Their successes. Their failures. Those they left behind. When I died, which could be sooner than later, would it be with dementia? Ineffective legs? And who might read *my* obituary? What would they think about it? That word again—*legacy*—came to mind.

The crinkle of the newsprint reminded me of the dementia poster and the SAGE exam. How in the hell could you tell the difference between a disease and getting old? After all that had happened in the last few weeks, did I really want to know if I had it? *I guess so.* But if I thought Angie had it... Well, I wasn't quite ready to confront that beast.

I thought back to the evening before, when I'd snuck up behind Angie as quietly as I could with a walker and a chaperone and kissed her neck as she stood at the stove, stirring the bean soup.

She'd slapped me away. "Don't do that! How many times have I told you not to...touch me like that?"

"But you're my wife."

"I know, but...this." She gestured toward the stove.

"And tomorrow you'll be making candy or filing or gardening or whatever else you decide to do in a day. I'm not asking for much..."

The blaze in her eyes cut me.

I knew that look. The one that said not to cross her. What the heck had I done? I couldn't be sure, so I did what I did best. Changed the subject. "Do you need me to set the table?"

"Yeah, sure. Use the good bowls, will you?"

"Which are the good bowls?" They were all the good bowls. Why did everything have to be so complicated?

"Really, Frank? You don't know?"

"Never mind. I'll figure it out."

With Dee's help, I shuffled across the kitchen and opened the cabinet I thought held the bowls she meant. First try and I was right. We needed four—only Nico was coming over that night plus one for Dee—and I placed them on the counter's corner. Angie may have mumbled "lucky guess" under her breath, but when I turned to face her, a peaceful look graced her face. I moved to find the linen napkins and then the silverware, trying a few drawers before I found the one that housed the best cutlery we had. On top of it sat the kitchen television remote control. What in the heck was that doing in a drawer?

"Uh, honey? Why is the remote in the silverware drawer?"

"I don't know... I didn't put it there."

"Well neither did I."

"Maybe it was one of the...boys."

That's right. Cam and Eli had been in and out the last few days, but why would they have hidden it? Hadn't I turned the television off right before they came in? Was I the one to put the remote in the wrong place? *Oh God, had I?*

I stepped back and leaned against the counter, my hand to my hammering heart. This was it. The moment I'd been afraid of. The moment where I misplaced an item, just like the stories of Alzheimer's patients. A lump grew in my throat; I swallowed against it. "How long is it until dinner?"

"About ten minutes."

"Okay," I whispered. "I'll be at the computer."

I opened a browser and keyed in my question. An online site listed the symptoms of Alzheimer's or dementia or... Oh hell, what was the difference between dementia and Alzheimer's, anyway? In the kitchen, the peal and plink meant Angie was still puttering around, but the ladle's clamor against the metal soup tureen created a sense of urgency. I pulled up the list and sat there, staring at it, until she called me in for dinner.

But I'd had time since then to do more thinking about that remote. I was certain I hadn't put it there, which begged the only logical question: Had Angie?

Now, Marissa popped out onto the porch, clean sheets in her hands. "Dad, I'm helping Dee with a few things before dinner, so I'm going to make your bed with the new sheets. Which color do you prefer?" She held up light blue plaid and pale green polka dot sets.

The sheets contrasted with her red-rimmed eyes, but I didn't point those out. "New sheets? What are they for?"

"Are you kidding? When was the last time you had new sheets? With the amount of time you spent in your bed recently, I thought it would be good to change them. Mom said you didn't have any sheets, so I bought two sets yesterday after work."

"Sheets? We have plenty of sheets in the other room. In the drawer of that long dresser."

"Oh. Maybe they don't fit your bed."

"Maybe not."

"Or maybe Mom is losing it."

"Don't say things like this about your mother. She is not *losing* it. She's *fine*."

Marissa moved to the chair opposite me and slumped into it, sheets on her lap. She pulled her hands through her hair and looked at me with her eyes wide. "You're right. I shouldn't use that terminology. It's rude. But Dad, she is *not* fine. You know where we went the other day?"

"No."

"To see your piano teacher."

"Okay. So?"

"She couldn't tell me how to get to his studio, but she showed me. And when we made it to the building, your teacher happened to be outside."

"So?"

"And she said, 'Hi, Roger. Frank is...' and then she looked to me for help. She couldn't tell him what happened to you and why you wouldn't be back for a while."

"Well of course not. This has all been very stressful on your mother. But I'm doing well. The stress should let up soon." Having a notion that something might be wrong with your wife and voicing that concern were not the same thing.

Marissa wrinkled her nose and brushed a hand across her forehead. She spoke in a low voice, which never boded well. "You're doing okay because I'm here, because Dee is here, because of Nico! We've nursed you back to health. We've gotten up in the middle of the night—how many times—to give you meds, to make sure you have healthy food. I'm so grateful for Dee because for a bit there, I put my life on hold to come here and take care of you. But if neither of us had been *there*, you wouldn't be *here*!"

"What are you saying?"

"Come on, Dad. Why did we have to hire Dee? Mom doesn't wake up to remind you of your medicines. She doesn't cook you more than an egg at a time, or soup—one of three recipes. She's not *quite right*... How about saying *that* if you don't want me to say she's losing it? Can't you see it?"

I *could* see it, now, at least. The remote, the bank, our stilted conversations. The chores that piled up—laundry, weeding, cleaning. Something was different about Angie. But before that? I'd been wrapped up in my own world. Walking with friends, having coffee with the guys, being the retiree I wanted to be. And she'd been wrapped up in her own world, too, of chocolate and business orders. Our orbitals didn't always overlap. Marissa had to know that.

"We're getting older, Marissa. We can't do everything we want to do anymore."

"You think that's it? That she's just getting older?" she whispered.

Yes, and no, but the truth was too hard to face, and deep down, I knew we'd be okay. I said as much.

Marissa shook her head as she clutched the sheets to her chest. "I disagree, Dad. Give me a minute." She left and returned with a notebook in her hands. "Let me read you something."

She wouldn't let anything go soon, so I leaned my head back against the love seat and waited with my eyes closed.

"I have these notes. Here, listen. *Called Angie from the store to ask about what sort of juice Frank liked; call lasted six minutes, but she asked three times if I could pick up food for the boys. Told me multiple times she'd checked on Frank. Angie asked two times about sleeping arrangements—I had to remind her the kids weren't staying overnight. She asked three times in quick succession where I bought the pizza we had for lunch.*" She glanced up from the page. "And these are just quick notes. Do you want me to continue?"

When I didn't say anything, she kept going. "This was from last weekend, something I recently remembered. *Mom flummoxed by the estimated taxes and when they were due and didn't understand what quarterly tax meant. Adamant Dad hadn't paid the first installment, though the checkbook says otherwise. I told her three times to get the correct credit card for a purchase, and she never did.*"

Lifting my head away from the back of the love seat, I opened my eyes.

Marissa stood there, staring at me. "So?"

"What? What do you want me to say?"

"You don't know?" she asked.

"No."

"You find nothing in what I just told you odd? Off? A little concerning?"

"Well..."

"Let me say this: We've been working our asses off around here for you the last couple of weeks. Scheduled follow-up appointments for the coming months, appointments with PT and OT inside the house. Scheduled time for the social worker from the Department of Aging, ran back and forth from the pharmacy to the Bureau of Motor Vehicles, which, by the way, you have a hangtag, but you're not driving anytime soon—"

"Wait a minute. If I want to—"

Marissa stopped with a curt hand and pursed lips. "My heart thunders in my chest every time I'm here. And it's not from physical activity. It's from being overwhelmed. The minute details. Keeping everything in line. And I'm willing to bet that Nico feels the same when he's here. It's great we have Dee, but how much longer can we do this? I don't know. What I *do* know is that we need to do something about Mom."

"What? Why?"

Marissa sighed. "If you can't understand why anything I mentioned is concerning, then nothing I say is going to help. And if you think you can handle yourself from here on out, I'll leave you after dinner to your peaceful home with Mom and Dee."

If Marissa felt she needed to step out of the lineup, so be it. "Do what you need to do, Marissa. We'll be fine."

CHAPTER 41: MARISSA

Despite my anger at Dad, the revolving door continued for me that evening. Moving from one group to the other—Will, the kids, Dee, Mom—I made my parents' bed, helped prep the last of dinner, and assured Dee she was doing a great job. Leaving after dinner would be the best option, and maybe I *would* take a break from my parents for a bit, Mom's issues be damned. All I needed was a breather, just a little one, and then, with a clear head, I could figure out a plan. Or rather, *we* could figure out a plan. Will, Nico, Luke—we'd even call Gabe. As much as I wanted to believe Dad and Mom *would* be okay, I knew they wouldn't. Not if something was truly wrong with Mom. But if we all took baby steps... My gut clenched at those words, and I shoved the thought of that positive pregnancy test to my mind's dusty back room, where it joined the HR call.

Will jumped in too, offering to take out Mom and Dad's garbage and recycling. I wandered over to be with the boys, who romped on the floor with Nico, one attached to his back, the other to his leg. Our kids were introverted, but given the opportunity to wrestle, they shed their shyness like snakes molted their skins. Now, their laughter rang in my ears, and Will had returned, moving next to me. We stood there, witnessing the activity for a peaceful moment. My mind drifted to an image of one more little one playing with Nico, maybe on his knee, a girl with wavy brown hair and big brown eyes, and I placed my hand over my belly. I turned to Will, who glanced at my hand and smiled as he slipped his arm around me, pulling me toward his warmth. "Nico's got enough love for another one. I'm sure of it. And we do too, Mar."

I nodded. "Remind me to tell you about the conversation I had with my father."

"Oh, we're there today, are we? Father?" He smiled, then turned to Nico. "It's great to see you playing so effortlessly with these two scoundrels. They can tire you out. Let me shake the hand of the man who might tire *them* out!" Will held out his hand and stepped forward toward Nico and the boys, all three of whom stared up at us expectantly.

Nico laughed and extricated himself from the tangle of limbs then rose to meet Will's hand. Two strong arms, opposite one another, pumped up and down. If I hadn't been looking directly at the two men before me, if I didn't know them both so well, it would be difficult to tell whose arm was whose. I'd never noticed how similar their builds were before, and I chuckled. Nico resembled Dad and Will resembled Nico and therefore Will resembled Dad and oh... *Stop, Marissa. You chose well.*

"Good to see you too. Our paths haven't crossed as much lately, have they?"

"No. You've been crossing with everyone but me." Will smiled. "And thanks for all your help. Even with Dee bearing the brunt of things now, Marissa wouldn't be able to do it all without you. Of course, someone has to be with these kids. And it's such a hardship, you know?" Will winked at the boys, who giggled.

Nico tugged at his skewed shirt, adjusting it across his shoulders, and smoothed his hair back off his forehead. He still had that youthful exuberance to him, the kind Will and I lost when the kids had come along. He tipped his head in my direction and whispered, "Ever think of having any more?"

In my mind, the whole room stopped, then Will pushed forward, leaning down to tickle the boys and insisting on an arm-wrestling match over the coffee table. Nico rose a brow at me, and I shook my head, thankful that he chose not to push.

"Oh, and it's a good thing I arrived when I did." Nico glanced at the boys, now poised to "beat" Will. "I heard everything about the butterfly garden." His eyes widened. "Hope all goes well there, you know?"

"I do too," Will said. "It's been...interesting. Fingers crossed and all that, eh, honey? If not..."

I shook my head again, hoping to send a silent message. "We can talk about that another time, you know, later." *When the boys aren't around.* Doubts about my ability to hatch a butterfly still plagued me. Doubts about my ability to be a mother still plagued me and now... The potential for another little one? *Oh God.*

"It's been fun, boys," Nico said and winked at them again. "But I'm thinking that it's close to dinner time, isn't it?" He rubbed his hands together and then patted his stomach. He'd always eaten like a horse. Maybe that's why Mom loved him; she could show off her cooking skills when he was around. Come to think of it, Luke had a big appetite too. Mom would bring him into the fold with no trouble. Dad, now, who knew? He still held to the belief that romantic love meant one thing: feelings between a man and a woman. Even after Nico divulged his "secret," he'd kept his love life private, never answering Mom's or Dad's questions, never caving to my demands to let me in.

The soup ladle *clinked* against the tureen, reverberating in my ears. *One of three recipes.* "Sounds like it's close to time. Are you staying?" I sniffed, and the pungent scent of peppers and roasted corn irritated my nose. "That corn chowder. The boys love it, you know."

"Hmm. I do too. And it's far better fare than anything I'd put together."

Cam chose that moment to launch himself at Nico while Eli practically took down Will. The boys, still in a heap, wiggled and giggled, until finally, Will glanced at me, a slow smile spreading across his face. He directed his gaze toward my belly, then reached a hand to Eli before jumping up and grabbing my hand too.

My husband had definitively spoken, told me once again how he felt about the possible new addition to our family, our own little cocoon. He tugged me closer to his body, and then shackled his arm around me before kissing me on the top of my head. The comfort in his touch was exactly what I needed right then. *You're loved. You're wanted. You're home.*

That's when Luke walked in, and Nico's face flamed the color of the stripe on the red admiral butterfly. I said nothing, just ushered everyone to the kitchen and helped Mom dish out dinner. Who knew what would happen around the table?

CHAPTER 42: FRANK

Dee sat me at the table and took the chair next to me. She was a good kid. Okay, probably not a *kid*. But a teacher or lieutenant or commander or parent would be proud of her. Damn proud. She knew what she was doing. She was gentle. And while I normally felt comfortable with her there, the discussion Marissa and I had prior to dinner hadn't set well with me. My stomach jumped and turned like it did when I kept secrets. That's what I was doing, wasn't it? The bank issue—which fell under Marissa's definition of "losing it"—was another secret to add to the line of other secrets. An ache clawed deep inside as I thought back to the information I'd read about dementia. God, maybe we both had it because I felt like I had to for sure: going through the same motions over and over. The same thoughts. Like a broken record.

"Can you give me a minute?" I said to those around the table. Cam and Eli hadn't come in yet.

"What do you need?" Dee asked.

"Can you help me over to the living room?" Dee had set up a Chromebook there, and I'd bookmarked the search I'd started a few days ago. The number of hits on "Alzheimer's disease" had astounded me then: 22,400,000 results in 0.33 seconds. Back when Angela and I had first met, I'd never heard of a disease called Alzheimer's. Now, in the blink of an eye, I could find more information on it than I ever thought possible. So much information, but I couldn't be sure one of us had it or not. What the hell?

"I'll give you five minutes, Frank," Dee said. "I think Angie's tired, and I reckon she'd probably like to see everyone head home."

The first link brought me to the page for a medicine called Namzaric. The site read, "NEW NAMZARIC is the only treatment for moderate to severe Alzheimer's disease. It combines NAMENDA XR˙ (memantine HCl) extended release and donepezil HCl—two proven medicines—in a single, once-a-day capsule." I scrolled down the page to the statement that followed: "To date, evidence does not exist to suggest that NAMZARIC prevents or slows the underlying mechanism of Alzheimer's disease." *Then what the heck is the point of taking such a medicine?* If one of us had it, would this even be useful?

The second link brought up The Wexner Medical Center at *The Ohio State University* page. Now that one held promise: OSU wasn't that far away. In fact, with Dee's help, I could take a trip out there if necessary. The page came up in scarlet and gray. Had to give it to them—scarlet and gray to the core. "Established in 1993, the Memory Disorders Clinic at The Ohio State University Wexner Medical Center is one of Ohio's most comprehensive centers for research, evaluation, diagnosis, and treatment for patients and families affected by Alzheimer's disease and dementia." *Dementia.* Would Marissa bring up her concerns with dinner? Had I asked her not to? I couldn't remember—

"Frank! It's time," Angie called, and Dee came in to help once more. She eyed the screen and whispered, "Listen, y'all are going to be fine, Frank. You hear?" She patted my arm and ushered me back to my seat, even extended her hand to mine under the table. Would it be fine? I didn't feel fine. My legs, my mind, Angie's mind. And then—

"Dad, what is this about you having dementia? Mom said something. What's going on?" Nico asked.

"You know what? I don't feel like talking about it right now."

"And why not?"

"Because I said so." A spoonful of my soup, and my mouth was full, which meant talking couldn't and wouldn't happen.

Nico threw back his head and laughed. "That excuse flew when I was eight, but right now? Not so much."

"Grandpa? I'm gonna be eight someday! What does that mean?" Eli asked.

"Do you want a piece of bread with your soup, honey?" Marissa stood to get the breadbasket on the counter. Always the peacemaker, always diplomatic. A smile spread across Eli's face, his question forgotten.

And the conversation continued, flowing around me but not settling. I had little to say, just watched my kids interact with one another. Cam and Eli punched each other in the arms. Will tucked a hand behind Marissa's back. Angie scraped the bowl's bottom. Nico draped an arm over the back of Luke's chair.

What?

My belly grumbled, and I dipped my spoon into the soup. "So, Luke, now that you're back, how are you keeping busy? Working lots of hours? When are you going to find yourself a nice girl? We'd love to see you more around here now that you're back."

"Dad," Nico said. "Leave him alone. Maybe that's not what he wants." Nico glanced at Luke, then Marissa, and he pursed his lips. The look on his face right then? Classic Antonio. And like Antonio, he had a habit of answering for other people.

"How do you know? Are *you* Luke?" I asked.

"Frank! Is it that...memory thing again?" Angie stood.

"How did we go from Luke to a 'memory thing,' Angie?"

"Well, you seem so...worried about it. I thought—"

"You thought wrong!" I pushed up against the table, my legs faltering a little, and Dee grabbed my arm, securing me in my stance. "Everyone needs to stop being so damn nosy. So I'm done here. Dee? Can you help me?"

Dee didn't need to be asked twice; she placed her napkin next to her bowl and ushered me from the room. Still at the table, Cam whispered about my use of the word *damn,* and Eli giggled before Marissa and Will shushed them both. Dinner would go on as it might on any other day we had everyone here, just without me. Dee helped me into the armchair, placed a blanket over my legs, and asked if I needed anything, her hands warm against mine.

"Nothing you can help me with, Dee."

Undisturbed, I sat there until long after everyone had left. Angie had gone up and probably sat in bed, propped up against the frilly white pillow, tucked into the soft, light summer comforter, television on. Maybe she was right. Maybe not being able to recall a few items didn't matter in the grand scheme of everything. But we might be on the cusp of something catastrophic and severe. Maybe *she* was. Maybe life as I knew it was about to crumble. I didn't want to miss out on anything— any clues, any cues—because if I did, I might fail her in a big way. I'd already failed too many people, and what kind of legacy would that be?

CHAPTER 43: MARISSA

"He didn't even say thank you to me!" I strode across our family room, pacing in front of the butterfly garden, grateful the kids were in bed. Luke and Nico had heeded the call to come to our house after the family dinner. They sat with Will, lined up on the couches like children receiving a punishment, and Gabe was on the phone. I could tell they didn't want to interrupt, so I kept going.

"Of course he looks and feels great! He's had a twenty-four-hour housekeeper/nursemaid who's done everything possible to get him healthy. How many times did I go to the store for them? How many trips to the pharmacy did Nico make? The only reason he eventually pooped is because I came in and not only put a suppository in, I helped with an enema—"

Will snorted. "You did not."

"I think she did," Gabe said.

Nico and Luke looked at one another with amusement written all over their faces. I pointed at the two of them. "You bet your asses I did!" That response sent them into a fit of laughter, and I had to admit that the unintentional pun *was* funny. "And he has the gall to say 'we'll be fine'? I hope he is because I'm not going back there to help them. And that's final."

Throwing myself onto the chair, I crossed my arms over my chest. I probably looked as juvenile as the men had, and I didn't care. At all. I was finished with my parents. Let them try to take care of themselves. *I. Was. Done.*

Will was the first to speak. "Are you okay, honey?" He stood, walked over, and kneeled in front of me, passing a hand over my forehead and down across my cheek.

The roughness of his palms somehow comforted me. The days I'd spent with my parents—I'd missed his laugh. His smile, his eyes, the way his arms wrapped around me at night. His hands felt familiar, and I needed familiar right then. "Yeah, I'm okay. I needed to get that out. I don't mind helping. They *are* my parents, but I put my life on hold. My family on hold to help them! My job might be at stake, for crying out loud! And to think that he'd be fine if I hadn't come in? What the hell is he thinking? Is he that selfish?"

On the line, Gabe interjected. "I don't think he gets it, Marissa. It's always been about him. He *is* selfish, plain and simple, and always has been. When he was home for dinner, what was the conversion about? Him. And what about now? On the phone, what does he talk about? Usually, it all loops back to him. We'll see what happens next. Dee can help, but she can't cure his impulsivity. Or his selfishness, if that's what it is. And what's this about your job?"

I filled my brothers and Luke in on the HR call, and I agreed not to panic until necessary. Gabe gave me a pep talk, and then Nico brought the conversation back to Dad.

"Gabe's right." Nico stretched his arms over his head. "There's no way he's back to normal. Not yet. He can walk with that walker pretty well and a bit by himself, but they still don't know *why* he fell, do they? Aside from being thoughtless. You know, that's what he would have called me years ago, right? 'Use your head, Nico.' 'Think it through, Nico.' God, if I only had a dime. Anyway, if they don't know what's causing the weakness in his legs—Parkinsonian-like or not—then it could happen again."

"That's all we, I mean, *you*, need," Luke said. "Anything I can do to help?"

Nico, Will, and I looked at each other, then at Luke. Same old guy, pitching in when necessary, and he'd already stepped up admirably. Nico needed to grab onto him and not let him go.

But I didn't want to go there tonight. My boobs were sore, the rest of me fatigued, and I still hadn't wrapped my mind around this pregnancy. Getting Mom off my mind was step one. Then I'd worry about everything else. "I can't answer that yet," I said, "but let me show you all something." I pulled the notebook out of my bag and asked Will to read a few entries that Dee had provided aloud. "You need to hear this."

Will cleared his throat. "This is what we have: *Angie was confused about the St. Vincent de Paul donation receipt. Thought we needed to give them a donation. She could not keep appointments straight (nurse at 11 a.m. Saturday and eucharistic minister at 10:15 a.m. on Sunday). When recounting her experience, she said 119 instead of 911. Went out and got the mail she forgot to get on Saturday, and thirty minutes later went out and checked again. Asked about taxes again.*"

I lifted a hand, like a student in school. "Those taxes have been sent already. Each time I visit, she asks about those taxes, and each time, I show her the check register."

Nico held up his hand in return. "You recorded all this?"

I shook my head. "No, these are Dee's notes. But when I was at the house a couple of times, Mom did some weird things. Things that seemed off, for lack of a better word. But I have so many balls to juggle, I think I shoved what I noticed into a compartment and didn't want to dwell there." Blame the pregnancy brain, too, which had already bloomed. But no one needed to hear about that yet.

"You are one brilliant woman," Nico said. "Honestly, I had no idea."

Luke laughed out loud. "I told you I liked her for a reason."

Will pushed against Luke's shoulder, the way Cam and Eli would have. "Hey now—"

"I know. She's off limits. It's fine. I—"

A quick lift of my eyebrows. "You found your soulmate?"

A blush rose in both Luke's and Nico's cheeks, and Will flicked a glance my way, a small smile on his face. Peppering them with questions ate at me, but now wasn't the time or the place for it.

Gabe's voice sounded on the line. "Am I missing something? Because it sure sounds like—"

"Will, can you go on? I think you need to read a little more," Luke said.

Will's voice filled the silence. "Here you go: *Had to explain about supporting Frank if he's vomiting. Had to show where medication was and explain (again) what Zofran was. Found what Angie thinks is an old cane, but then she tried to find the new cane, and she looked for at least twenty minutes, checking all the places she'd already been. Asked about the physical therapist, who was scheduled to arrive at two o'clock, six times.*"

"I have one thing to say," Nico said as he rubbed a hand over his chin. "And that would be...oh fuck."

Luke shook his head and closed his eyes. "I was going to say that, but I was looking for something stronger."

"What's stronger than fuck?" Will said.

CHAPTER 44: HER

A lot had happened over the last few weeks, and it was good that her daughter had been around. Last night—or was it the night before that?—she'd come back, just for dinner. She had enjoyed having her daughter there. Made her feel lighter, happier somehow. Perhaps the next time she came over, she'd pull her aside and give her a hug big enough to say what she wanted to say. Stirring the chocolate over the double boiler, she hoped that even if the hug didn't say it, these candies could. If she set aside the tray today, they'd be ready for her daughter's next visit.

What kind was her favorite? She dug around in the containers for what she knew were there: caramels with peanut butter, caramels with nougat. She placed a few of those on her favorite tray—the one that made the ensemble cast of chocolates look like a garden filled with those colorful things. She then pulled over several pieces of molded milk chocolate, dark chocolate, and white chocolate. Her husband used to complain about the white chocolate. "It's not chocolate at all, honey. Why do you include it on the tray?" But at least one of the kids enjoyed biting into a creamy white chocolate truffle. Oh yes, and the truffles! How could she have forgotten? Taking in her stock, she realized she'd need to make more of her favorite kind, the ones with the double dark chocolate and the toasted...crunchy pieces. To save time, she could add those toasted pieces to the double dark chocolate she'd already begun.

She wandered to the pantry but didn't find the crunchy pieces. *No worries*, she thought. *There might be a bag, a backup of sorts, in the office.* And if not there, maybe the neighbor—Bea? Betty?—had some. Her belly grumbled, and her mouth watered. It had been years since she'd made those toasted truffles. She couldn't wait to taste them.

CHAPTER 45: FRANK

A light mist began a few minutes after I headed out for a very slow walk with my neighbor. The pace and cane didn't matter to me: I was walking, and life was looking up. Dee had been so useful in the week that passed since the blowout with the kids. With me. The laundry. Keeping the peace with Angie. Having Dee around made me understand I could have conveyed my gratitude to Marissa and Nico for their service, but after Marissa's spiel in the living room the day she left and the words at the table with Nico, I didn't have the heart to bring it up. They were right, of course. I could see it now—how much they'd helped.

The mile we walked was slower than any I'd done in a long time, but it felt great to stretch my legs and be out of the house regardless of the dampness. Angie was irritating me. Ever since I'd fallen down the stairs, she seemed more distant and concerned with things that didn't matter to me. And scattered. The other day, she couldn't find the hair dryer. There it was, sitting in the drawer it was supposed to be in. She passed off her actions as not seeing it, but I knew better. Facing that truth, the real truth, of what was in front of me would take courage. I wasn't ready for that yet.

I opened the sliding door. The kids had agreed to come over for Friday night dinner as an early celebration for Fourth of July. They'd decided to grill and bring sides so Angie and I didn't have to take care of anything or ask Dee for help. Angie was on the phone with her back to me as I stood on the stoop, hands clinging to the doorjamb. With the phone on the speaker setting, the entire conversation reached me.

"Okay. By the way, where is Dad?" Marissa's voice boomed.

"He's walking with the man across the street."

The man? Since when did she refer to Bill like that? What was that all about? We'd lived here for years. Never had I heard her call him "the man."

"Did they walk outside today? It's raining here now... Sort of spitting. How about over there?"

"No...not outside." Angie ducked her head into the fridge, then pulled it back out and closed the door, her hands empty. "They headed over to the place...where you can walk inside."

She meant the old strip mall. We'd considered heading inside, but the time driving wasn't worth the mile we'd do. And why didn't Angie use the proper word? Was Marissa picking up on this? Should I interrupt and try to ask her? I stood, rooted in my spot, an uneasy feeling in my bones, and I shrunk back, hoping Angie didn't see me.

"All right. Tell him I called. If you need me to pick up anything else, let me know."

"Will do. Talk soon."

Angie placed the phone back on the cradle and then moved to the kitchen sink for a glass of water. She gazed out over the backyard's expanse. What did she see? What was she thinking?

Because I didn't want to confront Angie, I texted Dee, who came around and helped me as I crept toward the side of the house to the garage entry and lumbered to the den. After Dee left, I fired up the computer and sat down, pulling up my bookmarks. That dementia symptoms list appeared on the screen. It hadn't even been that long ago that I first accessed it. Time had somehow sped up and slowed down all at once.

At the top of the Association for Alzheimer's Research and Education list I read: "Memory loss, in particular, recently learned information, is a common sign of Alzheimer's disease. Other signs include asking repeatedly for the same information; forgetting significant dates or events; needing to rely on memory aids (e.g., reminder notes, calendars, or electronic devices) or family members for things they used to handle on their own."

I'd gone over this before. Both of us couldn't remember things like we used to, and I relied more on my planner for my appointments, but had Angie exhibited this symptom? I closed my eyes, searching and searching and suddenly—

Angie said she kept more lists these days. If she couldn't find the list, she couldn't remember. Lists would be considered a memory aid. *Put a check next to that one.*

The second symptom listed said, "Some people experience decreases in the ability to work with numbers or develop and follow a plan. Recipes and monthly bills can be especially difficult to follow or maintain. Concentration can be a problem, and they may take longer to do things than they did before."

Shit. That odd feeling, a coiling of snakes, crept back into my stomach. I didn't know about her recipes. Angie had always kept her business to herself. But the checkbook? Oh, the pain the checkbook had been recently. Several arguments about errors ensued, along with a quick, "that's not what happened, *Frank*." And the tax bill? The proof was written in front of her, and she couldn't even remember that. Then my mind jumped back to the bank. My conversation with Joseph.

My fingers shook as a possibility slammed into me: *she couldn't understand.* Closing my eyes again, thoughts bombarded me. The time to speak had come. To her, the kids, to anyone who would listen. But what would that mean for us, our marriage? Would I lose my wife? My friend? What would happen to our family? Visions of the life I thought we'd have in retirement—happy family, financial security, time to travel—burned and floated to the floor as ash. And one final thought: What would happen to me?

I was about to go on to the third symptom when Angie walked through the door.

"You're back? What...what are you doing?" She squinted at the screen and then moved closer. "Oh no...not again. You do *not* have a problem!" Her eyes flashed with anger, and she shook her head. Marissa would have said that a negative energy pulsed in the room.

A boldness belted through me. "I don't think that I do either. But *you* might."

Bright red spots emerged against Angie's otherwise pale cheeks. She puffed air out of her nose and turned away from me, fists clenched against her hips. As she left the room she muttered, "There's nothing wrong with me!"

Either she didn't know, or she didn't want to face the music. Been there, done that—another expression courtesy of Marissa. My bold moment gone, an exhaustion worked its way through my body. I'd never been so glad to have the kids coming for dinner.

CHAPTER 46: MARISSA

Over a week had passed, and I hadn't gone to check on Mom and Dad. I couldn't—I was still too angry. Nico said he'd go, Will said he'd go, and of course, Luke decided he should give it a go too. I suggested Will stay home, citing that the kids and I needed him. It wasn't entirely true, but we'd already been wrapped up enough in the madness, and Will was easy to convince.

But behind the scenes, I still worked my magic, mainly to help Dee: a few calls to the pharmacy during my lunch smoothed over the gap in medication refills; a chat with the occupational therapist on the way home from work ensured that the proper rails were installed in the master bathroom; a video call during a begged-for extra thirty minutes of leave allowed Dad's clearance for moving about the county. Though I'd cleared everything up with HR—an overzealous newbie had gone on a power trip—the clinic still needed me to step up when possible, and the threat of no job lingered, no matter what my boss said.

"You know your dad will never thank you for all this, right?" Will said the evening after I'd spoken with the pharmacy. "He has no idea that these tasks even need to be done, and he certainly doesn't know you're balancing them with your job and the kids. I hate to tell you this," Will leaned over and kissed my cheek, "but you'll never get his approval either."

"Is that what you think this is about?"

Will gave me a cup of tea, stepped away, and leaned against the counter, crossing his arms over his chest. "Isn't it?"

"No...I...want to help him, and he's family, so it's the right thing to do. But no matter what I do—I could literally save his life—I'll never measure up to what he wants."

Will nodded, a thoughtful look on his face, then sighed. "Mar? None of that matters. It's not about him or your mother or your brothers. It's not about seeking approval and getting it. It's about you. Who you are, what you want. That's what it's about. What do you want?"

What I wanted had always been a tough question to answer. True love and happiness? The ability to understand my family and their motives? A family that loved me for the person I was? I couldn't answer Will, and his question nagged me as I did my business. But those questions and my parents haunted me all the time, thanks to Dee: she'd jotted her observations in that notebook like a doctoral student in the sciences.

So when she called me one afternoon and said, "I encourage you to say something soon, Marissa. I can't. I work for Frank and Angie, and it's not my place since they have you and the boys. But say something. Soon," I didn't get angry—I got thoughtful. And I called Nico, who came over that night.

"Dee can't be the only one observing," I said, hoping we could figure things out before summer ended and well before my belly expanded. "We need to address this, and we might want an overall picture to present to the physician. Can you head over one day to check in?"

He balked at having to take notes. "I do enough writing during the day. Who wants to take notes after school?"

"Dictate them on your phone then, Einstein. I don't care how it's done, you know. Be creative!"

Nico nodded at my suggestion and put a finger to his chin. "Okay, okay. Something a little different from what the rest of you might do."

He narrowed his eyes and then widened them. "Perhaps I'm being a little like, oh, I don't know, could we call it...a renegade?"

I waved my hands in the air in surrender before covering my ears. "Don't sing it. Just *don't* do it. It's been all over the radio these days, and I don't need this right now."

"I know you love me, Marissa."

"I do. But I don't need to feel any more angst! I've got enough of my own these days."

My statement held true: even though I wasn't at their place, the strain from Mom and Dad's situation hovered in the air at our house, too, and I didn't like the feelings being projected. Cam and Eli had picked up on something. They knew Grandpa was still recovering, but the hushed whispers told them something else was going on as well. They weren't old enough to understand everything, but after speaking to Will about the whole situation, I realized that if I brushed my thoughts under the rug and kept them from the boys, I would do exactly what my parents did: hide from the truth. But what would the truth do to the boys? Keeping my family intact was important, paramount even.

So before we headed over to celebrate the Fourth of July, I pulled the kids into the backyard and asked if they wanted to play in the sandbox. A departure from their incessant checking on a possibly dormant chrysalis would do us all some good. Two resounding yeses meant I'd have at least part of their attention for a while. We sat in the octagonal oak structure, constructing castles and moats, bridges and quarries to the best of our abilities.

Cam had always been my intuitive child. As he poured water from the bucket into the box, he looked up at me and said, "What do you want to talk about, Mom? What's wrong?"

I felt my brow furrow. Will and I hadn't been great about hiding our conversations, but was I that transparent? "How'd you know I wanted to speak with you?"

"Usually, you send us out here together and *then* you come out and play." He placed a rock in the middle of the puddle. "Today, you're out here the *whole* time. You must want to be with us."

"Can't I be with you without wanting to talk about something?"

This time, Cam's brow furrowed. He spent a moment in thought. "You can, but it's not your MO." He placed a second rock next to the first.

I laughed out loud. "MO? Have you been talking to Uncle Nico?" I felt my smile widen at the thought of Nico and his antics and that my almost seven-year-old child had used the term MO properly in a sentence. What a hoot. "You're good, Cam. I do want to talk to you. About Grandma and Grandpa."

Eli looked up from the truck he'd been moving back and forth on the sand. "Grandma and Grandpa? When are we going to their house again?"

The kids knew nothing of the evening dinner plans. Despite what Dad believed, he still wasn't fully recovered, and I didn't want to overwhelm Mom, so I'd tell them instead of making it a surprise; they'd be more subdued when we visited this time.

My phone buzzed. A short text about a backed-up order for cotton swabs. I held up a finger to the boys, silently asking them to wait, and made a brief call as Eli watched me and Cam focused on the airplane flying overhead.

The call ended. "We're going over for dinner, boys. You'll get to see them and spend time there. But remember that Grandpa is still getting better. He might be tired. He might stay in his room more often. And Grandma has been...more stressed out."

Eli's face scrunched up in confusion. "What does that mean?" He lifted the truck and spun the wheels, forcing sand to fly over our knees.

I wiped the sand away. "It means she's had a lot to do around the house since Grandpa can't do it. Even though Dee has been there, Grandma might feel tired and upset too. And," I looked at them and got their attention by placing a finger under their chins and tipping them up, "I think Grandma is having trouble remembering things."

"Like what?" Cam's mind was always on the go. He loved details, and I should have been prepared.

"Well." Did I have any good examples that they would understand? "Oh, like remembering what Grandpa eats for lunch. I asked her that when I was visiting, and she couldn't remember."

"That's easy, Mom. He eats turkey lunchmeat with Swiss cheese on rye bread, and he likes to put mustard on it. The kind that looks and smells funny." He stuck his finger into the wet sand. "It's like this color, Mom."

"You must mean brown mustard. You know, it's kind of grainy like sand."

"It is?" Eli said as he thrust his fingers into the wet sand, too, and rubbed the grains between them.

"Yes. And how do you know that's what he eats?"

"I just do," Cam said. "Every time we eat lunch with him, that's what he has."

Give that kid the notebook! But he was my *child.* I didn't want to involve him any more than he already was. "All right. Well, you see how easy it was for you to remember that? I think Grandma doesn't have that capability anymore, and it might make her upset. So please, don't pester her too much."

"We won't," the boys said in unison.

And then Eli piped up. "Is Uncle Luke going to be there?"

"I'm not sure, honey. I don't know."

A few days after the last family dinner, Luke had stopped by the office with a grim look on his face.

"I'm not sure about this, Marissa. I'm not sure."

"About what?" I had no idea what he was talking about. We'd all agreed on what Mom and Dad needed.

"Nico. Me. Nico *and* me."

Concerned, I ushered him in and shut the door, then leaned against my desk and gestured for him to sit in the chair. "What do you mean? Did something happen? Don't take this the wrong way, but why are you confiding in me?"

"You're a good listener, and you *care.* But nothing happened. Nothing bad, anyway. I mean, there's too much going on in your family right now to be honest about Nico's and my relationship. Your parents, they...they might not..."

"What?"

"I get the feeling that if anything, they expected you and I to be together! What would they say about Nico and me instead? And your dad...he's a conservative for fuck's sake." Luke almost hissed the words. "For all his flaws, and we all have them, I love him like a father. I guess maybe I don't want to disappoint him."

Well shit. Apparently, Luke Butterfield was like the rest of us—full of insecurities that no one saw. "Do you love him? Nico, I mean, not my dad."

That telltale flush moved up his neck as he replied, "I do."

I leaned over and reached for Luke's hand, squeezing it as hard as I could. "Then I hope you'll let me officiate someday so I can hear you say those words to him. Because you and he both deserve all the happiness in the world."

We hadn't had more time to chat that day, but I would have understood if Luke skipped the family meal this time. He had to come to terms with his own life before he expected anyone else to accept it. And where was he in that journey? I didn't know.

A bit of sand flew as I glanced at the kids, who were still waiting for me to expand on my answer. "Uncle Luke has a lot on his mind right now, so we'll have to see. Okay?"

With not a care in the world apparently, the boys got back to digging before creating a monster truck rally and then a race across a flattened, windswept desert (I provided the wind). When they asked about checking on the butterfly, I didn't have the heart to say no. The last few months had taken a toll on me, bruised and cracked my heart, but a few moments with those two stitched it right up. And in that moment, I felt it: our new addition—still a secret to everyone else—though surprising and unexpected, would be welcomed, loved, and cherished. We had enough love to go around.

•　　•　　•

Will had said he'd occupy the kids so I could get to Mom and Dad's early. Being the grill master at our house, I'd brought the chicken breast for Cam and Eli, the hamburger for Nico and Luke, and the veggie burgers for Will and me. We had enough of all of them, so everyone else could pick if they wanted something different from their usual choice. I was hoping Nico and Luke would remember a side dish. At home I'd put together a potato salad that usually went over well, but I had plans to bake a pan of brownies once I got to Mom and Dad's. Mom kept a clean household for Cam's sake, something for which I was grateful, but if anyone thought deeply about my cooking, my secret would be out: pregnancy brought out the cook in me, and they knew it.

After hauling all my items into the house—only dropping the bag of favorite condiments once—and making sure I hadn't left clutter in my wake, I went to the kitchen, brownie ingredients and meats in hand.

Mom looked up as I came in, giving me a big smile and a quick hug. "You're early."

"Yep, I thought I'd come get everything situated before everyone descended. I know how chaotic it can be when we're all here."

"It's okay. I...like when you visit."

Was she for real? I'd always felt like we were a bit of a bother when we were at home, as if being there was too much for her to handle. And now she said she liked it? Pressing the issue made no sense, so I didn't. "Well, at least we all won't be here long. Just dinner and dessert, and we'll be on our way. Speaking of which, can I borrow a bowl?"

She moved to one cabinet, opened it and closed it and then moved to another cabinet before pulling out the salmon-colored Pyrex bowl from my childhood. So many batches of cookie dough and brownie batter had been mixed in that bowl. Its sides were scratched and worn, the salmon color less vibrant than when I was a child, but it still served its purpose.

"Thanks." I pulled out the ingredients from the paper grocery bag.

"What...what are you making?" Mom picked up the sugar box and flour bag, then put them back on the counter. Her finger trailed over the brown letters on the unsweetened cocoa carton.

"Brownies. The kids love them, and so does Will. And I think gooey brownies will be a good dessert for a cookout. Don't you?"

She nodded. "But...my stove doesn't work right."

I stopped moving the ingredients around and looked at Mom. "What? The stove or the oven or both?"

"Well, no, the oven...it doesn't."

"Wait, you have a business to run. Don't you use the oven?"

"Not really. I just don't use it."

Even if wrangling the right words occurred, I wasn't certain I could remain calm. Against my better judgment, I entered the icy waters as I put the ingredients back into the bag. "So your oven doesn't work, and instead of having someone come fix it, you don't use it. Is that right?"

She shrugged.

Shrugs only meant one thing to me: indifference. No concern at all. Like if she ignored the problem, it would go away. Did Mom *think* that would work? And did Dad know? The whooshing of my blood increased in my ears, and my fingers tapped a steady beat against the countertop. "Why didn't you call a repairman to come fix it?"

At that moment, Nico walked in with a grin on his face, his mouth poised to say something. He stopped, looked at us, cocked his head, as if contemplating the barometer of emotions, and walked right back out again.

I took his action as permission to keep going. "All right, Mom. Tell me..." I pulled out a tray she used for her confections, the one she used most often for a business function. For years, she'd placed the same candies in the same spaces. Even I knew what went where. "Tell me what goes in this spot." I waited as her eyes grew wide. "And this one?" My finger jabbed at the indentation on the tray. I pushed it away when she said nothing. "And how do you make your toffee fudge? Can you tell me that?"

"Well...I have the recipe right here..." She reached over to her cookbook, well used and yellowed, covered in stains, paper notes sticking haphazardly in all directions. I practically ripped the book from her grasp.

"You don't use that! You haven't had to use it for *years*. Doesn't it mean something that you rely on the recipe book now? And what day is it, and don't you dare look at that calendar!" I slammed my fist onto the granite countertop. "I'm sorry, Mom, but can't you see what's in front of you?"

"Stop...stop shouting at me!" Mom turned her back to me. "I've been busy, and I can't...remember everything."

"Oh come off it, Mom! You can't remember *anything!*"

Pushing past her, I stomped out of the room, through the utility area, and out the side door, letting the old wooden screen slam behind me. The summer air whipped at my hair, matching my mood, and storm clouds hovered in the distance, gray and menacing. Humidity accompanied me as I walked toward the old cherry tree, its limbs plump with fruit no one had harvested. *Check off another box on the list of forgotten tasks.*

Nico's presence there didn't surprise me. This old tree had witnessed countless rounds of angry, bitter discussions that usually involved our parents. He'd known by the tension in the kitchen what I'd need. Slumping to the ground, I pulled up my knees and rested my head on them, my face tilted toward him. Two minutes passed, and then I spilled the tea.

"Nice job, M. Now you're the one she'll be mad at instead of me." I looked up at him. "What did *you* do?"

Color flushed his cheeks. "It's nothing. Nothing that can't wait."

Maybe he meant his relationship with Luke. Maybe he didn't. It didn't matter— "You know... Who cares? I don't think she'll remember any of this in the morning."

My gaze held steady with Nico's until the weight of everything caused tears to fall. For Mom's forgetfulness, Dad's refusal to confront his present, his denial, my inability to hold everything together and fix everything, my fear for the future, for the boys, for my unborn child. For *Mom*. My imagination had always gotten the better of me, and there I sat, trying to piece images together of events that hadn't yet happened. And why? To soothe my soul? Keep control of my surroundings? I pressed my face to my knees and sobbed.

Nico scooted over and pulled me in for a hug. The comfort he could give me wouldn't be enough. That I knew. And it was the only thing I was certain of that day.

CHAPTER 47: FRANK

Billowing white smoke from the burning charcoal wafted toward the kitchen; the kids had started dinner preparations. With the grandkids, life would be infused into this house again, at least for a little while. Their cackles and footsteps always echoed through the halls, loud at first and then quieter as they moved from room to room. Like Antonio. He'd moved quickly, as if he didn't want to miss any opportunities in life. And yet...

As usual, Angie was in the kitchen. She checked something off on the calendar and then moved to the sink to wash dishes. That woman had such trouble standing still. She'd always been that way. The doctor once said that people who were depressed and anxious sometimes felt better if they were busy. They felt more useful, as if they had a purpose. Maybe Angie felt that way. I'd never taken the time to ask.

Dinner would be a grand affair. Despite her distance lately, Marissa had outdone herself organizing everything, and she brought her famous potato salad. I wasn't supposed to eat too much of it, so I would stick to a few tablespoons. Nico and Luke had supplied some well-deserved wine and beer as well as fruit salad and veggies. My mouth watered at the thought of such a tasty meal.

Marissa's words about Angie's "three recipes" rang in my ears. All easy. All soup. And those family dinners? Sometimes, the kids would pitch in, which cut down on any sort of work on Angie's end. How had I missed so much?

Will and Marissa would give me an honest answer, so I headed to the porch, slow but mostly steady, better at using a cane now that I'd worked with Dee for a while. They were deep in conversation with Nico, and a notebook sat open in front of them on the wicker coffee table. I edged my way in—no one stopped me—grabbed the notebook and read aloud from the pages: "This is from Sunday after dinner: *When Frank was in the bathroom and she was supposed to be watching him, she got mad that he made a mess with the mouthwash. Left him in the bathroom to fend for himself. She came down into the kitchen, where I was getting the meds, and I said, Is Frank in bed? She said, Probably. I said, What do you mean by probably? You're supposed to help him. She said, Yes, he's there. That conversation didn't sit well with me.*"

What in the hell? I looked at the kids and Will, who all stared back at me. I went back to reading: "On Monday: *Same thing about appointments. Was confused by when the social worker was coming and didn't communicate well with the social worker...*"

Without finishing Monday's words, my gaze bounced ahead to the next one. "Wednesday: *Bothered that we didn't park in the same place for church. Didn't answer How is Frank? adequately when a man asked her. Didn't remember stories she used to tell the kids about Melinda and Belinda. Could not explain what a mailing label was used for.*"

That ghastly feeling took root inside me as I scanned the pages again. Not reading, not seeing. Just feeling. "What is this?" I whispered.

"These are notes. Something is wrong with Mom," Marissa said. "As in memory issues, we think, and we need you to confront her. See if she'll get help."

Will's gaze drilled into me. "Frank, memory issues, dementia or not, aren't things to take lightly. Today it might be lost keys or a lost watch, tomorrow it might be someone calling her on the phone and swindling her out of her credit card number."

Had I slipped and told them about the bank fiasco? I didn't think so. Maybe Angie had said something to Marissa.

"Or worse," Will continued. "Eventually, she could leave the stove on or wander away from the house or try to cross the street without looking—"

"No... We don't know... Not yet."

Nico touched my forearm, and I bristled, backing away to the wall as carefully as I could with my cane in hand. Falling now would do no good at all. But Nico followed, finally putting a hard hand on my shoulder. His gaze held steady with mine, but his eyes were too much like Antonio's, and the pain there, though different right now, reminded me again of him. I looked over his shoulder at the neighbor's house.

"You can't ignore this, Dad. Not this time."

The silence disturbed me, brought my attention to my heart's rapid beating. I placed a hand on the wall behind me to keep myself steady against the judgmental stares coming from my children. "I can for now. At least until after dinner. Maybe Sunday. Let's not ruin a celebration. And I only came by to ask about the dessert." *One white lie never hurt anyone.* "Your mom says a plate of goodies is around here somewhere, and she wants everything set out before dinner."

Marissa sighed and pointed to the corner, where Angie's chocolate garden sat, covered with plastic wrap and cold packs. "It's over there. I figured the kids would know to look for it in the kitchen. Trying to outsmart them is a full-time job." She placed a hand against her back then said, "I'll help you bring it out, and then we'll join you."

With slightly shaky steps, I followed Marissa, who placed the tray on the picnic table and went back into the house. I uncovered the candies and looked at them. Each piece in its proper place. An assortment of "delights" as Cam liked to say. Yesterday, the smell, the thought of their creamy goodness would have tempted me because when all was said and done, Angie was a fantastic candy maker. That was the truth. But now, the images of that notebook, those words, lorded over any thoughts of sweetness.

Cam ran toward me, arms outstretched like he planned on hijacking the entire tray, unlit sparkler in hand, and Eli jogged behind him. We hadn't eaten yet, but a little dessert before dinner would do no harm. "Take what you want, boys. But only one." I lowered my voice. "And don't tell your mother!" I winked at them.

They didn't have to be told twice. Eli shoved his choice into his mouth and bolted, chocolate dribbling down the sides of his small chin, evidence he'd need to clean before Marissa saw it. Cam took his time: he scanned the choices, picked up a chocolate, inspected it, then placed the edge in his mouth, chewing slowly. He seemed to savor the morsel, just like I would. As he opened his mouth to take one more bite, though, his face paled, and he reached for his throat as he gasped for breath and dropped the sparkler.

"Marissa! Will!" Those were the only two words I got out before Cam crumpled to the concrete patio.

CHAPTER 48: MARISSA

A single toasted walnut truffle—no, scratch that, one *bite* of a toasted walnut truffle—had taken down my son, and I paced in the hospital room as Cam breathed with the help of machinery that beeped and whistled. My blood boiled, and my mind raged, and the urge to smack my mother rushed through me, but anyone or anything would do. A stack of blankets on the side table drew my fists until Will came in. He grabbed my wrists, held my arms against his chest with one hand, and wrapped his free arm around me. I placed my head against him and wept.

"I'm sorry." Wiggling away from the circle of Will's arms, I wiped my hands across my eyes and sniffed. "I've tried to stay so strong. I realize Cam is probably going to be okay. No, he *will* be okay. But I'm so angry. So angry! Dammit! She knows not to put walnuts into her chocolates. She *knows* Cam is allergic. Where the hell did she get those walnuts? That house has been clean for years. *Years!*"

Will pulled me back in, tightened his grip around me. "Shit yeah. You *should* be angry, and I'm angry too. She made a mistake, a big one. But—and please don't think I don't have your side, because I do—I think that's what this is. She didn't mean to put those walnuts in there. My guess is she fucking forgot."

Pushing back once more from Will's embrace, I focused on the words on his shirt, some tagline from his favorite show. "I'm still pissed! At her for not doing anything about anything. At him for not doing anything. They're not doing anything about what's going on endangered our son's life! You know that, right?"

A silent moment, and then Will exhaled, and I looked into his eyes. Love. Truth. Patience. All of those swam behind his gaze. This man was mine, and he had my side—always and no words needed. I took a deep breath. "You're right. It's... I understand what you're saying. But I'm still angry, at myself, too, for not even thinking about it! For not being more proactive! How could I not foresee that she might put our child in danger? And I'm scared. *This*. This piles on the self-doubt that already exists in concert with motherhood. If I can't keep the two I have already safe..." A sob ran through me as guilt overpowered me, and Will hung on, ever the calm one. After a minute, my breathing regulated. "I love you. So much. That's a given, but right now, I'd love to know what they're thinking about. Do they get what happened? What they did?"

"As far as I know, Luke's talking with your folks. Or trying to."

A third wave of rage spilled over, stomping on my logical side. "Do you know where they are? I need to give them a piece of my mind. She could have killed her own grandchild. *Killed* him!" I wanted to hit something again, but I pulled my fists behind me. "Maybe I should tell her that. See if they might own up to what's happening with her."

Will rubbed my arm and tugged on it, forcing me to look back up at him. He pointed his finger at me. "You do what's best for you. If talking to them now is what you want to do, go do it. I'll stay here with Cam."

Hesitation rose within me. I wanted to be there for Cam when he woke up, but I also needed to get to my parents. "Is this what a tug-of-war feels like?" I said.

"He'll be fine, but it's your decision." Will kissed my forehead and hugged me once more.

I looked at my oldest son in the bed, pale cheeks, tousled hair. I couldn't leave him. Not yet. But an hour later, Cam awoke. It was time.

"Luke is still with your parents, and I'll text if we need anything. Try to stay calm, Marissa. You give so much to so many people, and that's one of the qualities I love most about you. But sometimes, you have standards...and well, I'm not sure everyone meets those."

A light kiss to my husband's lips, a smile and a smooch for Cam, and I left the room. My hands trembled against my sides as I wound past the nurses' station to a small room off to the side. Mom sat in a chair, that ever-present fucking purse against her chest. A carbon copy of the days Dad had been in the hospital. Dad sat beside her with a hand on her shoulder, the other on his cane, as if he was ready to rise and leave at any moment. Both with wan faces, like they were at death's door, probably mirroring my own visage. Luke stood before them, one hand on his hip as he raked the other through his hair.

"Luke," I started. "I'd like to speak with my parents, alone, if you don't mind."

"Sure." He leaned in and gave me a peck on the cheek, then pulled me close in a side hug. His warmth comforted me—it always had—but Will's hug from a few moments ago made me feel like I was home. Maybe Nico and Luke had found that same feeling. "Thanks," I said.

After Luke left, I stared at my parents, unsure of what to say to them. A weight hung in the air like a damp blanket, too heavy to move past. Dad swallowed and patted Mom's arm, then tried to speak, but nothing came out.

He tried again. "Marissa...we're sorry." His voice wavered, and he brought his hand up to his face, swiping at his cheeks like he was trying to wipe away something. His guilt perhaps?

"*Sorry*? That's what you have to say?" My inclination to lash out had me moving toward them. "I told myself to remain calm and come in here and speak to you both in a civilized manner, told myself I'd put on my NP hat and clinical side and speak to you both like I would a patient or their family. But I'm finding that so difficult to do right now. I'm livid. I'm *scared*. You almost killed my child!" Tears pricked at my eyelids, and I grabbed at the fabric of my shirt to ground myself.

"She didn't mean—"

"You know what, Dad?" A stern but steady voice erupted from within me. "I think Mom can speak for herself." I threw a pointed look her way and willed Mom to speak with my forceful glare. Intimidation wasn't the point; I wanted to hear the lame-ass excuse of an explanation that would come out of her mouth.

"I forgot," Mom whispered. "I forgot he was... That he can't have...those crunchy things."

Whoosh. Any remaining sense of reasoning fled without looking back. "*Those* crunchy things? Tree nuts, Mom. He can't have *tree* nuts, and walnuts fall into that category. But to simply say you forgot? That's it? Well thanks for being honest, but honesty doesn't make up for the fact that your grandchild is lying in a hospital bed having trouble breathing because you forgot about a life-threatening allergy. And it's not just that you *forgot*—it's that you've refused to see that you *are* forgetting, that you *have been* forgetting. I don't have a clue how long that's been going on. And don't say it's not true—"

"Marissa. I—"

"No, please let me finish. Everyone in this family has a fucking bad habit of interrupting people." I took another hard look at my dad, who was the worst at it. "I understand memory loss. It sneaks up on people. I know this, and I clearly missed it myself, and I'm beating myself up for it right now. That's a weight I'll have to carry for the rest of my life. But I even told *you*," I pointed to Dad, "about my suspicions. You refused to see—or maybe acknowledge—what was happening right under your nose! And you," I directed my finger toward Mom, "printed out all those articles! Bought those memory supplements in the cabinet? Yeah, I know about those. What the hell, Mom? Why didn't you tell anyone? Ask for help? You could have been on medicine this entire time. It wouldn't cure you, but the meds help slow the decline!" I slapped the side table in anger, then turned to Dad, my hands now on my hips. "*You* were so troubled by the possibility of your own dementia. How long have you known it's Mom's problem and not yours? All this time—you ignored me, dismissed my concerns. You know what that fucking feels like? Do you?"

My parents simply stared at me, and my rational side took over. *I'm scolding someone who lacks the ability to interpret the situation. Hadn't Mom proven that by not calling 911?* While it might make me feel better in the moment to continue the rant at the two of them, eventually someone on the hospital team would come find me and give me something to calm me down, which wouldn't help the baby. I needed to be lucid while I spoke to my parents, not sedated. Plus, I had to acknowledge my role in this debacle. Having known that Mom was forgetting. I *should* have been more careful about what Cam was exposed to at their house. In truth—I had too many things on my mind to even think about something I thought wasn't an issue. Add pregnancy brain to that, and...

One deep breath. Two. "So here's what we're going to do." Now, it *was* easier to put my NP persona on. I was in a hospital. My son was being taken care of. We weren't going to mess around. "We're going to make sure that Cam is okay. And while I'm sitting by his bedside—and he could be here for a few days, I don't know—I'm going to make a few calls. We're going to get the both of you into a senior specialist. Someone who can evaluate you and your health and your behaviors and let us know for sure what's happening."

"I don't know what's happening," Mom whispered.

"I realize this. And I know it's scary. It might be nothing. You've had a stressful few months. But it might be something." *And I'm pretty sure it is.*

"Stressful? Yeah. But...my whole marriage has been stressful," Mom said.

I looked at Dad, wondering where this conversation was going, but he only shrugged.

Mom rose from her chair and paced the room in the same way I just had. Her eyes took on a slightly glassy appearance, and her voice lowered. "You know, I didn't always want to get married. I had plans...so many other plans... I wanted to be a nun." She paused for a minute but continued walking back and forth across the room. Her head fell into her hands, and then she looked up, her eyes wild. "I should never have gotten married!" she said, and the sneer that crossed her face told me she believed, in that moment, what she said. "I shouldn't have gotten married, and I certainly never should have had kids!" Mom fell into the chair and sat, weeping.

Who was this talking? The real mom I'd known for over thirty years, or the one I thought she was becoming? And where had the words come from? So resolute, so deliberate. So unlike what she'd been capable of lately.

But my sympathy was close to running out. "Yep, Mom." I crossed my arms over my chest, my heart thumping a beat against my wrist. "You wouldn't have me pestering you, and you wouldn't have your awesome grandkids. None of them." *And this isn't the moment to tell you I'm expecting.* "I guess this incident wouldn't have happened. But chances are, even if you'd never said yes to Dad, even if you went into the convent, even if you'd lived another completely different life from this one, you'd *still* be where you are, sitting in a chair crying over abnormal memory loss."

The words left my mouth before I had time to think about them or how they'd be perceived, but once they were out, my belief in them held firm. And clarification descended: She wasn't crying for her grandson or because she'd hurt someone she loved. She was crying because she had a major problem, she'd have to deal with it, and she didn't know how. After all this time, she'd have to be honest with herself, and Angie Raffaelo had never, not once in her life, faced brutal honesty like that. Focusing on that last piece, I realized the situation's extreme sadness. To be so scared of the truth that you ignore it? That you endanger your loved one? Mom sat hunched over in the chair, spirit broken.

Her words had barely hurt me, *this time*, and I'd allowed my anger—maybe ripples of fear, a defense mechanism—to do the talking. I knew this as clearly as I knew Will was the one for me. And somehow, that truth softened me and my next words, at least a little, because I hadn't meant to be cruel, only honest. Maybe I had work to do on my part too. "I could stand here all day and give you my anger," I said, lowering my voice once again. "But that won't change anything about Cam."

"No, it won't." Dad's eyes brimmed with tears. "Can we...can we see him?"

"You can come with me to see him once I check back in with the doctor. While you're sitting with him—quietly, please—I'm going to start on calls, or maybe Nico or Luke will. I'm not sure when we can get evaluations, but we're going to schedule them as quickly as we can."

Those "calls" led to a friend who pulled strings, allowing us to schedule Mom an appointment five weeks down the road. Dad would have to wait a little longer, but I wasn't really worried about his memory anyway.

"I'm going with her," I said to Dad as he sat in Cam's room with me. Mom had left to use the restroom. "I don't know if you should be there or not. It might cause stress. I'm not sure she understands *why* she's going—maybe she's still in denial, I don't know. I'll know more when we get to the evaluation."

"You have to do what you have to do, Marissa. Again, I'm sorry."

And he was, but his apology wouldn't change a thing. He and Dee would have to help Mom for the next month until the evaluation could take place. Who knew how those thirty days would go?

As I said my goodbyes to them, Mom nodded, her face haunted, pale. A veil of sadness, in knowing the road we were going to be heading down, stationed itself on one shoulder, but an enormous sense of relief landed on the other.

CHAPTER 49: FRANK

Cam's accident. One of the worst days I've been through, and that's saying a lot. The fear that shook me didn't hold a candle to anything but my experience with Antonio, and the rotten feeling had lingered. A churning in the gut. A burning in the heart. Knowing that your *grandchild* could have died at your *wife's* hands. Now that was a TV movie for you, but Hallmark wouldn't show it, unless it had a miraculous ending.

Miracles. As I riffled through the coupons at the kitchen table a week after Cam came home, I stumbled across an advertisement for holy water—the images in the page blurred at the edges, like the printer hadn't lined something up properly—and my mind stopped on that word, *holy.* Years of being Catholic meant I believed in miracles. But the question was—was I worthy of a miracle? For that matter, were *we* worthy? Cam had recovered easily, mostly because of quick action by Marissa and the epi pen, but Angie... We needed nothing short of a miracle. Maybe she'd go to the evaluation and find out that her memory issues were something that could be cured with a good diet—

Angie came into the kitchen, opened the fridge, and then looked at me.

"Everything all right?" I asked.

"Yes...thinking about eating."

"I can make you something." I rose carefully from my chair and moved, still slow but mostly steady, toward the cabinet. "What about scrambled eggs and fruit? We have Big Sky cinnamon bread. That would all make for a good meal."

Angie nodded. "I can do it myself, but that's fine..." She exhaled loudly as I put the skillet on the stove, then anger flared in her eyes, and she lowered her voice, probably so Dee wouldn't hear. "You used to let me cook, Frank."

I bumped her with my elbow, lightly. "I've got it, hon."

Silence as I grabbed the eggs, the already cut-up watermelon—Dee's handiwork—and the butter. Added a few splashes of milk after I'd cracked the eggs into the glassware, just like Angie had taught me years ago. Now wasn't the time for an argument over cooking technique. "I know you didn't mean to hurt Cam, Angie. But—"

"But what?" She glared at me, lips pursed, eyes narrowed.

Did she even fully understand what had happened? Letting it go would be easier; letting it go had always been easier. "Nothing. Go and sit. This will be ready in a minute."

When the eggs had finished cooking, I slid them onto a plate next to the fruit bowl. The toast would be ready soon. "Here you go." I placed the plate on the table.

Angie picked up her fork, stabbed the eggs. "Fried eggs. Tomatoes on...the side. Can't you do...what I want?"

I sat next to her, defeat weighing me down. "You said a minute ago that scrambled eggs would be fine. They aren't fine?"

"No."

"Why not?"

"Because I like fried eggs better. These...are not fine."

Despite her prowess as a candy maker, Angie had never eaten well, ever. Fried foods, too much chocolate, not enough vegetables. Later, Dee and I would get to the store and stock up on more healthy, fresh foods, those to help Angie's brain function. But now? A distraction, maybe.

"What about the toast? You want that?"

"I do not." She stood, moved to the counter, and pulled out the checkbook, then flipped through the pages, a scowl on her face.

"Angie, I told you Dee and I would take care of the bills. You've done it all these years, and now it's my turn. I like to get out, anyway, and Dee will help me get to the bank, the store, you know—"

"I'll do it!" She turned toward me, her cheeks pink, lips trembling. "I'll do it! I did it before. I'll do it again. There's nothing going on...in my brain. I'm fine, dammit!"

What about Cam? That day's details, the ruddiness of his face, the labored breathing, the medicinal hospital smell... Reminding her of all that would be too cruel, too below the belt.

Without a word, I turned my back to her, cleaned up the dishes, put the butter away, and washed my hands, then left the kitchen on shaky legs. Out on the porch, the sun was just beginning to peek around the roof, shedding light on the dusty floor, the scattered stink bug carcasses, the decaying leaves that had rained down with the wind from the night before. I dropped into the swing and tipped my head back. Closed my eyes. Something had to change. But what? How could I get around this mess? Which friends could I call on? I hadn't been on the golf course since the big fall. My walks with Bill had dwindled. Times like these with me, Dee, and Angie—I missed Antonio. Fifteen years with my brother wasn't enough. Close as we'd been... If he were here, we'd still be that way. If he were here, I could call him up, tell him the problem. If he were here, he'd know exactly what to do. Relationships like that— sibling or otherwise—they *mattered*. And who did I have?

A gust of wind rustled the crushed leaves at my feet, chilling my ankles. The wind would give no answer. I pulled my phone out of my pocket and called Gabe.

"Everything okay?" he said.

No hello. No, how are you? Marissa would say he sounded just like me. "Everything is fine—"

"*Fine*? You said that like it's not all fine. How's Mom?"

"She's okay. It's been a little tense here."

"What do you mean by that?"

"I don't want to talk about it. I only need to know where to go from here."

A buzz sounded over the line, and I checked my watch. Gabe would be at work right now. Unless the kids were sick again. They'd had a rough go of a virus earlier in the year.

"Here? Doesn't Mom have an evaluation coming up?"

"Yes."

"So what do you need?"

A miracle? A do-over? Reassurance that the carpet wouldn't be pulled out from under me? "I don't know."

Gabe sighed. "Dad, I can take leave time if you need me to. Or talk to Nico or Marissa. I'm pretty sure Marissa has most of this handled. Appointments set. That sort of thing. Is that what you're talking about?"

"I don't know."

"Well, that's not helpful. I'm not trying to be insensitive. It's... I'm not *there*. I can try to help as much as possible. I *will* help as much as possible—will check in with Marissa and Nico later, and I'll get back to you. You're not alone. We'll get through this. Hang in there."

Hang in there. The service had taught me how to do at least that. We chatted a bit more, and his kindness helped smooth things over for the moment. After we hung up, a voice murmured at the back of my brain as I went in search of a cup of coffee. *Do something*, it said. *Do the research. Take Angie to the doctor. Find the answers.* Then the chair beckoned, and I let my gaze coast across the kitchen to an old stuffed dog Eli had pulled out when he stopped by the day before. It lay beneath the dining room table on its side, like it was exhausted. "Let sleeping dogs lie." Wasn't that the expression?

I pushed the chair back away from the table and placed my confidence in Marissa. She'd get everything done. She always did.

CHAPTER 50: MARISSA

Dad, with Dee's help, of course, had taken care of Mom for a month. I tried to step away from them, keep things going at work and at home with Cam and Eli and baby number three—though we hadn't divulged the news to anyone yet—and spend time with Will. Luke and Nico had come over several times—as a couple—though they also hadn't announced anything to Mom or Dad yet.

"Dad has enough stress in his life right now, doesn't he?" Nico said each time I mentioned any forthcoming notice.

"How fair is that to Luke? To you? And you don't think they think it's strange that you both show up to family dinners?"

Despite Mom's outburst and impending appointment, dinners continued, weekly now, though they looked a little different. We all helped cook and clean up. And everyone made sure that food was safe for Cam. During those times I'd been around, I'd taken a few more notes on Mom's behavior, and I was glad we were going to have her evaluated. I'd caught Mom doing her usual, looking at the calendar and crossing off what day it was, but other behaviors had also cropped up. The day before we went to see the specialist, she came up to me and whispered, "Sometimes, I think people are getting into this house and moving things. I can't seem to find anything I want."

My eyes teared up at that statement. Here she was, already showing signs of paranoia. I didn't know enough about dementia to categorize where she was in the stages, but that statement told me all I needed to know. Mom had a problem, and the senior specialist would confirm it.

So it was no surprise that in mid-August, on the morning Mom and I left for her appointment, she asked me again about where we were going and why.

"Well, we need to get you looked at," I said as I steered her toward the car.

"Why?"

"Because Dad fell, and you didn't call 911—"

"I called the neighbor."

Always the neighbor. Never his name. Never realizing what she *should* have done. Those instincts, judgment calls, already caught up in Alzheimer's plaques and tangles?

"And you forgot about the tree nuts. Something that you've known for a long time. It's a safety issue now, Mom. Cam could have died. We want to make sure that you're okay."

She didn't argue. In all the years I'd known my mother, Angela Raffaelo had never taken a seat and gone with the flow. She stood up and argued, whether or not it was right to do so. And Dad had told me that her anger was at high tide the last few weeks, at least with him. Was all the stress causing her to be silent? Or did she not comprehend everything that had been going on?

We sat for a while in the stuffy, wood-paneled reception area—Mom fiddling with the textured butterfly key chain the boys had given her—while the staff got ready for us. I handed them the papers we'd filled out before, page upon page of medical history and personal questions. The papers included a set of signatures about who, other than Dad, could access Mom's medical records. All three of us—Nico, Gabe, and I—had signed it. Mom had signed off on it too, which was another odd thing. All these years she'd never opened up to us about anything health related, and if we tried to talk to her or ask about her doctors, she would shut us down. But she'd agreed to Nico's request without a fight, no questions asked. That behavior alone spoke volumes.

When Pachelbel's "Canon in D" had looped back to the beginning, Amy the nurse practitioner came to get us with a kind smile and soft voice, explaining what would happen: she'd take vital information, blood pressure, weight, and heart rate and then move on to a more thorough questioning. Mom nodded as if she understood. The vacant look in her eyes told me otherwise. How long had she looked like this? Had I noticed that sooner, I'd have pressed more for Dad to say something earlier. To get her assessed before everything had gone so wrong. Guilt rushed through me again—I'd been caught up in my own life just like everyone else and had missed so, so much.

After ushering us to the table and chairs in the corner of the room, Amy rearranged a stack of papers. "Are you ready?" she asked, tapping her pen against the tabletop. "I have questions for you, Angie."

"I think so," Mom said as she positioned herself in the chair and looked at me. For what? Approval? Confidence?

My heart cracked inside my chest, and I placed a hand on Mom's forearm. "You'll be fine, and if you don't know something, it's okay. Got it?"

Mom nodded.

Amy looked at me. "And if you don't mind, remain silent unless I ask you specific information. It will be clear when that happens." She flashed a small smile, noted the time on the paper, and began addressing Mom. She asked what her name was and the year, which Mom answered. Then, "What is your birth date?"

"April...April something." She tapped her nail against the table.

"And what year were you born?"

"After my sister. But before my other sister."

Amy jotted notes on the lined yellow legal pad in front of her. "Great. I was going to ask you about your family. You have sisters... What are their names?"

Mom looked at me, then shifted her gaze back to Amy. "There's Carmie and...Nina...and..." She shrugged. "I guess I can't remember."

Can't remember? This is worse than I thought. The mother I knew would have been angry and frustrated at her inability to recall the names. The mother I knew would have stood up, pounded her fists against the table, and stormed from the room. The mother I knew would not have remained seated at the table with a resigned look on her face. The stressful day could add to some of the memory loss but... Who was *this woman?* Tears burned at the back of my eyes, but I blinked them away. I had to, for Mom's sake.

"And the names of your grandchildren?" Amy asked softly.

Mom sniffed and looked down at the paper. "Cameron and," another shrug, "Ian. His name is Ian."

Having been given all the family names and relationships earlier in the week, Amy had to have recognized Mom's error and that Mom didn't mention Gabe's kids, but her clear, steady gaze never wavered from Mom's. "Let's switch gears, Angie. I want you to sketch a clock." She placed a piece of paper in front of Mom with a large circle drawn on it and then handed her a pencil. "First, draw the numbers of the clock."

Mom picked up her pencil, thought for a minute, and drew numbers around the circle. 1, 2, 3, 4, 5, 7, 8, 9, 10, 12. She smiled, then put the pencil down.

"Good. Now can you show me what the hands on the clock look like if the time is three twenty-one? Where would the hands be?"

Mom picked up the pencil again and confidently drew two lines: the large hand pointed a little past the 5, and the small hand pointed to the 2. She'd drawn something closer to 2:31, not 3:21. Mom blinked expectantly at Amy, waiting for the next question.

For the next hour and a half, Amy asked Mom about the season and where she lived, had Mom recall a series of words, prompted Mom to spell a word forward and backward, and showed her objects that Mom had to name. Amy inquired about recent events and if anything significant had happened in the past few months. She talked about Mom's diet (heavy on fats, light on vegetables) and exercise habits (nonexistent, except for walking in her kitchen from the stove to the refrigerator to the pantry and back again), her past and present smoking habits (a pack a day for at least thirty years). Amy covered Mom's sleep habits, drinking habits, and any other habits she could think of. Mom answered what she could, and Amy sometimes looked to me for input. And the entire time, Mom complied. No anger. No frustration. No *emotion*.

As the visit wrapped up, I knew what I expected to hear but thought back to what Will had said to me before I left that morning.

"Wouldn't that be a cruel joke if your mom *doesn't* have dementia?"

I understood what he meant. Dementia wasn't a condition I'd wish on my worst enemy, but if we had a diagnosis in hand, then it would serve two purposes: provide proof to Mom and Dad that something was wrong, *and* it would allow us to get Mom on medicine, which might slow the decline. There would be comfort in the knowing, and the uphill battle with my parents might ease a little.

Mom and I waited in the reception area for forty-five minutes before Amy called us back to the room again. This time, the room details stood out to me: the blonde, walnut paneling, the floral wallpaper, peeling at the edges, a few dusty baseboards. Old, worn, much like I felt. Much like Mom must have felt as we took the same seats we'd vacated less than an hour before.

Amy took her glasses off, directing her gaze at Mom. "I can't give you a definitive diagnosis right now, Angie. We'll need to get an MRI to confirm any possible brain changes... But my findings here today," she placed Mom's file on the table, "support the idea that you have cognitive changes consistent with an Alzheimer's diagnosis."

Expected words sometimes still have immense power, and I placed a hand to my chest as a palpable weight landed there and my breathing hitched. Mom nodded her head, like she'd done the entire time we'd been in the office. I waited for the words to sink in for her, waited for a storm to brew behind her eyes, her cheeks to flush, something to let me know she understood what the nurse practitioner had said to her and would argue.

The fire, though, never caught. Instead, Mom blinked. "Can we go home now?" she asked. "I'm...tired."

Amy and I exchanged glances, and she nodded.

"Sure, Mom. Let's go."

Amy extended her hand, and I told her we'd be in touch about follow-up procedures, then I guided Mom out of the office, through the reception area, and out the front door. As the fine rain droplets hit my face, Mom tugged on my arm and turned to me.

"How'd I do? Did I do okay?" A smile flickered across her face. Calm, gentle, peaceful. One I'd rarely seen. One I'd remember for years to come.

I wrapped my arm around Mom's shoulders and pulled her close, tucking her into my side, trying to keep the chill away. "You did fine, Mom. You did just fine." Turning my head, I focused on the black swallowtail that had taken shelter in the eaves of the office building, hoping the rain might camouflage my tears.

CHAPTER 51: HER

The woman in white had been relaxed, with a kind, easy smile and soft voice, and when the woman asked if they were ready, she nodded. The sooner they did this, the sooner they could go back home and get some orders filled.

This woman told her what to expect, which was nice. Knowing what was to come always seemed to take the sting out, at least a little. That's what she used to tell the kids. So she listened to the questions—about her sisters, her children, her husband, her. What year it was and where she lived. So many questions! Things she hadn't thought of for so long, really, some of them, anyway. And she had an answer. For every single question. Didn't she? Even when the woman in white extended a pencil, she drew what the woman wanted.

And then, the questions stopped. *Thank goodness*. Her brain was tired. So, so tired.

She drew her hand across her forehead, surprised at the stickiness there. Maybe the questions had been stressful, but the smile on the woman's face and her daughter's face had been so genuine, so calming. "You will be fine," they said.

The weight of the secret had been so heavy for so long. A sense of relief settled in, and for once, she trusted them.

CHAPTER 52: FRANK

Angie and Marissa came home a few hours after they departed. The usual push and pull didn't simmer off them, and they arrived with grins on their faces. Perhaps the visit had been a good one. Maybe nothing was wrong with my wife. The more I said it, the more I convinced myself it was true. Angie put her purse on the counter and then went to check on something in the freezer. Marissa pulled me to the side and said, "Let's go talk in the living room."

Just like the porch, that room had been a place for the kids to do their chatting. Filled with fluffy couches and my sitting chair, I read my paper there each morning when the weather was too cold or rainy for me. The kids had brought many friends through the room. We'd taken countless Christmas and birthday photos against the backdrop of the fireplace. I'd thought fondly of Antonio in that room. It was a *nice* room. A room full of pleasant memories. Adding to those memories today didn't sound like a good idea.

I looked out the large picture window at the gray sky. The sun tried to peek out from behind the smudged clouds, but it couldn't do it. The raindrops only formed a fine mist—not enough water to bother me. Maybe Marissa wouldn't want to feel the dampness, but so much news had come to me on that porch. "Let's go to the porch."

Marissa grabbed a light blanket from the edge of the couch and followed me outside.

As always, I chose the swing, my back against the coolness of the wooden slats. The rain misted, and moisture pelted the air. Maybe the news Marissa had to share would be more positive than the weather.

She snuggled into the blanket and sat back against the wicker chair she'd decided on. At that moment, footsteps sounded on the concrete drive: Gabe, Nico, Will, and Luke. Even the existence of Gabe, who I hadn't seen in months, couldn't squash the horror, and I swallowed it back as my gaze connected with each of theirs. "No," I said, to no one and everyone at the same time. "No."

Gabe took up residence next to me while Nico, Luke, and Will each chose chairs across from me. Everyone looked at Marissa.

"I'm not going to beat around the bush, Dad." Marissa's brown eyes, usually warm and kind, held a steeliness to them. "Mom has cognitive changes consistent with Alzheimer's."

My stomach caved, like the time my best friend had punched me in the gut, and the years rolled back to the day I'd learned about Antonio. "It can't be," I whispered. Then and now. Tears formed in my eyes, and my words clogged my throat. Despite the changes I'd seen, despite Angie's huge mistake with Cam, despite all that had happened and the evidence the kids had told me, I never thought I'd hear that word. *Alzheimer's.* Deep down inside me, I wanted to attribute her changes to simple aging. *This couldn't be happening...*

Gabe got up, stood next to me, and placed a hand on my shoulder, and I covered it with my own.

"I know what you're thinking, Dad." Marissa's soft voice held authority. "It's not age. The NP, Amy—she got it right. She'll confirm with an MRI—something we need to set up in the next few weeks. But I was there. Mom's not simply getting older. Her brain is deteriorating. It's *dying.*"

I closed my eyes. A montage of images shuffled past my eyelids. Angie in the gold dress at our twentieth anniversary party. Gabe in her arms on the front steps of our first house. The smile on her face as she stood before the Sistine Chapel. The ever-present chocolate smear on her right temple. She and the kids jumping in puddles as they dashed through the thunderstorm in St. Louis. Life, energy, sustenance. And then: Her favorite coffee cup, cherry red with sturdy handle, clean and overturned on the drainer, waiting to be filled once more. The coolness of the empty sheets next to me in bed. One toothbrush—not two—in the plastic holder by the sink.

"And, I think it's a good thing if I tell you what you need to do," Marissa continued. "You need to know that you will step into the role of caregiver, at least for a little while."

Shit. "Caregiver? What does that even mean? And how would I know what to do? I'm air force, not a medical professional."

Marissa smiled. "It means you need to be there for her. Not just as a pocketbook. You need to be there for her emotionally *and* physically. You'll need to read up on what this disease will send her way and yours. Find ways to help her cope with her memory loss. Invest in sticky notes while she can still read so she has reminders. Play her favorite music when you're at home and dance in the kitchen if your legs will let you. Walk with her when she's agitated and rejoice with her when she's not. Help her manage life, essentially—"

"How?"

"Drive her to her appointments, be sure her medications are filled. Listen when she's angry or depressed, take her out for dessert just because. And hold her when she needs to be held. We don't know how long the process will take, so spend your time *being* the two of you. Just be, Dad. Because eventually, you'll get tired, and you'll need to go back to the role of husband, not caregiver."

"What do you mean?"

Marissa placed a hand on my knee and squeezed it. "This is an awful disease. You'll see and do things you never thought you'd see and do, but someday, probably soon, you'll be in over your head, and you'll have to rely on Dee to take care of bathing, toileting, dressing, and more. Because it's going to grate on you, Dad. A lot. Beyond that, we'll need to think of nursing facilities and twenty-four-hour care."

I blinked a few times, unsure of what to say, so I closed my eyes. "Not sure I can do that, Marissa. I've never been the nurturing type. And besides, I never imagined my retired life to be this way."

Luke spoke next, his words steeped with kindness. "We never know what's around the bend, Frank. We'll be there to help you. You know that. And like Marissa, I'm not going to mince words. This is going to be hard. Harder than anything you've ever—"

My eyes flew open. "Harder than anything? Harder than losing Antonio?"

"Antonio?" Luke's face crumpled with confusion.

Gabe said, "Dad's brother. He died when he was fifteen."

"Died? He didn't die. He was killed." My mind jumped there, to that night at the lake's shore. "They killed him because...he was gay! And I did nothing to stop it. Nothing!" I slammed my free hand on the chair's edge, wincing at the pain that shot through it.

Marissa scrambled off the seat and kneeled in front of me, grasping my hands. "What are you talking about? Maybe this conversation should be for another time, but I thought... You said—"

"I said what I said so you wouldn't know. All these years, the guilt—"

"The guilt? Did you at least love your brother? Is that why you've been so aloof with me?" Nico said, his jaw clenched. "Because I'm gay? You couldn't stand to have another one of *those* in the house?"

"That's not it, Nico. I swear it's—"

"It's what, Dad? This discussion has been a long time coming. You know why Luke came back? Do you know *why* he's been here more often?"

Something in Nico's tone, his posture; he stood defensive, like an armed... No. He and Luke...

"Sure, he had a job lined up and it was a great opportunity. He looked into that job specifically because *I* live here. *Me.* Of course, he means something to all of us, but Will, Gabe, Marissa—they don't love him like I do. Luke loves me—"

I gasped. "What?" I never thought... Well, I guess I missed that one. Like I'd missed everything with Angie.

"That's right? *He. Loves. Me.* And I love him. Romantic love. Just like Antonio once loved someone. Luke's back, and he found a job here because we're getting married. Whether or not you like it—"

"Why would I not like it? I love you. I love Luke."

Marissa stood. "Not that I want to interrupt this conversation, but can we please stop cutting everyone off? I can barely keep up here, and it's rude. And what about Mom? We need to get back to her, don't we?"

Gabe leaned in and high-fived Marissa.

"Seriously?" Nico said as he glared at his siblings, all who had the decency to blush. "*This* isn't easy." He gestured between him and Luke, then turned to Luke and extended his hand. "It's not about you, you realize that, right, Luke? I love you. I just said it, put it out there. It's that...all these years," Nico turned back to me, "the shit you gave me... I didn't know if *you* loved *me*. How the hell *would* I know if you didn't say it?"

That porch had witnessed so many significant conversations, but that didn't mean it could help me craft a proper response. I shrugged.

"That's it? That's all you're going to say? One of your sons questions your love, and you have no response? How classic, Dad. What the fuck?"

Marissa squeezed my hand. "Nico, we've opened a lot of wounds here, and I'm not faulting you, but give him time to come to terms with everything, especially considering what we know about Mom. And would now be a good time to tell you all that I'm pregnant?"

"You're what?" That conversation had turned too quickly. I'd be a grandfather again? What an emotional rollercoaster. When was the—

"Playing the peacemaker again, eh?" Gabe chuckled. "I, for one, didn't know I was so out of the loop with you all. That's what I get for living so far away. Maybe the three kids have something to do with it. And now you'll have three too. Holy shit."

"You got that right," Marissa said, but a smile crept across her face as the rain picked up, setting a steady rhythm, both of which prodded me to be honest.

"Marissa, Will, we'll talk about that another time, but congratulations. That's thrilling news." I gazed at Nico. "I'm not sure what to say or what you want me to say. There's a lot here. In this conversation."

"Then start at the beginning. What happened to Antonio?" Nico asked. "The truth this time, as we seem to only have bits and pieces. And I'm not pushing Mom to the side." He glanced at Marissa. "We've been waiting all summer to discuss her, so she can wait a little longer."

Blunt. Concise. Just like Antonio.

The words rolled out. My brother's charms, our relationship, his woodworking skills, and dreams. Growing up in a Catholic family, the shame that Antonio would have thrown at us if he'd been honest with everyone. How the newspapers covered up his death as an accident.

"Were you there? When it happened?" Gabe asked. He still held my hand.

"No. But I should have been. He needed me, and I wasn't there. That guilt has gnawed at me for years, featured in my dreams, or nightmares. I thought maybe going into the service would help, but it didn't. And before you ask," I glanced at Nico, "those were different times. Had I said *anything*, had my family gone against the guy who did it, who killed, murdered really, Antonio, we'd have been ruined. I couldn't do that to my family."

Marissa rubbed my knee again. "But how about Nico? I can't pretend to know what he went through growing up, but you two *always* butted heads. Always. What was that about?"

Antonio's tortured face flashed before my eyes. "I feared *for* him, for Nico. That he'd end up like Antonio. Even before he told us about being...gay, something seemed different. And when he told us, my mind froze on the past. I couldn't go through that again. I just couldn't."

"As if it were all about you," Nico mumbled before turning and walking away.

"I'm not saying it was the right thing to do..."

Luke threw a sympathetic glance my way, then followed Nico out into the rain. They moved into the car but didn't leave. I tipped my face up and focused on the swirling clouds. A walk in the rain might cleanse me, but my thoughts and emotions bounced around. I dwelled on the past: Antonio, Nico, Angie. How many more mistakes would I make? I'd been selfishly unaware of everything, and guilt weighed heavy on my chest, cold, hard, impenetrable. Rubbing at it didn't seem to do anything, but I did it anyway.

CHAPTER 53: FRANK

That first day following Angie's diagnosis hit me hard, though she seemed to be unaffected by it. She went about her business as usual, apart from me hovering like those helicopter parents the newscasters reported on. Angie performed the same actions over and over. Checked the calendar incessantly and folded the kitchen towel repeatedly. Moved to a cabinet for something, couldn't remember what it was, sat for a minute, and then went on doing something else. Strode to the mailbox on a bright summer day and then not even thirty minutes later, did the same thing. Scrubbed at the spot on the granite counter that looked like a stain several times a day. I said nothing, not a word, just watched and inwardly grieved.

As the month of August blew past and September rolled around, the kids warned me of what would happen, that life would get tougher to handle.

"She's going to repeat stories, Dad. Over and over. And it's going to aggravate you," Marissa said one night at dinner. She rubbed her hands over her expanding belly. They hadn't had their first ultrasound yet, but they kept referring to the baby as Farfalla. Like the pasta, farfalle. I hadn't asked why, but something in the way Cam and Eli whispered it—there was a story there.

"It already does," I admitted. "Every day. Multiple times a day. I wonder where we'll go from here."

That answer arrived soon enough a few days later when Angie forgot to turn the stove off. With Dee out for the morning, I came back from a slow walk to feel an unfamiliar heat in the house. When I confronted Angie about the stove, all she said was, "I don't remember leaving it on." Of course she didn't. Deep inside, I recognized her lack of fault, but the fear that came from knowing we could have burned the house down was too scary to bear.

"You can't leave her alone," Marissa said when I told her what happened. "Dee mentioned that last week. You just can't. At this point, Dad, you need to have Dee switch gears, place more attention on Mom. You've got most of your mobility back anyway." She was right, but her next words didn't sit well with me. "Have you thought about moving yet? And how about the car? Have you taken her keys away?"

Gabe reinforced that same sentiment when I spoke to him later that day. He'd returned to Germany but was scheduled to head back again soon for a visit. "Dammit," he said. "What do you need me to do? It's going to be difficult, Dad, but those keys—you need to take them. Before she kills herself...or someone else."

Stripping someone of their autonomy held no appeal. I'd seen enough of that in the service years ago and that summer with my falls. And yet, how would I live with that guilt if something dire happened? First Cam and then...possibly something worse?

I called Marissa at home—it was one of her days off. She'd given us her schedules—all the kids had—to make it easier on me and Dee. "Your mom is mad at me. I told her I was going to sell her car."

"Did you tell her why?" Marissa asked.

"Well, no, but what's done is done. Do you have the time to come by?"

In the background, Cam or Eli called for her. She whispered something, then got back on the line. "Give me a few," she said.

A half hour later, I let her in the door. Cam and Eli raced in while she placed both hands against her back. Eli, watching his mom, moved toward her, rubbed her belly, and whispered, "Farfalla," before giggling, which sent Cam into a fit of laughter too. Then he held up the chess game he'd brought and pointed to Eli's stuffed llama, which would probably serve as game spectator. Happy to oblige their wishes, I said, "Let's sit in the living room," and led them away. We were close enough to hear the conversation between Angie and Marissa.

"You're not going to believe what happened," Angie said.

The bar stool scraped against the tile floor and a quiet *thud* followed as my daughter sat.

"Your dad sold my car!"

"Yeah, I don't think he did yet, but he told me he was going to. Do you know *why*?"

"Um, no... Why?"

Bile rose in my throat. She thought I already sold it, which I had not. And no? How could she not know— *She doesn't understand what her diagnosis means.* Placing a finger to my lips so the boys would know to stay quiet, I quietly moved to the corner, hoping to peek in at Angie and Marissa. They sat next to one another, faces close, with Marissa's hand on Angie's arm.

Sorrow laced Marissa's voice as she said, "You have Alzheimer's disease, Mom."

Angie looked at Marissa, her brow furrowed.

"I know you know what that is, somehow. Your mom had it, your uncle too. And well... You have it, and you cannot drive anymore. It's the safest thing for everyone, and you might as well let someone else do it, let someone else take care of you. Okay?"

"Okay," Angie whispered back, tracing a finger along the fold of the napkin on the counter. Then she cocked her head. "Anything else...I can't do anymore?"

"There are," Marissa said. "But we'll take that one day at a time. How's that sound?"

"Good. It sounds...good." Angie placed an arm around Marissa's waist and tipped her head against Marissa's shoulder. "Do you...know how, how glad I am to have you here?"

Marissa and I had never been close, and her relationship with Angie? Difficult at times. If I knew anything about my daughter, that simple statement was exactly what she needed to hear. Though it wasn't directed toward me, I needed to hear it too.

CHAPTER 54: MARISSA

Two months after Mom's diagnosis, the boys and I dug around in my parents' garden, pulling thistle and rearranging rocks before fall hit us hard. Well, I managed what I could. Five months into this pregnancy, and it was throwing me for a loop—a big one. The fatigue this time around surpassed anything I'd experienced with either Cam or Eli, but as Will was so quick to remind me, I carried far more responsibilities now. As Eli collected random sticks and twigs from the mulch, Cam stood back, assessing our work.

"Looks good so far, Mom. But I think—" He gasped and pointed. "Look, there!"

An eastern tiger swallowtail, only a few inches wide, perched on a large rock on the west side of the flowerbed.

"Shh," Cam said as he crept toward it. "Can you believe it?" Eyes wide, cheeks flushed, Cam clenched his fists at his sides, trying to curb the excitement. "Finally! We get to see one in action." Sadly, despite all our efforts, the caterpillars in our hands never morphed into butterflies.

Eli moved toward me and grabbed my hand, still unsure of the insect. Anything with wings, while fascinating, still held the unknown for him. I tugged on his chubby fingers, moving him as close as I thought possible to the enchanting creature. "See the colors on the wings? Look, not quite white, not quite yellow."

"Like those old photos Grandma and Grandpa have of Great Uncle Antonio."

I smiled. Dad had finally shared a handful of good stories about Antonio after our major blowout, letting us form a genuine portrait of his brother. He'd taken out pictures, compared them to photos of a young Nico and Gabe. Gabe had Antonio's nose, but Nico? Nico's entire being seemed to mirror Antonio. The resemblance was astounding and sad at the same time. The boys loved to look at those photos, carefully holding them with their tiny, freshly washed fingers.

"Those photos are precious." I snapped a picture of the butterfly with my phone then sent it to Will. He'd know exactly what we were doing. "Maybe later we can put them into a better album for Grandpa. He'd probably like that."

Cam turned, placing a finger against his lips. "Mom!" he whispered. "*Please* be quiet. And let's add that picture of the butterfly. Grandma would love it!"

She would, but for how long?

We sat in the sun and planned for next year's butterfly garden, which we'd start after the baby arrived, talking about what we could do differently to produce a better outcome until the butterfly fluttered its wings and took off, looping by the hydrangea and past the Norway spruce at the corner of the house. All three of us tipped our heads back and followed its movements, gazes focused on the rhythmic beating of its gossamer wings as it moved through a low-lying cloud. Inside my womb, the baby fluttered too.

•　　　•　　　•

I left Will, Nico, and Luke to dinner preparations that night at my parents' house, knowing they'd do fine. A peace had taken hold of me over the last few weeks. A recognition that only a minute amount of control rested in my hands, and no matter what, not everything could be fixed. Further, not everything could be fixed by *me*. Plus, it didn't matter if dinner was a little heavy on meat and light on vegetables as long as everyone was happy. As usual, Dad sat on the porch swing, gently moving the seat back and forth with his legs, its creak a metronome to his life. The seat next to him called to me.

"All right, Dad. I want to know how you're doing. Really. Be bold, pretend we had another blowout. Give me and the baby the goods."

He stroked a hand across my belly and smiled, then looked up at me and took his hand away. "I guess I should have asked before I did that. Sorry."

"It's no bother." I placed his hand back on my belly as Farfalla kicked. "She's active right now, so it's a good time to put your hand there."

"A girl? You're having a girl?"

"Actually, I don't know. Will and I—we don't want to know. But I have this feeling. Mother's intuition, I guess."

He smiled. "You're not going to name her Farfalla, though, are you? Like the pasta?"

"No, I wouldn't do that to my child. But let's not get distracted." I smiled and squeezed his fingers. "What do you need from me?"

He shook his head and looked out over the front yard, vibrant and lush, at least for a little while longer, his constant: even when life gave you lemons, the grass still grew.

"I guess I keep going back to my life. That this isn't what I thought retirement would look like."

Sympathy *and* irritation flickered inside me. "And neither did Mom. Neither did we. But we can't worry about what we don't have control over, Dad. What we can do is adjust how we react to everything, and that's where we are now. We're reacting. And families take care of one another, right? I just wish we'd thought more about the possibility of this happening after Grandma was diagnosed, you know?"

Dad huffed. "You know how your mother is. Always right. Always defiant. In the end, it wouldn't have mattered."

What had made Mom like that? Depression and anxiety? Would her behavior be defined by a disorder forever? Would fear continually hold her back? We'd never know, and all that history would be lost now, stuck in the tangled, sticky web of a brain no longer able to do what it needed to do. Asking the questions was meaningless; answers would never come.

"Okay, well, it is what it is, as they say. So let's think about our reaction, try to be as proactive as we can be. Let's get her that MRI and get her on meds, and we'll go from there." I stood to go back to the kitchen. Nico and Luke were thinking of leaving right after dinner. They'd put a down payment on a house and were expecting the results of an inspection to come in. Hearing their good news about the number of bedrooms and bathrooms and whether a house had a good backyard lifted my soul as I waded through the particulars with Mom and Dad each day.

"What's that going to cost? The MRI, the meds, all that, I mean."

Turning back, I shook my head, aghast and yet not surprised at all. With every step forward we made with Dad, we moved backward at warp speed. "Dad, we went through this before. And I'll tell you the same thing I said then: You need to get her the meds and think about moving out of this house. *You* aren't out of the woods, and she'll start to wander. And who's going to cook, clean, keep house, do the bills? Help her when she can't dress herself or go to the bathroom? That's where you're headed. Dee can help now, but she won't be able to serve you twenty-four hours a day. And you're uneasy about the cost?" Anger never got me anywhere with Dad, so like every other time I spoke to him, I lowered my voice, softened my words. "Remember that wedding day you like to reflect on? The red ranunculus? Almost fifty years ago, you said for better or worse. *For better or worse, Dad.* I'm sorry to be the one to say this, but this isn't even the worst yet."

He swallowed but refused to meet my eyes. "I know," he whispered.

"No, I don't think you do. What's this really about? *Is* it the money? Because that's so...so abhorrent. Honestly."

Dad pursed his lips. "I worked long and hard for that money, as did your mother, and I want to leave you something when I go. Is that too far-fetched to think about? Leaving a legacy to my kids?"

Didn't he get that if he and Mom were happy and healthy—at least as much as they could be—none of us cared about the money? Money might be important to him, and yes, I thought about it, especially with a new arrival in the mix, but we'd be fine. We were some of the luckiest out there. Life wasn't about material goods and things or about money and prestige. It was about tickling the boys' bellies and holding Will's hand and watching Farfalla grow with each new ultrasound and witnessing Nico and Luke's love bloom and ushering Mom through her new chapter. "Legacies come in all shapes and sizes, Dad. They don't have to be concerned with money, you know."

Mom chose that moment to stick her head out then. "Do you know...where the checkbook is?"

Did all dementia patients hold to one item the way Mom seemed to hold to that checkbook? "I'll help you find it in a few. You okay otherwise?"

"Yes. Why?"

"You learned recently that your brain is showing signs of probable Alzheimer's disease. And I kind of wanted to know—how does that make you feel?" The words reminded me of that person who interviewed the celebrities and asked about Disney World, but I wanted to know. Truly.

"Well... What, what can I do?"

Mom had been so adamant that nothing was wrong, and she'd battled us her entire life to see things her way. Where did this "acceptance" come from? I didn't buy her behavior, but I didn't know what to do with it either.

Placing my hand on her arm, I said, "Not a whole lot. And Dad is going to take care of you now."

She lowered herself into the chair, pushed her hair out of her face, and sighed. "It's about time," she said.

●　　●　　●

Later, under the ombre tones of the setting sun, Will and the kids found me on the porch with Nico and Luke, who had opted to stay though Dad and Mom had long gone in. Luke sat in Dad's spot on the swing, and Nico rested next to him, his head in Luke's lap, an easy smile on his face. Luke played with Nico's hair while Nico mindlessly fiddled with the edge of Luke's shirt as they listened, earbuds in, to music.

Nico caught my eye, pulled out an earbud, and said, "Lots of changes, you know, since yesterday...with...everything." A smile broke out across his face as he hummed a few bars of Taylor Swift's "Everything Has Changed."

"That's one of my favorites," I said. "It could never be an earworm because I love it, so do your best."

He shook his head, popped his earbud back in, and smiled up at Luke once more. Then he winked at me.

Seeing them both so content despite our chaotic summer brought joy and hope to my heart. Cam slid next to me while Eli scrambled on my ever-diminishing lap, tucking his head into my shoulder before leaning over to kiss my belly. Both kids brought the sweet scent of baking with them, and I looked up at Will.

"Was she baking?"

"She was. She asked us if we'd help with a recipe, and we all made cookies. Nothing too special—dark chocolate with chocolate chips, tree-nut free—but they turned out great. Might want to grab a few before Nico and Luke eat them all."

I shook my head. "They can have them. Those two are good for each other. Don't you think?"

Will picked up Cam, sat next to me, and adjusted our squirrelly son on his legs. "I do. It's good to see them both so happy."

"I never would have guessed, you know. Not about being gay; love is love. But Nico and Luke? Together? They're two lost puzzle pieces that finally found each other and yet...I never realized they belonged to the same box."

Will laughed. "I'm not sure that comparison works, but I get what you're saying."

Down by my knee where the kids couldn't see, I flipped him the bird. "I'm a clinician, honey, not a writer. Remember that."

A car pulled in the driveway, and the boys ran to the edge of the porch. Will rose from the seat, moved to the boys, and placed his hands on their shoulders, holding them back. The boys had always been so excited to see visitors. The year before, Nico hadn't even stopped the car and the two of them had careened forward. Now, they wiggled against Will's hands as they waited for the car to stop and the door to open.

Gabe stepped out of the car, an enormous smile on his face.

"What are you doing here?" Will called. "And where's the rest of you?"

Gabe comically scrunched up his face. "The rest of me?" He patted his pockets and looked down his shirt. "I'm all here, aren't I?"

Cam and Eli howled and glanced at Will.

"Go, you little scamps! Permission granted to leave the porch!" Will patted them on their bums, and they took off. Then, he moved back to his seat next to me and placed an arm behind my back. "No idea where Sarah and the kids are, but my guess is we'll find out soon enough."

I nodded.

"And you know what else we'll know soon enough?" he asked.

"No, what?"

"How your dad will do. If he'll step up." Will took my hand and squeezed it. "I think he's going to be okay."

"You do? How can you say that? Did you not hear any of the conversation I had with him this afternoon?"

"I did. But he and I chatted later, and, get this, he took notes. He asked me what I would do and how I would handle things. He wanted to know what the cost of nursing facilities—"

"The cost? You see—"

"Mar, you're doing what you say everyone does to you. Just listen for a moment."

God, he was so right. How was he right all the time? I drew a line across my lips with my fingers.

"He wanted to be sure that he set aside enough money for her care. We talked about investments and who to see to manage them and then, he called Nico and Luke in too. The four of us drank beer, and while the conversation never totally lightened—how could it, you know?—I'm confident he can do this. He'll need help, for sure, but he'll do it."

"How can you be certain?"

"Because the truth is, he loves your mother. He loves you and Nico and Gabe and all of us. And if the only legacy he leaves is a love that finally understood how to find its voice, then I think we're pretty lucky. Don't you?"

CHAPTER 55: HER

The woman opened the long cabinet at the rear of the kitchen. She was looking for a bowl for the corn they'd popped. The snack had a lot of that grease on it, so she didn't want to use the wooden one the man had placed on the counter for her. Maybe a shiny one would be better. She stood in front of the cabinet, her eyes scouring each shelf for something that might work. One piece here, another there, she moved them, hoping it wouldn't take her too long—she preferred eating the corn while it was still warm. And she guessed the picture show might already have started.

Out of the corner of her eye, something moved, and she looked out the kitchen window. A creature hovered near the windowsill. Orange and black, like those vegetables her grandsons carved for that holiday when they went door to door for candy. One beat of its long wings, then two, and the woman turned back to the cabinet.

She picked up a small pitcher and moved it to the side. Behind it, she glimpsed a tiny reflection of the kitchen lights, one that might be produced by the bowl she wanted. Her fingers clumsily groped toward the back of the cabinet as she lowered her shoulders and stretched her arms forward. Her hands encountered a hard, cold object, one that felt unfamiliar, and yet... She pulled her arms back, carefully bringing with it whatever it was her hands had found.

She gasped at the treasure, a beautiful object of art, right there in the kitchen. A tray shaped like a flower garden—hard, sturdy—one that would serve as a wonderful addition to the clear glass and plastic trays she used for the muffins and cookies she served when friends and family came over. Where did she get this? And why did it now seem so familiar at the same time? She gently placed it on the top shelf of the cabinet to continue looking for whatever it was she needed. *I'll come back to that tray later...*

"Honey? Are you coming?" Behind her, his voice echoed across the space and then, his arms wound around her waist, warm and comforting. Pressing his lips against her hair, he whispered, "You go and sit, and I'll finish up the popcorn. The movie's almost starting."

The woman sighed and closed the doors of the cabinet before glancing one more time at the creature now resting on the windowsill, the evening light illuminating its wings.

THE END

NOTE FROM THE AUTHOR

The Raffaelo family stems from my imagination, but they were inspired by my family's experiences. During summer 2015, my sisters and I helped our parents manage Dad's ocular shingles, diabetes, leg weakness, and multiple falls. Mom's reaction (or lack thereof) to one particular fall led to an evaluation and diagnosis of probable Alzheimer's disease. Of course, my sisters and I knew long before that Mom likely had a problem, but it wasn't until that summer we had something definitive in hand to help push for answers.

As a scientist, I was academically interested in Alzheimer's, but after that summer with my parents, two things became clear to me: 1. I needed to tell at least some semblance of our story as a means of processing my feelings, and 2. I wanted that story to differ from what was currently available in terms of dementia fiction so that others could be prepared. Thus, I started *The Weight We Carry*, which focuses on turmoil that can come *before* an actual diagnosis and the toll it can take on the entire family. I hope readers understand that missing signs and symptoms of dementia is typical (especially by those closest in proximity to the affected), that denial is common, and that sometimes, you have to strong-arm your way into keeping your loved ones safe and healthy.

This book ends where many others pick up, and readers might wonder, what comes next? For us, we faced another uphill battle. Both

Mom and Dad denied the existence of what was right in front of their eyes, and they fought my sisters and me almost every step of the way. My father insisted a miracle would occur, and Mom shrugged off every mention of dementia, even as her capabilities dwindled. Soon, neither of my parents could deny they needed help, and after living with my sister and a false start at a facility in Michigan, my parents moved to Ohio, where Mom lived for almost three wonderful years. While it might seem like an odd thing to say about someone living with a terminal disease, Mom found an unconventional happily ever after with the staff and residents of The Carlyle House in Kettering, Ohio. Sadly, she passed in October 2022, almost a year before this book was published.

The World Health Organization (WHO) states that over 55 million people worldwide have dementia, and according to the Alzheimer's Association, as of this writing, 6.5 million Americans live with Alzheimer's disease. Right now, there's no cure, though medications to slow the disease are available, and certain healthy behaviors (diet, exercise, etc.) can minimize the risk. Information is power, and it's plentiful. If you suspect that you or a loved one might have abnormal memory loss, seek help. The sooner you do so, the better.

Related Reading and Resources:

The 36-Hour Day: A Family Guide to Caring for People Who Have Alzheimer Disease and Other Dementias, by Nancy L. Mace, MA and Peter V. Rabins, MD, MPH

Alzheimer's Through the Stages: A Caregiver's Guide, by Mary Moller, MSW, CAS

My Two Elaines: Learning, Coping, and Surviving as an Alzheimer's Caregiver, by Martin J. Schreiber and Cathy Breitenbucher

What to Do Between the Tears...: A Practical Guide to Dealing with a Dementia or Alzheimer's Diagnosis in the Family, by Tara Reed

Alzheimer's Association: https://www.alz.org/, 24/7 HELPLINE 800.272.3900

National Institute on Aging, Alzheimer's Disease and Related Dementia: https://www.nia.nih.gov/health/alzheimers, 800.222.2225

ACKNOWLEDGMENTS

Mom: Always and forever. I wish you were still here with us, but I truly believe you're somewhere even better, surrounded by butterflies, books, and hot buttered popcorn. I miss you each and every day.

Dad: Our journey the last several years has been interesting, to say the least. Thank you for always asking how the writing is coming along. Little nudges made all the difference.

My sisters: My words of thanks will never be enough for all your support during the summer of 2015, the years following, and especially the days surrounding Mom's passing. While I had already submitted this book to the publisher by then, I'm certain I would have never put the story on paper without your unwavering support.

The Plot Sisters—Cindy Cremeans, Jen Messaros, Ruthann Kain, Jude Walsh, and Traci Ison Shafer: You read a good number of these pages years ago now, and I'm certain that your influence is found there still, even after revision. Plus, I have to thank you for your encouragement this last decade. I would not be doing what I'm doing without all of you.

The beta readers—Jen Messaros, Erin Flanagan, Cindy Cremeans, and The Spun Yarn: Your invaluable feedback sculpted this book into the story it is today. Thanks for helping me break it apart and build it back up again.

CCBs—Erin Flanagan, Katrina Kittle, Meredith Doench, and Sharon Short: Our writing retreats provided energy that kept my momentum going even when I didn't feel like working. Thank you for all the positive vibes and words of wisdom.

Kelly Hansen: Without the Hansen House Writing Retreat, this book would still be in the draft stage. Your generosity of spirit is second to none, and I feel grateful that we crossed paths. I owe you so much!

Christina Berry: Just knowing you're on my side makes all the difference. Thank you for your unwavering support.

Edward Stiffler, Tex Thompson, and Laurel Leigh: I stumbled across you (Edward and Tex) almost by accident, and I'm so glad I did. Your edits and encouragement kept me moving forward. And nothing compares to your thorough read and no-nonsense comments, Laurel. You're my go-to editor, and I consider myself lucky in finding you.

Kim Wilson of Kiwi Cover Design Co.: You stepped up when I needed you most! Thank you for your generous spirit and creative eye.

The Black Rose Writing team: I appreciate all your support and for giving this book a home.

The late Mary Oliver: The inspiration for the title of the book comes from your poem "Heavy." Each time I read it, I find something new to love about it.

The Carlyle House staff, past and present: All of you played a unique role in helping Mom find happiness in her last few years on this earth, and you made a tough situation easier to digest. Your empathy and grace, kindness and positivity make a difference in so many people's lives. Your actions will never be forgotten. A little shout-out to Ashley, Beth, Becky, Bryan, Deborah, Dee, Janessa, Leighann, Lynne, Meredith, Paula, Robert, Shy, and Sonya for your big, big hearts.

Zoe, Talia, Aaron, Melina, and Tim: Every book will have you listed last in the acknowledgments because you are the most important people in my life. And every book will have a variation of the same sentiment— I'm not sure how to articulate my love and gratitude for you. You as individuals. You as a collective whole. There's no other way to say it: I love you all. Thank you.

ABOUT THE AUTHOR

Christina Consolino is a writer and editor whose work has appeared in multiple online and print outlets. Her debut novel, *Rewrite the Stars*, was named one of ten finalists for the Ohio Writers' Association Great Novel Contest 2020. She is a former senior editor at the online journal *Literary Mama* and freelance edits both fiction and nonfiction. Christina lives in Kettering, Ohio, with her family and pets.

To keep up-to-date with the latest news, check out her website at www.christinaconsolino.com or follow her on social media.

OTHER TITLES BY
CHRISTINA CONSOLINO

CHRISTINA CONSOLINO

NOTE FROM CHRISTINA CONSOLINO

Word-of-mouth is crucial for any author to succeed. If you enjoyed *The Weight We Carry*, please leave a review online—anywhere you are able. Even if it's just a sentence or two. It would make all the difference and would be very much appreciated.

Thanks!
Christina Consolino

We hope you enjoyed reading this title from:

BLACK🌹ROSE
writing™

www.blackrosewriting.com

Subscribe to our mailing list – *The Rosevine* – and receive **FREE** books, daily deals, and stay current with news about upcoming releases and our hottest authors.
Scan the QR code below to sign up.

Already a subscriber? Please accept a sincere thank you for being a fan of Black Rose Writing authors.

View other Black Rose Writing titles at
www.blackrosewriting.com/books and use promo code
PRINT to receive a **20% discount** when purchasing.

Printed in the USA
CPSIA information can be obtained
at www.ICGtesting.com
LVHW041300151023
761121LV00001BB/208